all best!
Sarah St Peter

MURDER.COM

The Dark Side of the Net

Sarah St. Peter

Dageforde Publishing, Inc.

ISBN 1-886225-41-9

Cover design by Angie Johnson Art Productions

Library of Congress Cataloging-in-Publication information applied for

Dageforde Publishing, Inc.
122 South 29th Street
Lincoln, Nebraska 68510
Phone: (402) 475-1123 FAX: (402) 475-1176

Visit our Website at
http://www.dageforde.com
email: info@dageforde.com

Printed in the United States of America

10 9 8 7 6 5 4 3 2 1

For Darwin Brown, my brother and trusted mentor
and
Darlene Brown, my mother and faithful friend.

Onward through the fog...

Acknowledgments

I would like to thank the many people who assisted me along the way as I wrote this book.

A multitude of thanks to Darwin Brown, Darlene Brown, and Kathy Wright. Your input and support through this project has been invaluable.

Thanks to Linda and Amy at Dageforde Publishing, Rod Colvin, and Fritz Limbacher for all their help. And Gail.

Thanks to Detective David Pontarelli of the Denver Police Intelligence Section, Denver's Chief Deputy Coroner Michelle Weiss-Samaras, and Epidemiologist Penny Studebaker of Colorado's Department of Public Health and Environment, for taking time to answer my technical questions.

PROLOGUE

She stared, amazed, at the dead man's body sitting in the driver's seat next to her. His mouth hung open; his dark eyes stared straight ahead. He looked surprised. His hand gripped the bottom arc of the steering wheel as if making a phantom effort to escape.

Elizabeth peered down at the gun still lying warm in her hand. *My God...I killed him.* Tears welled up in her eyes and the overflow slid down her cheek. Suddenly, she became aware that she wasn't breathing, and pulled air deep into her lungs. She grabbed a tissue, stuffed the gun back into her purse and latched the flap, then carefully wiped down any area in the car she might have touched.

Wrapping the tissue around the door handle, she let herself out into the night. The car door swung shut with a quick bump of her hip. She pulled off her boots and started to run with abandon. She ran until her lungs ached and forced her to stop.

God! I actually killed him. What do I do now?

Elizabeth stared up at the clear night sky, as if seeking answers. It all seemed to start with that phone call; that's when her life began unraveling.

CHAPTER 1

She cinched the belt of her white cotton terry robe. Toweling her hair dry, she strolled over to the caller ID unit to see who had phoned while she was in the shower. The electronic display read, "C H Strong," and a phone number. Her childhood home phone number. She grimaced.

The red light on the answering machine blinked at her like a winking demon. Reluctantly, she pushed the play button and braced herself, while her heart pulsed like a nervous tic.

"Hello, Lizzie? Are you there? Lizzie? Well, anyway...this is your dad. I have to talk to you. I want to apologize. I quit drinking and I want to set things straight with you. I mean it this time, Lizzie. You there? Pick up if you are...Lizzie, please... It's been a year since I touched a drop, I swear to God. I am so sorry for everything. Please call me back. You know the number. At least you used to. Bye."

Glaring down at the machine, she clenched her teeth. "Shit! Shit! Shit! What's he doing calling here? That sonofabitch! He's got some nerve calling here, trying to tell me what to do."

She stalked over to the mahogany credenza, jerked open a small drawer, and grabbed a matching gold cigarette case and lighter. Both were elegantly engraved with her given name, Elizabeth. Flipping open the case, she pulled out one of two hoarded cigarettes. She made it a point never to have more than that on hand. Even these two were in the house strictly for occasions like this, when her stomach threatened to bolt into her head.

Elizabeth sped out to the terrace to smoke. Shaking, she lit the long menthol sliver, and with trembling lips took a long pull from it. Leaning her forearms on elegant railing, she looked eastward to a balcony several floors down to a long-haired blonde woman sitting outside on a patio chair playing a flattop guitar and singing. Elizabeth strained to hear the words, but couldn't. The openmouthed chantress reminded her of a hungry baby bird perched high in a cement nest.

Scanning the skyline of Denver, she noticed a greenish translucent cloud hovering around the slick shiny skyscrapers, as if someone had sprayed a tall crystal garden for mosquitoes. She preferred looking at the skyline at night when she couldn't see the smog.

In the dark, the buildings looked like those in a porcelain Christmas village; the windows were lit up, but no people could be seen inside. She usually felt snug and safe inside her concrete cocoon, one of two opulent twelfth floor penthouses in an exclusive downtown apartment building. She didn't feel safe now.

As her therapist had suggested she do when she got anxious, she took a deep breath, and tried to calm herself by counting to ten aloud. Angry thoughts ripped through her concentration as she counted. "Four, five, six..." *What does he want from me? Dad, my ass. And my name is Elizabeth, not Lizzie, asshole.* "Seven..." *Burn in hell, you bastard.* "Eight...nine... ten."

Frowning at the billboard across from her apartment building, she took another deep drag off her cigarette. She detested billboards in the downtown area, and this was the last straw. The advertising irritation's latest display was the caricature of a popular rock jock on KRAS radio, wearing a diaper and horn rimmed glasses.

Cute. Real cute. Elizabeth shook her head in disgust, and flung the cigarette over the balcony to the cement drive below. She watched it fall for as long as she could see it, then went back inside.

Feeling a bit more restrained, she sat down to her computer to answer some correspondence. Her composure didn't last long. She clicked on "Send New Mail" and began to type. "*To:* My father. I HATE YOU! I HATE YOU! I HATE YOU!" With nimble fingers, Elizabeth typed this phrase over and over again, hundreds of times, until she filled up the electronic page. It didn't make her feel any better. It wasn't enough.

CHAPTER 2

Sunday was Elizabeth's favorite day of the week. No one expected her to be at home, so the phone rarely rang. Privacy and time were precious commodities, and she guarded both ferociously.

Elizabeth dropped the heavy Sunday edition of the *Rocky Mountain News,* and its accompanying heap of sleek sale supplements, on the floor beside her bed. Pulling the puffy white down comforter up over her feet, she stretched out full length on her back, atop luxurious, pale blue Egyptian cotton sheets. They felt cool and smooth on her skin, and her head was snuggled into fat feather pillows. She felt herself getting deliciously drowsy.

Staring up at the ceiling, she examined the texture of the jaggedly painted white swirls, thinking they looked like big thumbprints. She contemplated new blinds or curtains to keep the light out when she wanted to take a nap.

Her long, graceful fingers hit the CD play button on the small stereo unit on the nightstand, and the peaceful piano music of Jim Brickman quietly filled the room. She gently placed a white silk eye pillow full of lavender and other soothing herbs upon her closed eyelids. Taking in a deep breath, she placed her hands down at her sides and began to count slowly backwards from five hundred. Instead of the serenity this exercise usually brought, disturbing thoughts of yesterday's phone call from her father crashed into her awareness. Agitated, she turned onto her side and the satiny pouch tumbled off her eyes onto the mattress.

That bastard! Her mind raced. She shifted fitfully, trying to get comfortable, and tried counting backwards again. Somewhere near three hundred she fell asleep. Soon, the horrible recurring dream assaulted her peace.

In her nightmare, little Lizzie was huddled under her twin bed to avoid him. This was the time of night he usually came in. Maybe if he didn't see her in the bed, he would forget—but deep down she knew he never forgot. She'd lie curled up as tight as a frightened baby mouse. The hardwood floor felt chilly on her cheek.

Her breathing became shallow and labored as she whispered assurances to herself and to the Chatty Cathy doll resting beside her. Chatty, nearly as big as Lizzie, was placed as a barricade between her and her father. Somehow, she thought Chet might be so drunk he would think the doll was her and leave her alone. That was her wish. She was glad Chatty had agreed to help her out.

Mama's music box soothed her some, and the alarm clock on the scratched blond nightstand ticked like a heart. She wound them both every night before she went to bed to hear the comforting sounds. Lizzie dozed off a few times before she heard him approach.

"Oh, Li-i-i-z—i-e..." The doorknob turned from the outside.

The frantic, barely understood but solemn prayer burst from a frightened child's heart. "Our Father, which are in heaven, holwed be thy name." Lizzie tightly shut her eyes and put her tiny hands in a steeple in front of her mouth.

"Where are you, you little slut?"

Lying still as death, she saw the overhead light come on and point to her whereabouts. The music box lid slammed shut. She heard Chet drop to his knees, then saw him bungle with the thin pink chenille bedspread. Lizzie thought his face looked like one of those horrible reflections from shiny Christmas tree ornaments.

She turned over on her back, stared up at the underside of the mattress and pretended he wasn't there. Reddish-brown stains dotted the back of the black and white striped fabric and she wondered where they came from. She formed another steeple with her hands and finished her prayer. "For Thy is the kingdom, power, and glory forever, aman." Lizzie's eyes began to water.

Chet grabbed up Chatty Cathy clumsily and squinted at her staring blue eyes. "Whaddayalookinat? Don't she talk or somethin'?" Bumbling, he turned the doll around and found the pull cord in the back of its neck. He jerked the string out and listened intently to the scratchy, artificial voice.

"I love you."

"Ha! Yeah right, Sweetheart, they all do...what else you gotta say?" Chet giggled goofily and tugged the line again.

"What's your name?" A crackling noise surrounded the doll's voice.

"Fuck you! I thought you just said you loved me. Now you don't even know my name. You're just like all those other bitches!"

Grunting, he hoisted the heavy doll up over his head and hurled it across the room. It made a loud crash when it hit the wall and Lizzie began to tremble. From under the bed, she could see that Chatty had landed on her stomach with her arms completely backwards and sticking up in the air. Her head was turned towards Lizzie and the lifeless sapphire orbs gaped at her.

It scared Lizzie to see Chatty that way. She felt the tremor rise from inside her stomach like an earthquake. Heavy tears splashed on the hard floor.

"Now, get out here, Lizzie! Don't make me come in there after you! Lizzie...I mean it! Come 'ere!!!" His right arm frantically swept back and forth under the bed looking for her." Goddamn it, Lizzie! Get out here! You make this so fucking hard on yourself."

She shrank against the wall, pressing herself tightly against the baseboard. "No, daddy, not again, please. Please!"

"Shut up. SHUT UP! I will come in here anytime I want to. Don't you ever say that word to me again...no! No, my ass. I MADE you—and I will do with you any fucking thing I please! Now, come over here!"

"NO! I won't!" Lizzie lay still and rigid, barely breathing.

When she felt his wrist clamp around hers, a red rage flashed through her and she bit him as hard as she could on the tender side of his forearm. Yowling with pain, Chet jerked her out from under the bed by her arms, and pinned her slight body on the bed. His face glowed crimson and the veins popped out on the side of his mottled neck as he glared at her with fury. His breath stank like dirty, beer-soaked socks.

Lizzie struggled hard to get free, kicking blindly in the air, managing to catch him solidly in the ribs a few times. He growled as he reared back and slapped her across the face. Gritting his teeth, Chet gripped her around the throat with his huge, calloused hands and squeezed until she thought her head was going to pop. She couldn't breathe. There was a bunch of red and white flashy lights inside of her eyelids, then everything went dark.

A vision of her mother, nervous and beautiful, floated softly across the screen of her mind. Her yellow hair was long and shiny, floating around her face like a gentle breeze was blowing it. *Mama! Mama! Where did you go? I haven't seen you in so long! Mommy!*

Her mother wore a beautiful long white dress. Smiling and ethereal, she blew her daughter a kiss and turned to go. Her mommy had wings! Beautiful white wings. "Mama! Come back! Take me with you! I want to go with you. Don't leave me again!" The image faded quickly as Lizzie heard a deadly hissing in her ear.

"I can kill you...and I will...if I have to. Now, shut up. I mean it. I *will* kill you." Chet's teeth bared as he spoke.

She beat on his arms and screamed. "Kill me, I don't care! I want to be with Mommy! I want to be with Mommy! Mommy! Come back! Mama...come back." Lizzie's sobs rose violently from the pit of her stomach.

"Don't you *ever* mention her again, you ungrateful little bitch! I'll show you. As a matter of fact, I'll show you what Mama *really* used to like! " He slapped her across the face hard. Lizzie tasted blood in her mouth. She lay completely still, defeated.

When he yanked her nightgown up and over her head with cruel hands, she started counting to herself and tried to go away to her special place. The pretty place in her soul where she was safe and only she could visit.

Elizabeth felt the scream boil up from her stomach and pour out of her mouth like lava. The soulful wail vibrated through her veil of sleep and jerked her awake. Sitting bolt upright, still shaking, she threw her legs over the side of the bed and sprung up. She stood for a moment, gathering her senses, and glared at the bed like it was her betrayer. Her knees threatened to buckle under with her weight.

"Jesus..." She put a hand on the wall for support and concentrated on her breathing. Her heart fluttered like the beating wings of a desperate moth against a porch light.

Elizabeth stumbled into the dining room and grabbed the last cigarette from the small drawer of the credenza. Not bothering to go outside, she quickly lit the smoke, inhaled deeply and made a mental note to bring two more cigarettes in from the car today. Obviously, she was going to need them.

CHAPTER 3

By 6:30 Monday morning, Elizabeth was sitting at her desk at Cleardrive, Inc., with a *USA Today* and a strong cup of coffee. Attendance was mandatory at the weekly planning meeting on the Mondays she was in town. The mail that had accumulated while she was working in Detroit last week was stacked neatly on her desk; her phone messages were arranged chronologically in a tidy pile. Checking her voice mail, she sipped coffee and tapped her pen on a scratch pad, occasionally doodling while she waited for the recorded callers to get to the point.

Maggie, the office manager, kept Elizabeth's correspondence organized while she was out of town on assignment. Maggie was one of the few tolerable people at Cleardrive. She cringed when ladies from the sales department would periodically poke their heads in her door, trying to chit chat. Having to smile while listening to meaningless drivel nearly drove her mad.

When she could, she planned her office visits either before the day staff came in, or after they went home. Normally, her office door was kept shut and she usually didn't see anyone without an appointment. These eccentricities were tolerated because she was very good at her job, easily taking the honors at the annual Christmas party for top salesperson four of the five years she had worked there.

The only office party she attended was the combination awards banquet and Christmas bash. The evening was usually reasonably predictable. John Mohr, the department vice-president, would get oiled up on spiked egg nog before his infamous "Next year is going to be the best year ever!" speech. Those who did not show up for this slurred masterpiece were not considered to be part of his inner circle, to whom generous raises and bonuses were granted. Elizabeth thought of it as the annual brainwashing ball.

As a reward for her attendance, she bought herself a ridiculously expensive dress every year that made her runner's body and long shapely legs look stunning. She attempted to smile at the right people during the evening, especially John Mohr. He was like most men; show them some cleavage and a little leg and they turn into lap dogs. Elizabeth wasn't the least bit interested in John Mohr sexually, just teased him enough to keep him polite and generous.

The pay was excellent and the corner office was a nice perk. She drove a black 1995 Mercedes E320 Cabriolet, compliments of Cleardrive. Management had offered to lease her a new company car numerous times, but she loved this car, and they didn't make them like this one anymore. It could do 0-60 in about 7.5 seconds, top end about 150 miles per hour. Not that she ever drove that fast, but it was nice to know she could if she wanted to.

Her west office wall was made up of several large windows, capturing a gorgeous view of the Rockies. Many times, when she had faced a difficult problem at work, she turned to the mountains as a tool of divination. Solutions and new ideas came often to her with uncanny certainty.

Being a corporate software sales executive was perfect for Elizabeth; she got to travel, be her own boss, and work with computers. Computers were logical and fairly predictable. They weren't inconsistent like most people she knew. Her closest friends were people who she had met online through the internet, specifically technological chat rooms and message boards. These types of friendships suited Elizabeth best since she didn't have to interact face to face with people. She could communicate on her own terms.

Luckily, she didn't have to be around too many people, and when she did, the type she had to talk to were mostly intelligent, busy people. When she went out to sell a system, it was usually a done deal. Most of her clientele did not like to waste time either.

It had been two weeks since she had been in her Denver office. Elizabeth had been on assignment in the Detroit branch office, helping to install a system for a huge client from Lansing, an account that she had helped to land. After turning on her computer this morning, she was met with a surprising pop, then black smoke billowed out from the back of the hard drive tower.

What the hell? Tech support probably won't be here for another two hours, either. Damn. Snapping off the power bar, she called for Gregory, the supervisor of Cleardrive's in-house tech support crew. Of course, he wasn't in yet. She left a message for him to come to her office as soon as he got in, and started through her mail.

After suffering through the Monday morning staff meeting, Elizabeth came back into her office and saw Gregory hovering over her computer. His dark good looks were disguised with thick horn rimmed glasses that made his eyes look very large.

"I see you got my voice mail, Greg. Thanks for coming right up. You know what's wrong with it yet?" She threw her memo pad down on the desk and sat down.

"Fried a board. Happens all the time. It'll be fixed soon. Used to be a time when you had to know something about computers to fix 'em. Now, it's all modular. You just pop out the bad board, and pop in a new one. Simple. Even I can do it." He laughed a little.

"What's that noise?" Elizabeth leaned in a little closer with an ear turned to the tower.

Gregory paused to listen. "That? Oh, that's just the fan. I got the cover off. That makes it louder than usual."

Elizabeth knitted her eyebrows. "A fan?"

"Oh yeah...you got to have a fan to blow air over the circuitry, that's what keeps it cool in there. See back here? This little vent? Put your hand up here." Gregory took her hand and guided it to the vent in the back of the computer tower. She had to stand up to reach it. "Feel the air coming out?"

"Yes, I do." After feeling the cool air pour over her fingers, Elizabeth retrieved her hand from his grasp. "That's why there was smoke everywhere when I turned on the computer. What would cause the board to burn up?"

Gregory put some silver tools back inside a small clear vinyl case. "Oh, it could be a lot of things. Has it been sitting long without being turned on?"

She sat back down in her high backed black leather desk chair. "A couple of weeks, I guess."

"Well, sometimes when computers sit idle a while, they build up condensation, then when you turn them on, it causes a power surge, and boom! Then sometimes they just go, for no earthly reason. Planned obsolescence, if you ask me. A few well-planned weak links in the chain to insure Michael Dell's bright financial future."

"Michael Dell?"

Gregory looked appalled at her question. "You know, the filthy rich computer nerd that makes stuff like this." He held up the circuitry board for her to see.

"Yes, Gregory, I know who Michael Dell is. My, aren't we the cynic?"

Gregory's eyes looked the size of pancakes through his glasses. "That's like the pot calling the kettle black, from what I hear." Flashing his right eyebrow and huge smile, he laughed.

"Are you about finished?" Elizabeth shifted some files around on her desk. "I have a shitload of work to do." She suddenly felt irritated at Gregory's bluntness and idiotic attempts at flirtation.

Gregory's smile diminished at her sudden aloofness. "Will be soon. I've got to go get a circuit board from supply and I'll be right back. You'll be up and running within thirty minutes, how's that?"

"Perfect."

Gregory's lanky frame crossed the room and soon left Elizabeth alone. She took the opportunity to peer at the brains of the computer tower. Studying what Gregory had told her about the tiny fan, she observed how it worked. Air blew straight over the circuitry, through the vent, and out into the room.

CHAPTER 4

"Chet. This is Elizabeth. I got your message on the answering machine and am returning your call. Did somebody die or something?" Elizabeth drummed her fingernails impatiently on the desktop and stared out the window to the foothills of the Rockies. Spring rains had painted the vegetation a lush forest green, and it made a striking contrast to the white snow that still covered the mountain tops. Elizabeth longed to be hiking through the towering pine trees, watching nature come back to life.

There was a long pause before Chet replied. "You could call me Dad, you know, I am your father."

"I'd rather not. How did you get my number anyway?" Elizabeth turned back to her desk and began doodling on a yellow legal pad. She drew boxes with outlines so dark, her pen sometimes tore through the paper.

"It's common knowledge around town that you've done well for yourself there at the Cleardrive company. Then, your secretary gave me your home phone."

Elizabeth paused, and made a mental note to have a serious talk with Maggie. Now she would have to get her home number changed. She jotted a reminder to herself on her open *Far Side* desk calendar.

"What do you want? Money?" She really wished she had a cigarette.

"No, I didn't call for money. Jeez. I just want to see you. I need to talk to you."

Elizabeth felt her face flush and her heart race. "What about? We have nothing to talk about that you can't say on the phone. This is as close as I ever want to get to you, Chet. I mean it." Her tone was absolute.

"Don't be like that Lizzie, I am trying—" Chet whined.

Never call me that again. If you ever call me that again, I will hang up in a heartbeat! I mean it, you bastard. My name is Elizabeth. It's the name my mother gave me, you asshole, use it!" She clenched her jaws.

A few moments passed before Chet replied. "Elizabeth, then. Let me talk, will ya?"

"Don't ever try and tell me what to do, Chet. Those days of you bullying me around are long gone. You can never, ever, tell me what to do again, *Chet*." She stood up and paced back and forth behind her desk. Raw energy raged through her body.

"Elizabeth! Jeez. Look, I am only trying to apologize here...if you think that is easy—"

"Who gives a *fuck* what is easy or not for you,Chet? You are the last person on this earth I want to be talking to. Now or ever. You are not my father—you were just a fucking sperm donor."

"Damnit, Lizzie! Let me talk. Oh, forget it! You always were a selfish brat. I could never talk to you."

"Fuck you, Chet! Fuck you! Burn in hell, you sonofabitch!" She slammed down the receiver, grabbed her purse and dashed out of the office. She needed a cigarette and a drink.

Elizabeth zoomed by Maggie without a word.

Maggie urgently called after her. "Ms. Strong! Ms. Strong! There is a phone call on hold for you from a Mr. Armin from Data Links. He wants—"

"Tell him I had an emergency," Elizabeth retorted without missing a beat. The adrenaline coursed through her veins, making her feel like a locomotive charging through the elegant reception area. Grabbing the doorknob, she jerked the heavy entry door open, and turned suddenly.

"Oh, and Maggie."

Maggie stood up. "Yes, Ms. Strong?"

Elizabeth stared at Maggie like a mad dog. "If you *ever* give out my home phone number again, I'll have your job."

Maggie's eyes teared up as Elizabeth flounced out, solidly closing the office door behind her.

CHAPTER 5

Elizabeth walked as fast as she could without actually running from the office building to the bar across the street. The *Happy Hour,* it was called, a low overhead pit stop for the pissed off. Most of its patrons were stressed out business people ducking in for a short liquid tension reliever or two during the day. It was really no different than the seedy bars just a few blocks away, except that its customers had more money and briefcases parked at their feet.

She sat up at the bar and ordered a Bloody Mary. The silent bartender sat two drinks down in front of her; it was "twofers" all day. Drinking in the thick red liquid, she felt the saltiness grab at her tongue. She walked over to the cigarette machine while ignoring a hello from some bleary-eyed pencil pusher coming out of the men's room.

After quickly downing her drinks and having a smoke, she set out for the shuttle bus stop at the corner. Her eyes impatiently scanned the street for the next coach. She was relieved when she saw its approach, although it was still several blocks away.

A sidewalk preacher pranced around on the red paved brick, belting out his warnings from Revelations and waving a coffee can marked for donations. Elizabeth tried to ignore him, but he was soon in her face.

"Do you know Jesus?" His eyes sought hers.

Elizabeth ignored him and turned toward the approaching bus, willing it to hurry up.

"Tell me, do you know Jesus?" He repeated, and his steady gaze pinned her to the air.

Elizabeth met his gaze punitively. "Oh, yeah, sure, I know Jesus. He was over for dinner last night. He told me to tell you to get a job."

The man gave her a blank expression and moved on.

"Got de time?" A nearly toothless woman in a raggedy brown sweater looked expectantly at Elizabeth. A shabby red patterned ski cap was stretched over her head, leaving unkempt gray hair poking out all over.

"2:30." She replied blankly.

"Naw, lady. Gotta dime? I said you got a dime? Please?"

She took a deep breath. What? *Do I have a sign that says weirdo magnet pasted on my forehead?*

The street people bothered her, but at the same time, she admired the ingenuity some of them used to survive. She fished a dollar and some change she had kept for the vending machines at work from her suit pocket. "Here. This is all I have. Please go away now." She dropped the change into the weathered palm.

"T'ank you, lady. Bless you, lady."

"Sure, I'm a real saint. Go away now. I haven't had a good day."

"You need dis money back? Bad money day?" The calloused hand of the old woman offered back the bill and the quarters Elizabeth had just given her.

"No, no, it's not that. You go ahead. What's bothering me would take a little more than that to fix." Elizabeth smiled thinly.

"God bless you, lady." The little bent troll-like woman turned and hurried about ten feet away and stopped. She huddled over her sacks of recyclables like she was guarding gold coins, and stuffed her newly acquired loot into a red plastic coin purse.

The shuttle finally stopped. The bus was full and it was standing room only. Elizabeth found a few inches of her own and stood clutching a bar overhead, near the exit. The close proximity of strange people made her anxious, but as the bus accelerated, the gentle rocking motion and the groan of the engine soothed her jangled nerves.

Elizabeth was looking out the back window, watching the curb disappear, when she saw a well dressed man leering at the front of her shirt. His tailored crispness and posture oozed confidence and success. She looked down and saw that two buttons on her blouse had come undone, and her bra was clearly visible.

She snarled at the peeper heatedly and turned away. "Prick. Just like a man, always trying to get something for nothing," she muttered under her breath. Stepping over to the vertical pole, she braced herself against the erratic travel pattern of the shuttle and buttoned up.

Presentable once again, Elizabeth took a deep breath and sighed. She stooped in an attempt to look out the front windshield. Facing her, seated comfortably on a nearby bench, was the familiar cheerful panhandler. Noticing that Elizabeth had seen her, the crone flashed a gummy grin, her eyes twinkling. She had not noticed a street person being that alert before, let alone that happy.

"Hey, lady. You got to know where to stand to get a chair quick. I'll show you next time. It looks like you could use a friend."

Elizabeth found the old woman's smile infectious, and her eyes steady black dots that drilled right through her skull. The bus screeched to a halt and the doors flew open to Larimer and Stout. She hurriedly stepped down and walked quickly down the street. A little paranoid of her adoring fan, she glanced over her shoulder to make sure the strange woman hadn't followed her. Elizabeth relaxed some when she saw no sign of her perceived stalker.

God, Elizabeth, get a hold of yourself. Everything is going to be okay. Everything is going to be okay. It was a mantra she often used to calm herself. Elizabeth purposely slowed her walking pace as she had learned to do from her latest therapist. *Breathe. Slow down. Walk slowly and enjoy your surroundings. Look at trees. Taste different foods. Alter your routine.*

Elizabeth tried very hard to be interested in window shopping. To her, it just looked like an endless sea of *Sale Sale Sale* signs. She never wasted time and she didn't know how to shop without a purpose. *Maybe I should buy myself a new outfit. Maybe that will make me feel better.* Elizabeth considered the options. Checking the boutique names her eyes landed on a sign that read, Tan Lines.

She cut across the street and stopped in front of the shop's display window. The mannequin on display was outfitted totally in black, the skirt an extremely short, soft-looking leather mini. The top was a thin suede shirt that was cut to appear torn. It wouldn't cover much skin, but enough. Sleek high-heeled black leather boots climbed perfect plastic calves. The crowning glory was a billed black leather hat, cocked pseudo-sexily over one eye. It made the mannequin look like Cyclops, but she got the idea it might look okay on a real person.

Elizabeth imagined the outfit on herself; she had the legs for it. It would be nice to have big boobs like the mannequin, but she figured hers were adequate. Besides, you couldn't possibly wear a bra with that shirt. She entered the store.

A petite blond young woman approached her with a considerable smile. "Hi! I'm Tammy! Can I help you find something?" Cheerful enthusiasm rankled the air.

"I was wondering about that black leather outfit in the window."

"Oh, yeah!" Tammy squealed. "That is hot! That would look fly on you, babe."

"Fly. Of course. Do you have it in a size seven?"

"The one in the window is the last one I have. I think it might even be a seven! Let me go look. Wow, wouldn't that be something if it was? That would be cosmic! Like you were supposed to have it or something! Don't ya think?" Tammy hurried toward the front window.

Elizabeth crossed her arms in front of her. *A moment of kismet with a black leather mini-skirt. Great.*

The young girl checked the tags. "Yes! Yes! The skirt and top are both size seven. I got those boots in a bunch of sizes. What size shoe do you wear?"

"Seven and a half." She bit the inside of her lip. She considered leaving.

"Seven, seven, seven! You wear three sevens! Good thing you don't wear a six! That would be scary! " Tammy laughed loudly at her own joke.

Excellent marketing strategy. Elizabeth complained silently and longed for the door. The little chatterbox, although clumsy, had already wrestled the stiff model undressed. The sight made Elizabeth feel an obligation to try the outfit on, sans the cap.

She followed the perky peddler to the back of the store toward the dressing rooms. Her long blond hair was braided with leather strips and beads. While looking at the back of her head, Elizabeth noticed the metal backs of at least five earrings per ear.

"Here you go!" Tammy handed her two hangers draped with the black garments. "Try these on, and I'll go get your boots."

She dressed quickly and stepped out to look at herself in the three-way mirror. She pulled on the boots Tammy had set beside the dressing room door.

Tammy crossed her arms and nodded at Elizabeth with satisfaction. "You look fabulous! You have a great ass!"

She hoped that was a harmless compliment. "You really think it looks good, huh?" Elizabeth strained over her shoulder to look at her backside.

"Good? It looks great! I hope you got a hot date tonight. If you don't get lucky, it'll be your own fault!"

Elizabeth couldn't recall the last time she had been out . She only remembered a constant stream of meeting clients for drinks to discuss business in upscale rubber-stamped hotel lounges. Her social life was practically non-existent. There had been a few token dates here and there, but nothing even semi-serious. Since she had received her master's degree from the University of Colorado, she had thrown all her energy into her work, trying to widen the gap between her and her past.

"I'll take it. The whole outfit." Elizabeth smiled at her reflection in the mirror. She looked like a very chic biker chick. The illusion made her feel powerful .

Tammy wore a big smile as she questioned her. "Do you need to know how much they are? I can total them up for you real quick."

"I don't care. I have plastic." She handed Tammy her credit card.

"Yes, ma'am!" She ran excitedly to the cash register and began poking enthusiastically. "Let's see, with tax, that's six-hundred eighty-three dollars and seventy-two cents for everything. Sure you don't need that hat, too?"

"Positive." She studied the light bouncing off the two silver rings in Tammy's pierced nose as she slid the magnetic strip through the scanner. Tammy flashed her a goofy grin while they both waited for technology to do its thing and approve the sale.

"Wow!" Elizabeth exclaimed as she saw the total. "I guess I better get some good use out of these things!" She signed the credit slip and passed it back to Tammy.

Tammy took the slip and slid it discreetly into her cash drawer after putting Elizabeth's copy in her clothing tote. "Oh you will, Mamasita. You look really hot in that outfit."

"Maybe I will just have to go out tonight."

"You definitely should." Tammy handed Elizabeth her sack.

Taking the sack, Elizabeth flashed Tammy a smile. "I just might do that, Tammy… I just might."

CHAPTER 6

Elizabeth blearily eyed her reflection in the mirror with approval. The wild look the new black leather outfit gave her made her feel playful. Free. Emptying the remaining brandy from her glass for the third, or maybe even fourth, time since she arrived home that afternoon, she struck a few poses to see what she looked like from different angles.

"Not bad. Now, aren't you glad we run every day?" She remarked to herself as she turned to carry the snifter back to the refill station. "Seems like I have been visiting you a lot lately, Mr. Holy Gatekeeper of Vices." She grinned as she opened the sturdy door of the credenza and reached for the nearly empty liquor bottle. "Jesus Christ, I am talking to a cabinet. I think that rates a cigarette, too."

Grabbing the suit jacket she had worn to work today from the back of a dining room chair, she draped it around her shoulders, and hustled her cigarettes and drink out to the balcony. Sitting on a black wrought iron patio chair, Elizabeth stared at the lights of the city and smoked. And drank.

A little herd of marauding gangbangers passed by under her on the sidewalk adjacent to the building. They yelled obscenities to each other and to passing cars. There seemed to be a lot of honking going on tonight. Road rage. Impatient drivers, judicious and ironhanded in the safety of their steel shells, could not wait two seconds for another driver to do what they thought they should do. Zero tolerance levels out there.

Elizabeth pulled a long drag off her cigarette and considered her options. *I think I will go to Ransom's. I hear that is supposed to be a hot place to party.* She hopped up from the chair and was taken aback; her head felt floaty from all the brandy. "Whoa, baby. I better get out of here while I still can." She held on to the patio door and took in a deep breath. "And I gotta quit talking to myself." She giggled.

After catapulting herself back into the living room, she rang the concierge desk. Speaking tightly into the phone, she carefully enunciated her words. "William, this is Elizabeth Strong in 1201. Could you call me a cab, please? Thank you."

She walked carefully to the dining room, straight to the open cigarette drawer and grabbed up the case. It was empty. "Shit." She drained the contents of the brandy bottle into her glass, and went wobbling over to lean on the patio door jamb. Surveying the night skyline, she sipped from her snifter while she waited for William to call back.

An ominous feeling slowly moved through her like hot oil and gripped her stomach like a vice. Something wasn't right. Anxiety constricted her throat, and she began to feel the unnamed panic that paralyzed her when it struck. Suddenly, she didn't feel good doing this, going out to a bar alone. She weaved into the bedroom, yanked the Colt .22 out of the nightstand, and tucked it into her purse. Elizabeth kept it loaded all the time. There were never any small children in her apartment.

❖ ❖ ❖

Elizabeth finally secured a scarce place at the bar in Ransom's and clamped her feet onto the railing. She nursed a screwdriver while she inspected her surroundings, and quickly remembered why she hated to go to bars. It was the shiny, beady eyes, peering out curiously from the smoky darkness, reminding her of small rodents seeking food at dusk. Men. Watching. Always looking to steal something from her.

She shifted her concentration to the loose people dancing to the funky bass beat. The blinking dance floor looked to Elizabeth like an altar for weird mating rituals. It didn't take her long to figure out coming here was a big mistake.

A male voice startled her. "Would you like to dance?" A pudgy blond man, who had stuffed his potbelly into a pair of tight jeans anyway, faced Elizabeth with confidence.

"No. I don't dance." Elizabeth turned back to her drink, lit a smoke from her new pack, and willed him to go away.

"You don't have to be rude." The rejected romeo stood rooted to his spot.

"Look. I just want to be left alone to finish my drink, okay? Is that too much to ask?" She took a drag off her cigarette and blew the smoke in his face.

"Bitch." He turned and took that long, lonely walk back to his table, where his buddies were cracking up.

"Loser." Elizabeth drained her drink.

What in the hell made that smurf think that I would dance with him anyway? This was a bad idea. What the hell was I thinking?

Lurching off her bar stool, she aimed for the front door. She felt sick and dizzy. This was not good. She needed some fresh air. Fast.

After finally making her way outside, she quickly strayed off to the third row of cars somewhere at the rear of the nightclub. She threw up. After gagging a few times, she composed herself. Her shaky hand fished a tissue from her purse and wiped her mouth.

"Bad night, huh?"

She jumped at hearing the deep male voice. As much as dim light would allow, she followed the words with her eyes over to a dark-colored Camaro, a few cars away from where she was standing. She saw the outline of a man with his head tilted back, relaxing on the headrest. The glow of a cigarette made a trail in the air.

"Why don't you scare the shit out of me?" she blasted.

"I'm sorry. Why don't you come over here and sit down for a minute?"

"No thanks. You're not my type." She leaned on a car for support and held her head in her hands.

"Can't someone just be nice to you? I thought you might need a place to sit down until you felt better."

She tried to weigh the situation, but her head was clanging. "Well, just for a minute. I need to sit down out of the wind. I still feel kinda sick. And no funny business! I know Karate."

"Come on, give me a break! We'll just sit here in my car, like two adults, and just talk for a little while."

"All right." Elizabeth made her way to the car. As she got closer, she noticed there was a dent in the fender.

She tumbled into the Camaro and immediately smelled the sweet stench of marijuana. The vinyl passenger seat had a crack in it, and its jagged edges snagged her panty hose. *Damn.*

"You smoke?" He offered her a hit off his joint.

Elizabeth took a deep breath and looked at him defiantly. "No. I don't. How do you know I'm not a narc?"

"I figgered a narc probably wouldn't be barfing in a parking lot." He took a long draw off the joint and held in his breath.

"Oh. Well, no. I don't want any. And I would appreciate it if you would put it out while I'm sitting in here." She tilted her head out the open window.

He let the air out of his lungs. "God, you're uptight." He tapped the roach's fire out in the ashtray. "You need to learn how to relax."

"Mind your own business. I don't need you to tell me how I need to be, okay?" Propping her elbow in the open window, she rested her forehead on her hand.

"Sure, okay. What's your name anyways?" His dark eyes glittered in the low light.

"Does it matter?"

He let loose a short laugh. "Aren't we Miss Paranoid? No, it doesn't matter. I just thought it would make conversation a little easier."

She tried to lighten up a little. "Elizabeth. Elizabeth Jones. And yours?"

"Jesse. Jesse that's all. I don't do last names."

"Suits me. I lied about my last name anyway."

"I figgered."

His hand suddenly reached out for hers. Elizabeth snapped back, like her fingers had been branded with a hot iron.

"What the hell do you think you are doing? You said just talk. Men!"

"Whaddyamean? Men? Why do you say it that way?" Jesse was insolent. "You one of those ball busters? You hate men? You scream about equal rights and all that shit?"

"I gotta go. This was a bad idea." She shifted in her seat; her hand grabbed the door handle.

"Wait a minute! Stay! I'm sorry. Stay... please. " He smiled, and put his hand on her left arm, waiting for her to ease back into her seat.

She resumed her exit. "Look. Thanks for letting me sit in—"

Suddenly, Jesse rocketed his massive body over on top of her. His lips sucked at Elizabeth's mouth like a hungry carp. His breath had that two-day-old booze mixed with nicotine smell. It was the foul odor she had smelled a hundred times before on her father's breath.

Elizabeth turned her head and tried to push his chest away with all her strength. It barely budged him. "Stop it, you asshole!"

"Oh, c'mon! No more games, Lizzie. You know this is what you want, look at the way you're dressed. And you're the one that got in my car." His tongue sloshed around in her ear.

Even embroiled in anger and disgust, she was frightened. Obviously, she had underestimated the size and strength of this man. He was obviously a work-out freak, maybe even on steroids. She immediately changed her strategy. A red screen then a black one clicked in her brain.

"Hey, Jesse. Let's start over, okay? Let's act like people." Elizabeth spoke softly and melodically. "Let's talk first. We might even like each other, who knows? You're a good looking man. Just give it a little time, okay?" His grip loosened and consideration flashed across his face.

Reluctantly, Jesse settled back in his seat. He stared out the window for a few moments. "Okay. I'm sorry, Lizzie—you're right." He turned his gaze back to her. "Forgive me? It's just that you are so damn sexy."

In a flash, Elizabeth reached to her side, plunged her hand into her purse, pulled out the Colt and aimed it at Jesse's head. She squinted to make sure his forehead was in her sight.

"What the hell?" Jesse looked flabbergasted.

"Never, ever, call me Lizzie, you asshole." Elizabeth pulled the trigger and sat perfectly still as the loud crack sliced the air and slammed Jesse's head back. Growling, he pulled his head up for a moment to look at her and grope clumsily in the air. She shot again and hit him square in the forehead a second time. Jesse groaned and his body convulsed, then his head fell back against the headrest and was perfectly still.

The muted glow from the flood lights on the back wall of the club gave his face an eerie look. Two neat dark holes in his forehead poured out a dark liquid that cascaded over his nose and down his chin. Elizabeth gasped when he stopped moving.

Part of her was very alarmed. But there was another part of her that was morbidly fascinated. *He was here, now he's not. He was talking, now he's not. But he shouldn't have called me Lizzie. He really shouldn't have.*

She looked down at the gun, startled, and quickly stuffed it back into her purse. Elizabeth snapped her head back and forth to see if anyone outside was watching her.

There was one couple walking arm-in-arm, heading toward a row of cars parked in front of the club, but they seemed oblivious to her or what had happened. She nervously watched until she saw their car's headlights turn out of the driveway and up the street. Elizabeth breathed a sigh of relief.

Tissue in hand, she tried to remember what she had touched in the car. The handles and the dashboard, that's it. Looking down, she examined her garments and purse. Leather, there would be no clothing fibers. She had seen no one in the club she knew.

She stumbled out of the car. Home wasn't that far from here. The trip would clear her head. The whole evening felt surreal, and she couldn't remember ever feeling stranger—or more alive.

Her all black attire made her feel more a part of the night. She felt exhilarated and energized. She pulled off the high-heeled boots, yanked her panty hose off, and stuffed them into one shoe. Elizabeth tucked the boots under her right arm, and began to run hard, barefooted.

CHAPTER 7

Elizabeth was breathless by the time she reached the concrete bike path down by Cherry Creek. It was part of the route she usually ran every morning, but it wasn't the place for a woman alone at night, or anyone for that matter.

The gun gave her a sense of security. Hanging from her shoulder, the purse concealed her right hand clutching the cold steel, ready. It wasn't so hard, killing someone. She could do it again. Mostly drunks and homeless people roamed this corridor at night, and both could be unpredictable. She vowed not to be caught off guard.

Passing through a tunnel along the bike path, her nostrils flared as she sniffed a combination of urine, booze, and cigarette smoke in the air. It was a diverse microcosm down here after dark. Vagrants ventured out like vampires, as if the night were a friendlier place.

Elizabeth padded along softly, hypervigilant. Her perception was keen; the alcohol buzz had worn off quickly and the lingering ache in her head turned her ears into amplifiers. She felt as though she was both the hunter and the hunted, moving inconspicuously amidst precarious predators.

She heard the clank of a bottle hitting and bouncing on the cement somewhere in front of her, and she stopped—barely breathing. The darkness gave no clue as to the identity of its inhabitant for a few moments, and the wait seemed like an eternity.

"Is somebody there?" The gravelly voice had a note of loneliness, even fear to it.

Elizabeth sensed the man was not dangerous, just drunk, and resumed walking as quickly and quietly as she could.

"Hey! I know somebody's there. You got a drink? C'mon, buddy, I need a drink bad." The voice was trailing behind her now.

The tunnel ended and Elizabeth saw the outline of steps leading to the exit closest to her apartment building. There was a street light at the top of the stairs illuminating two human shapes sitting on a bench. She paused for a moment. It was probably just a couple of bums or teenagers anyway. There would just be more drifters at the next exit, and the streets were full of people dressed weirder than she was. No reason to think she would draw any attention.

Popping up at the top of the stairs, Elizabeth glanced toward the idle figures. Each woman had a grocery cart parked closely beside her, heaped with cans and sparse belongings.

"Hi lady! Remember me? T'anks for the money today. I bought me a grilled cheese at White Spot. It was real good."

The other Gypsy she shared the bench with bit into a Moon Pie, and chewed with her mouth open while she gaped at Elizabeth.

"Glad about the sandwich. See ya." She tried leaving when another stream of babble sprayed at her.

"You usually all dressed up fancy or in sweats when you run like a fool, but never like dat. You look like you been out walking east Colfax tonight! Ooooh, girl, where are your shoes?" The old gal and her companion howled with laughter.

"It's a free country," Elizabeth blurted out and silently cursed the hideous old bag woman and her damn weird red hat. The crazy hag couldn't possibly remember who she was and what she usually wore. Impatiently waiting on the curb for a break in the traffic so she could run across the street, Elizabeth heard the old lady call after her.

"Hey lady! Still havin' a bad day?"

CHAPTER 8

Elizabeth's eyelids popped open and she stared at the ceiling. Sighing, she turned her head to one side, and glanced at the oversized red numbers displayed on her alarm clock: 9:07. In her peripheral vision she saw black leather heaped up on a chair at the side of the bed. She turned back toward the ceiling. A sketchy recollection of last night's events came flooding back to her consciousness.

"Oh, my God," Elizabeth appealed toward the thumbprint swirls on her ceiling. Nerves whining like locusts and bile rising in her stomach, she tumbled out of bed, ran to the bathroom, and hovered over the toilet bowl. The dry heaves. There was nothing in her stomach. She couldn't remember the last time she ate.

Her whole body felt weak and drained. Sitting on the chilly marble floor, she put down the toilet seat cover, shut her eyes, and rested her cheek on the cool surface. It soothed her aching head.

The phone ringing startled her. She must have dozed off. Awkwardly pulling herself up, she headed towards the phone. The number displayed on the caller ID announced that it was her office.

Shit. I can't answer that. I have to think. Bowing over the answering machine, she anxiously waited for the caller to leave a message.

"Ms. Strong, this is Maggie. I'm calling to make sure everything is all right. It's ten o'clock and we haven't heard from you. You have a lunch meeting scheduled today with Mr. Salazar from Rolla Technowriters—"

Elizabeth snatched up the receiver. Her voice was very frail. "Hello, Maggie?"

"Ms. Strong?"

"Hi, Maggie. I intended to call in, but I fell back asleep. I have a really bad case of the flu. I'm thinking of calling the doctor. I can't come in today. Could you call Salazar and cancel for me, Maggie? He's just pitching a new software package for us to push. It's nothing urgent." Elizabeth rarely called in sick.

Maggie's tone was apologetic. "My goodness, of course I will. Do you need anything? A ride to the doctor? Chicken soup?"

Elizabeth was quick to discourage her. "Oh, no. Thanks, though. I just need to rest. I'll try to see you tomorrow, but it might be a couple of days. I'll call you. If you have any questions about anything, I'll be here."

"Oh, Ms. Strong, I wouldn't think of bothering you while you're sick. I'm sure the world up here can get along without you for a few days."

For once, Elizabeth was grateful for Maggie's supportive tone.

"Thanks, Maggie. I appreciate it."

"Oh, and Ms. Strong, I want to apologize for giving out your home number. I knew it was your father; he'd called here before. He sounded so serious. I thought I was helping."

"Oh, Maggie, don't think another thing about it. My father and I got everything straightened out. It was just a misunderstanding."

"Well, I will never give it out again."

"Thanks, Maggie, I appreciate the call. I better go. I'm not feeling so good."

"You take care, you hear? And don't worry for a second about what's going on up here. I'll handle everything. Please call me if you need anything from the store."

"Thanks, Maggie. Bye."

Elizabeth went back to bed and fell into a deep, dreamless sleep until five o'clock that afternoon.

CHAPTER 9

After taking a long, hot shower and managing to get some canned soup and saltines to stay down, Elizabeth started to feel human again. She couldn't even taste what she had eaten. It was cream of something, but she couldn't have cared less. She ate only for the strength it might give her.

Piecing together as much as she could remember of the night before, Jesse's lifeless face kept drifting through the scenes in her mind. Blood ran off his chin and dripped down onto his shirt, like rain off an eave. The staring surprised look in his eyes reminded Elizabeth of her Chatty Cathy doll from long ago.

Examining the black leather outfit carefully, she found specks of blood and gunk on it. Disgusted, she had stuffed everything, boots and all, into a heavy plastic trash bag and hid it in the guest bedroom closet until she could decide what to do with it. Her bed was carefully made and most everything in the apartment had been restored to its proper place. Order was important, and she had to get organized.

The morning newspaper was still outside Elizabeth's door. She brought it in and scanned it from cover to cover, looking for any information about the murder last night. Nothing. That relaxed her a little. There were no visible signs to remind her of last night. Order had been partially restored.

When she went to retrieve her cigarettes and lighter from her purse in the nightstand, she took the pistol out and peered at it, amazed. *God. I really killed somebody with this thing.* She turned the silvery gun over and over in her hand, studying it like a rare art piece. With her right hand she brought the pistol up, and carefully aimed at her reflection in the mirror.

"Boom." Elizabeth said quietly.

She replaced the gun in her purse, shut the drawer, and walked up to the dresser, where she stared deeply into her own eyes. Long black eyelashes veiled gold-colored flecks, shimmering inside chocolate brown pools, surrounding the two black holes that she searched into intently. "My God," she whispered to herself, "what have you done? Have you gone mad?"

Slowly the ends of her mouth turned up at the corners. Her eyes glistened and she laughed in a sinister tone. A dark voice from within chided her.

Mad, ha. You're not mad. That would be a luxury. The bastard deserved it! Forget it.

❖ ❖ ❖

Later that evening, she sat at her computer and read her e-mail. There was some important correspondence from clients that she had to answer, as well as mail from a few favorite net buddies. One more sick day off tomorrow, and she would do all that, plus figure out how to get rid of the clothes and the gun.

She logged on to the internet, accessing her favorite chat room to see who was there. None of the regulars she liked to talk to were in the TechChat room tonight. After making polite small talk for a few minutes with those who had greeted her, she logged out.

She grabbed her cigarettes and headed for the patio. As she leaned on the balcony rail smoking, her eyes panned across the street to the bench lit by the streetlight she had passed under last night. The same bag lady was sitting there again with her friend. Facing them was a scruffy old man, waving a tubular brown paper bag. He was obviously sharing an important opinion with his female audience.

Shit. That old woman. She saw me last night.

She felt a pang of icy terror spread down her spine as she remembered the words the crone had called out after her. Elizabeth watched the head that sported the red hat wag back and forth as the old woman talked. Smoking and thinking, she watched the trio for a long time. Elizabeth wondered what they were talking about, but more importantly, wondered what she should do about the odd little bag lady having seen her last night.

CHAPTER 10

The night seemed endless. Elizabeth alternated walking the floor, attempting to read, and playing computer solitaire. The instant the newspaper hit the mat outside her door the next morning, she planned to be there. There was so much to figure out she was overwhelmed, but she knew she had to gather more information before she could make a plan.

Her mind raced all night. Sometimes, the thoughts whirled around so fast that her body reacted with an anxiety attack. When the tension got real bad, all she could do was sit or lie down and wait for it to pass. When that didn't help, she just rocked and prayed. Several times, she couldn't catch her breath and she was sure her heart was going to stop.

When the attacks had first begun a few years ago, she had honestly thought she was dying one night, and called an ambulance. After spending eight hours under observation in Denver Health Medical Center's emergency room, she was sent home with instructions on how to use a paper bag when she hyperventilated, and a referral to a couple of therapists.

It was a humiliating night that Elizabeth had not discussed with anyone. She had not even turned an insurance claim into her company health plan for fear someone at the office might find out about it. She paid the entire hospital bill out of her own pocket.

The paper finally came. While the coffee was brewing, she spread the *Rocky Mountain News* out on the table and began scouring it for the article about the shooting. She scanned and flipped anxiously through the paper and finally, on the bottom of page six, she saw it.

Aurora Man Killed

Denver— An Aurora man was found dead in his car Tuesday morning with a sizable amount of drugs in the car's trunk. Thirty-six-year-old James "Jesse" Waller, apparently the victim of gunshot wounds to the head, was found in the parking lot of Ransom's, a Denver nightclub at 11412 W. Aldemere Street. A pound of marijuana and three pounds of street-ready cocaine were found in the trunk, leading Denver police to theorize the death was drug related.

Elizabeth sighed in relief. The police wouldn't be looking for her after all. She massaged her forehead with her fingertips, took in a deep breath and felt her heart flutter.

"Thank God." Elizabeth felt as if a huge, pressing weight had been lifted from her shoulders. Brimming with newfound energy, she thought about jogging, but if she planned to call in sick another day, she couldn't risk being seen out running. The office was too close.

Instead, she spent the day puttering around the apartment, cleaning things and doing odd jobs she rarely took the time to do—dusting tops of picture frames, washing her bedding, and cleaning the grout around the tiles of the shower. Several times she tried to make herself sit down to rest, but she would just bounce back up and start straightening and cleaning.

That evening, a calmer Elizabeth sat scrutinizing her computer monitor like it was the face of an old friend she hadn't seen in ages. She read an e-mail from her boss assigning her to Detroit again next Monday. Elizabeth welcomed the opportunity to get out of town and banish the nightmares of the last few days from her mind. She decided to take the blood-spattered leather clothing with her on the trip. She'd find a place to throw them away after she got there.

Elizabeth decided if the leather was cut up and put into several plastic sandwich bags, she could dump the pieces in different places around Detroit. It could never be traced in scraps over a thousand miles away even if they had been looking for her, which they weren't. The boots she would shine up and take to a Detroit Goodwill. She hadn't made her mind up about the gun yet.

Sitting in front of her computer, she logged into the TechChat room, and oscillated between cutting her two-day-old, expensive, black leather outfit into small pieces and tapping at her keyboard. It was oddly relaxing; like a form of woolgathering.

Chat rooms were great. She could enjoy companionship, yet be productive at the same time. Her nickname was "mouse." She didn't like to be conspicuous like some women were, flouncing around the chat rooms looking for men, with names like "Sweetie" or "Hot Lips."

One night she had been discussing broadband widths with Monroe, a regular in TechChat, when she received a private message from someone named Bambi telling her to back off, that this man was her online love relationship. Mouse told her she was pathetic and to get a life.

Anonymity. Fantasy. That's what the safety of a chat room gave her. The ability to express her true self. Living for the moment and being anyone she wanted to be, any gender and any age. It was fascinating stuff. Elizabeth had experienced more connection with some of her online friends than she ever had with people in real life.

Her favorite chat buddy was here tonight, his name was Chip. At least he said he was a man. Chip could be a six-hundred pound woman in Jersey for all she knew. It didn't matter to her.

Chip: Where you been, I missed ya. :-)

mouse: Workin' as usual...how you been?

Chip: Good. Did you watch that special on 20/20 tonight?

mouse: No. What was on?

Chip: They had a special on Germ and Bacterial Warfare. It is scary! Did you see where that guy was going to dump anthrax out of a plane over New York several months ago?

mouse: What's anthrax?

Chip:	It's this poison that is made into powder and you just blow it in the air. Just a little bit can kill hundreds of people.
mouse:	Man, what a nut! Where did he find something like that?
Chip:	He said on the internet!
mouse:	You are kidding!
Chip:	No, I'm not. He said you can get all kinds of poison and guns over the net. I saw him talking on TV.
mouse:	Wow, scary! Quit watching that stuff! It will make you neurotic. Well, I have to go. I have to be at work early in the morning. Take care!
Chip:	You, too! Check out my website, will you? I just finished doing a bunch of work on it.
mouse:	Will do. Bye!
Chip:	Bye!

Elizabeth decided to have a cigarette on the balcony before going to bed. This resurrected habit had to stop. After tomorrow, she would get back in her routine of running every morning. If she kept this up, even that weird bag lady would be able to outrun her. It seemed so ridiculous now, and she groaned at the thought of how scared she'd been of the grizzled woman's having seen her the other night. She had actually considered killing the old woman when Elizabeth had thought she could tie her to Jesse's murder. Now, she just felt silly and paranoid.

She went out on the patio to smoke and looked out over the city. It was cloudy. Short, intense thunderstorms had been sporadically passing through all day. The wind had blown out the smog, and the air smelled of clean rain.

Looking up at the stars, she wondered if Anyone was really up there. Elizabeth held a theory that the earth was probably Someone's plastic toy ant farm. Someone who could see all the tunnels at once to see who were the workers and who were the slackers. Someone who secretly knew all the ants' diligent work in the plastic tomb was a futile attempt at a natural civilization.

Watching the lights of an airplane overhead, she thought about what Chip had said about that guy dropping poison out of the sky.

Life was a crap shoot. You could be walking along, minding your own business and...wham! You're dead.

She walked back in, sat down at her computer, and typed *anthrax* into Net search. The screen returned tons of matches, and there was one entry that even had a phone number you could call to order the hazardous substance. *Wow.* She read about poisons and the availability of all sorts of weapons that a person could order through the mail. *Unbelievable.*

Elizabeth leaned back in her chair and stretched. Piles of cut black leather were lying on the desk in front of her. As she stared hard at the computer screen, a plan began to formulate in her head. A wry smile spread over her face. She looked at the internet screen filled with the anthrax information and pecked the print button. She picked up the phone and dialed her father's number. It was time for justice to be served.

CHAPTER 11

"Hello, my name's Chet and I'm an alcoholic."

"Hi, Chet." The voices in the room answered him warmly. The steel folding chairs filled with other Alcoholic Anonymous members were arranged in a circle. All eyes were upon him.

Chet looked down and pinched at the lip of his empty Styrofoam coffee cup, making indentions with his thumbnail. "I wondered if you guys can help me on Step Eight, the one about making amends for stuff you did to other people while you were drinking. Well, I called my daughter Lizzie the other day to apologize. She wouldn't even listen to me. She never even gave me a chance! I got to admit, she pushed my buttons." Chet grabbed at his ear. "I got real mad and said something stupid. I screwed it all up, and then she hung up on me. What do I do now? Can someone help me fix it?"

Darlene, the chairman of the meeting, spoke first. "Well, Chet, I'm sorry to hear about the bad luck you had with your daughter, but just because you've stopped drinking doesn't mean everyone is going to love you for it right away. Don't expect to be rewarded with praise and adoration for something you should have been doing all along. It's going to take some time for her to trust you again."

"Lizzie never did trust me. She never should've either. I've been a terrible person." Chet hung his head and held his face in his hands. "She'll never forgive me. I can't even forgive myself. I'll never forgive myself. I've done horrible things." Chet's voice started to tremble and his eyes began tearing up.

Darlene interrupted his litany of self-deprecation. "I'll tell you one thing for sure, Chet. If you don't forgive yourself, you ain't gonna stay sober anyhow. You got a sponsor yet?"

"No. I just been coming to meetings a couple times a week and listening. I'm trying to work the steps by myself." Chet accepted a tissue from the woman seated next to him and blew his nose.

"Well. First things first, Chet. Sounds like you need more than two meetings a week right now. And, you better get yourself a sponsor pronto. This program is simple, but it ain't easy. If you are going to stay sober, you gotta work the steps, and you're going to need some help. We help each other. Look for a man you trust in the program—a man, not a woman, with some sobriety. Ask a him, not a her, to be your sponsor. Then hang on to your ass, Chet, you are in for the ride of your life!"

Other members responded to Darlene's commentary with a knowing titter.

Darlene was quick to explain. "We're not laughing at you, Chet. We're laughing with you, because we've all been there." She flashed an honest smile. "It's easy to stop drinking, the hard part is to stay stopped. On the up side, kids can be very forgiving, and have a way of coming around after you prove you're gonna stay sober. They want to love you; it just takes some time. One day at a time, Chet. "

After the meeting, Chet was deluged with willing shoulders to cry on and caring ears to listen. Chet asked Bud, an AA veteran of twenty-nine years, to be his sponsor. Bud accepted. Chet cried until he could laugh, and felt much better by the time he left the meeting.

He arrived home to find the message light blinking on his answering machine. Grabbing his mail, he plopped down on the couch and sorted through it while his messages played back.

"Hello, Chet? This is Greta from the AA meeting at the church on Sunday nights. I wondered...well...if you might want to go out for coffee sometime. Give me a call. My number is 687-0243. Bye, hope to talk to you soon!"

Chet winced. Since he sobered up, he was getting attention from several women. Still six feet tall, he had a pretty good physique for a fifty-six-year-old man. He still had most of his hair and all of his teeth.

Any attention was more than he used to get, because now he actually went out in the evening once in a while. It's hard to meet women sitting drunk in front of a television set every night. Now, that was an exciting life. Chet had watched more first halves of movies than he cared to remember; he was usually passed out by the second half. But, he still wasn't ready for women yet; he didn't even feel comfortable with himself. He put the decision to call Greta back on hold as the next message came on.

"Hello, Chet. This is Ron. Just wanted to call you about that job tomorrow. Hope you're still available, I need the help. I'll pick you up at six in the morning. If I don't hear from you tonight, I'll figure that's okay."

Ron had a commercial painting business. Since Chet got sober, he kept him busy and in a little extra spending money by putting him on his overflow crew. Ron paid him in cash, that way it didn't interfere with the modest disability income Chet got from the government. He blew an eardrum while working on the flight line as an aircraft mechanic in the Air Force.

Chet stopped short and sat straight up, riveted, as he heard the voice of the next message.

"Hello, Chet, well, Dad, I mean. This is Elizabeth. I thought about what you said the other day, about you stopping drinking and all. If that's true, I guess we can talk. I'm sorry I hung up on you. I have to go out of town on business for a couple of weeks. I'll call you when I get back and we can make plans to get together and talk. Bye."

Chet was shocked. As soon as the message was over, he rewound the tape to hear his daughter's voice again. He played the message over and over, weeping with joy.

CHAPTER 12

Elizabeth dressed carefully the next morning while planning ways to restore order at work as well. While pulling on her nylons, she thought about Maggie. *You've been too hard on her. She's been nothing but helpful to you, Elizabeth, and all you do is keep her at arm's length.*

She decided to stop by the grocery store on the way to work and get her a plant. *Maggie likes plants, doesn't she? Maybe I'll take her to lunch.* She quickly dismissed that thought. No way could she spend an entire hour chatting inanely about nothing. A female friendship was taxing on her—or any relationship for that matter.

She did have a dog once, when she was nine, that she loved more than anything. Her father had gotten it for her in a weak moment after her mother died. She named it Beeper. It drove Chet crazy when she stood on the porch and called for her dog. Her father told her she sounded stupid, standing there wailing like a car horn. Of course, it drove her father crazy when she made any noise at all.

One night, she summoned Beeper and he didn't come home. Beep always came running to her when she called, knowing she would feed and pet him as soon as he got there. Elizabeth knew something was terribly wrong.

She had cried and begged Chet to go out and look for him. He refused. "You don't need no goddamned dog, anyway. I can't even afford to feed him. He eats like a damned pig. Relax. He's probably just off humpin' the neighbor dog. He'll come home after while. Go to bed."

Shortly after she finished brushing her teeth, she heard Chet's truck start up. From the bedroom window, a horrified child was watching her father take Beeper's lifeless form from the storage shed, throw it stiffly into the back of his pickup, and drive off.

❖ ❖ ❖

Elizabeth was working at her desk at the office, when Maggie lightly rapped at her door. She normally used the intercom.

"Come in." Elizabeth tried hard to sound cheerful.

Maggie walked in tentatively, holding her clasped hands in front of her. "Hi, Ms. Strong. How are you feeling today?"

"Much better, Maggie. Why don't you call me Elizabeth?"

"Oh, okay—Elizabeth. That feels funny to say that. I may have to work up to it." Maggie laughed cautiously.

"Anyway. What I came in here for was to thank you for the beautiful plant! I love it!" Maggie's voice became animated. "It's called an Ice Plant, did you know that? My grandmother used to grow it every year in her flower garden. It brings back some wonderful memories. Thanks again."

"I'm glad you like it, Maggie. I was thinking about us going out to lunch today. It would be my treat." Elizabeth couldn't believe those words came out of her own mouth. "Unless, of course, you have other plans. I know it's short notice."

Maggie's face lit up while she fumbled her acceptance. "No! No—I don't, Ms. Strong—oops, I mean, Elizabeth. That would be great. What's the special occasion?"

"I was such a bitch the other day. I'm sorry. I must have been coming down with that flu."

"Don't you think another thing about it," Maggie waved her right hand toward Elizabeth. "I'll see you soon." She scurried away with a lift in her step.

What the hell were you thinking, asking her to lunch?

Elizabeth nervously tapped her pencil on the desk and began to think of a way to cancel the lunch date, when the voice spoke. *Relax. You never know when she might come in handy. Suck it up. It's only an hour.*

Sarah St. Peter

After they had returned from Maggie's favorite Indian restaurant, Elizabeth was actually pleased with herself for making the effort. It was excruciating, but she had fawned over Maggie's pictures of her grandchildren and listened to far more information than she cared to about Maggie's financial situation. No wonder Maggie looked scared to death when she threatened to fire her the other day. At lunch, Elizabeth had apologized for frightening her and assured Maggie her job was secure. A look of blessed relief passed through Maggie's eyes.

CHAPTER 13

Elizabeth was glad to see Denver International Airport's tent-topped roofs, shaped to represent the Rocky Mountains, from her window seat on the incoming aircraft. Now, if she could only survive the baggage claim experience. A busy, stressful couple of weeks in Detroit was crowned with a tedious homecoming .

The passenger train that was supposed to take her from airport concourse B to the main terminal broke down somewhere in between, with her on it. Many weary and irritated passengers were stuck in the middle of a tunnel waiting for the wizard electrician to fix them up and send them on their way. The unreliability of the airport train was a local joke. In building the mega-airport, construction costs had gone several million dollars over budget, and there were still several quirks that refused to be worked out.

She sat quietly, staring out the windows at the many mining pickaxes embedded in the walls of the train's concrete corridor, obviously someone's idea of lending the decor a local flavor. Elizabeth visualized them as weapons, gouging the skin of the stalled railway system. As she waited, she tried to take her mind off her agitation by reviewing her trip.

The installation of the business software at Wright International had gone smoothly, but—as usual, employees fought against learning a new network system. One little red-headed butterball had announced, "I'd rather go to the gynecologist than learn this new thing on the computer!"

"Do you need to call the doctor's office first and see if they can get you in, Ma'am?" Elizabeth retorted to the friendly heckler, grateful to her for breaking the ice. The room lit up with laughter. Humor served as a valuable tool in getting people to listen.

The transition went much smoother when a trainer worked with employees for a week or two, until they got comfortable with the new software. Her impatient pupils wanted nothing to do with reading a training manual; they wanted her to show them what to do, and quickly, so they could get back to their regular routines.

Wright International was a huge new account, with excellent potential for future steady growth. Detroit was headquarters for many nationwide companies, and Elizabeth strived for rave reviews from the good old boys at Wright International. Rick Haynes, a bald and obnoxious vice presidential good old boy, had been ogling her for several days before he asked her out to dinner during a private after-hours training session he had requested. She had politely declined the inappropriate invitation, flashing the gold wedding band she always wore on out of town trips.

Haynes politely backed off, acting as if he hadn't noticed the ring before he asked. Elizabeth didn't have to mention the picture of him, an attractive woman about his age, and two beefy teenage boys on his desk. It was difficult for her to be tactful in these slimy situations, but necessary. A bruised, fragile male ego in management could easily blow a deal she had worked very hard on.

Leading training seminars for several departments each day, Elizabeth maintained an open-door policy, encouraging people to explore the new software system while she was there to help them with any problems they might encounter. One-on-one, she taught supervisors how to access and utilize help programs. After arming management with clear, simple training manuals, her phone numbers and e-mail address, they finally felt confident enough to take over after she left. At the end of two weeks, company users were wondering how they ever lived without the new network. That's when she knew it was okay to go home.

Mr. Mohr would be handing her a fat bonus envelope at the next Christmas party for bagging this sale; not to mention that her sales were up at least ten percent from last quarter. Financially, Elizabeth was doing better than she had ever dreamed. It was a far cry from where she came from, where she scrimped and scratched for every dime.

She had gotten rid of the blood-stained clothing in her treks around Detroit, a little bit at a time. She stayed at the Doubletree Hotel at the Renaissance Center, and each day as she made the journey over the skywalk to the business meetings in Cobo Hall, small sandwich bags full of leather disappeared into waste receptacles along the way. She would quickly reload her purse each time she returned to her suite, anxious to purge herself of the black leather albatross. If she ate at a fast food restaurant, she would throw away a small bag of leather strips as she dumped her tray on the way out. Bag after bag of the evidence disappeared into Detroit's disposal system.

It was easier to relieve herself of the boots. Elizabeth just drove to the rear of the Goodwill outlet on Grand River Avenue and threw them in the donation drop box. Soon, those very cool black leather boots would be hitting the pavement again. Elizabeth wondered who their next owner would be. Two weeks ago, she hadn't even owned them. Now, the boots had been present at a murder that she herself had committed, and their new occupant wouldn't have a clue.

On Sunday, she took the rental car over to Belle Isle. Its beautiful thousand-acre park along the Detroit River made it a popular tourist attraction. It had a small zoo and the nation's oldest freshwater public aquarium. A lot of the locals used the park for picnicking and fishing. She waited until dusk to go to the Belle Isle bridge. She would have gone at night, but it was much more dangerous than it was in Denver. There were people here who would set you on fire for your shoes.

Parking at the base of the bridge, Elizabeth got out of the car and walked up the sidewalk to the center of the structure. She reached in her oversized jacket pocket, and felt the outline of the pistol stuffed in a new athletic sock. She had spent at least an hour wiping it clean in her hotel room. Although she knew she was being compulsive, she still couldn't fight the urge to wipe off the weapon one more time.

Poised at the crest of the bridge, she waited for a noisy trio of garrulous teenagers to amble by behind her. Satisfied no one was watching, Elizabeth casually pulled the gun out of her pocket and quickly hid it in front of her, using her jacket as a curtain.

After taking one more glance around, she hung the sock over the railing and squeezed the gun out like toothpaste. It dropped from the top of the Belle Isle bridge straight into the dismal depths of the Detroit River. It made a quick plop and it was over. She watched the water run under the bridge and wondered how many other guns had made their way into the murky waters.

Darkness was falling fast; she hurried back to the car. She tossed the tube sock into a litter basket on the way, and drove back to the hotel. She took a long hot shower and scrubbed the last of the bad memories away. Order had been restored.

With a jolt, the airport passenger train began to move forward, and snapped Elizabeth out of her daydream. *Thank God. She sighed. All I want to do is go home.*

CHAPTER 14

Elizabeth was working at home, finishing up paperwork on the Wright account. In one efficient swoop, she rolled across the hardwood floor to the file cabinet and retrieved a folder. On the way back to her desk, she heard a loud snap under the wheel of her office chair. Looking down to see the cause of the noise, she saw that she had run over a computer disk and popped it open. She scooped up the pieces and placed it beneath her lit desk lamp.

Examining it carefully, she realized she had never seen the inside of a diskette before. It was so simple. She eyed the magnetic film and imagined thousands of tiny rows of information lying in her hand. Putting it back together loosely, she peered into the plastic square to see how much room there was in the corners, outside the film.

This disk had been an auxiliary backup of some client data. She would just make another copy. It must have fallen from the briefcase she had taken to Detroit. She backed up all her data daily on a Zip drive twice, and periodically made additional back-up disks.

Information was powerful and fleeting. It had to be treated properly. This was a point she repeatedly tried to drive home to her pupils at training seminars. She had little patience with people who cried the blues after losing all their data because of sheer laziness.

Putting the disk down beside her computer, she resumed working. Checking her calendar online, she saw that she had *call Chet* on her to do list for this week. The thought of it agitated her, but she had a mission. It was going to take a little time to accomplish, but it would get done.

This one's going to be for you, Mama. If it weren't for him, you'd be here with me today.

She remembered her mother fondly, but with some irritation that Mama could not have been stronger. Timid and shy, fragile Saundra had not known how to handle Chet's drinking and anger. Elizabeth remembered pleading with her mother so many times.

"Let's just leave, Mama. We can make it, you and me! C'mon Mama. Let's just go."

"Baby, I'm sorry. I just can't. I just haven't got it in me anymore. Please forgive me, baby." Saundra's eyes would look so sad, so haunted. The only time they twinkled a little was when Mama looked at her. Elizabeth remembered Mama biting her quivering lower lip and tenderly pushing long copperish bangs out of her eyes. "Please promise me, baby, that you will get your college education and get out of this hell hole. It's too late for me, but you, Elizabeth. You have a chance! You are really, really, smart. The teachers at your school told me so lots of times! Elizabeth, swear to me right now!"

"Okay, Mama. I promise." Elizabeth remembered her second-grade teacher, Ms. Hoag, asking her if she would take home a parental consent form so she could be tested for the gifted program at school.

Chet had told her to forget it. He claimed if public school was good enough for him, it should be good enough for her.

"Good. That's a good girl, Elizabeth. You are the only thing that makes your mama happy."

There were a few times when it seemed Mama was awfully close to leaving Chet. Once she and Mama had even packed a few things and took off while he was at work. Since Chet had the only car in the family, they had started walking to the bus station. They were going south to Texas somewhere to grandma's house to live.

Elizabeth had met her grandmother only one time when she was really little, so she didn't remember her. She hoped her grandma was nice. Mama said she was. Chet wouldn't let Mama call her mother even on special occasions. He said it cost too much.

Mama got three blocks away from the house that day and started sobbing uncontrollably. Neither female saying a word, they turned around and walked back home, with Elizabeth's tiny arms around her mother's waist, supporting her as best she could. The incident was never mentioned again.

Years of cowering in fear and crying came to a head when Elizabeth had come home from school one day and found her mother in the garage, hanging from a pipe at the end of a rope.

After frowning and staring at her mother for a little while, Elizabeth had gone quietly to the kitchen, and hung up her art on the refrigerator with an angel magnet. In her third grade class this afternoon, for her mother, she had made a watercolor picture of a fish dangling from a fishing pole. There was an envelope on the refrigerator, stuck behind a banana magnet. Elizabeth wondered why Mama hadn't used the angel magnet instead. Her name was written on the front, in her mama's handwriting. She took the letter from the refrigerator, stuck the envelope in a library book, and sat down in her usual chair at the kitchen table.

Elizabeth stared at the door that led into the garage, and not moving a muscle, waited for her father to get home. Even when she had to pee real bad, she went right in the chair as she sat motionless, in spite of knowing how mad it would make her father.

Her father had not come home until late that night, and when Chet did show up, he was dead drunk. Elizabeth had been sitting in the dark for a long time, flinching at every strange sound. Elizabeth kept watching for her mother's ghost to come and tell her everything was going to be all right.

Chet had staggered in the house and gone straight to bed and passed out. He did not hear Elizabeth screaming for his help. When he came lumbering out to the kitchen the next morning for coffee, she still sat at the table, paralyzed in her own urine. By then, all she could do was point, at the door that led to the garage.

CHAPTER 15

The wispy blonde called out an order of two eggs, sunny side up, with hash browns, extra crispy, to the short order cook at Otto's, a popular breakfast and lunch place in Derby, a small Kansas town south of Wichita.

"Hey, gorgeous. Any chance of getting a cup of coffee around here?" Chet teased her.

Saundra blushed. Chet had been coming in every morning to sit at the counter and flirt with her for about two weeks now. She had developed a huge crush on the trim, good looking airman from McConnell Air Force Base.

Chet was so charming in those days, so handsome. He sported bright brown eyes framed in long black eyelashes and a quick smile edging white, straight teeth. A spartan haircut tamed thick, chestnut hair, but didn't diminish his good looks. If anything, the short hair served to make his handsome face look even more sculptured. Saundra couldn't stop staring at his full, smooth lips.

While she was pouring him a refill of coffee that morning, he touched her hand. An electric spark crackled through her arm and grabbed her lungs, squeezing out all the oxygen. As Saundra listened to him speak to her softly, she trembled inside.

"Saundra, I have been wanting to ask you out for a long time now, but I was afraid you wouldn't go. Would you? If I asked you to go out, I mean?" Chet was using his convincing little boy look on her that he had used to get free pie a few times. He usually left her a big tip anyway, whether he got free pie or not.

"Well, I don't know, Airman, maybe you should ask me sometime and find out." Saundra shyly grinned at Chet and felt the heat exchange between them.

He always wore fatigues—with a name tape that said *Strong* over the pocket. She had teased him that she thought Air Force uniforms were blue, with white gloves and hat. He told her he had a real man's job, where he had to get dirty, a missile mechanic or something. Saundra still longed to see him in his dress blues, imagining he would look like a handsome prince.

He had dropped down to his knees, and in front of God and everybody in that diner, asked her to go to a movie with him that evening. Some of the greasy spoon regulars had actually clapped and cheered Chet on. Saundra couldn't remember ever being so embarrassed. It was the first time a man she liked had lavished so much attention on her.

She had been working two jobs trying to make enough money to finish her last year of college at Wichita State and hadn't had any time to think about meeting men. Chet just showed up one day, like it was meant to be. Maybe even destiny.

Chet had swept Saundra off her feet. They fell in love right away. She had never been all the way with a man before Chet and it made him very possessive of her. He was after her for sex all the time. At first she was flattered, but eventually he became so rough while making love, she found it neither romantic nor fulfilling.

Saundra began to dread it when he came near her with that look in his eyes. The more she rebuffed him, the more it seemed to turn him on. Saundra began thinking about breaking up with Chet.

Three months after they had been dating, Saundra found out she was pregnant. She considered having it "taken care of" and not tell Chet about it. The more she thought about it, the more she realized she could never do away with her baby, even if she had been able to gather up the money.

Considering her options, she knew that as a student, she could never afford to have a child and still go to school. Saundra considered adopting the child out to a good family so they both might have a chance. She discussed this possibility with Chet.

Chet would not hear of adoption. He was thrilled about the baby, and pleaded convincingly. "Marry me, Saundra. I'm ready for a family. I love you so much. I'm up for another stripe, and I applied for a transfer to Colorado Springs. It's really beautiful out there, Sandy. I can support you while you go to school and finish your degree. We can make it work, I know we can." Chet had crushed her tightly to him, and whispered softly in her ear. "Be my wife and the mother of my babies, Saundra. I love you so much."

Saundra felt glad for the baby that he was so receptive to the idea of fatherhood, but she had an uneasy feeling about the whole thing. She tried hard to love him, but her intuition nagged her that Chet's words didn't ring true. Saundra felt powerless to stop the impending chain of events.

The wedding was a forgettable ceremony in front of a justice of the peace. Her worried mother, Gladys, and a couple of Chet's Air Force buddies made up the audience. Shortly after the wedding, Chet received orders to Peterson Field in Colorado Springs. Saundra fell in love with the mountains the moment she laid eyes on them. In six months, Elizabeth was born.

After the novelty of having a new home, new wife, and baby wore off, Chet began drinking more often and not coming home from work until the wee hours of the morning. He was of little help to her or the baby when he was at home.

Saundra never returned to college. When she brought the subject up to Chet, he would get angry and accuse her of just wanting to be around other men. He emphatically and repeatedly warned her that if he ever caught her with another man, he would kill them both. Chet would usually use the opportunity to stomp out of the house and go get drunk. It was as good of an excuse as any, and she was glad when he was gone.

After a few years of arguing about it off and on, Saundra gave up on finishing her education and settled into a mostly fearful existence of raising Elizabeth and trying to keep peace in the house for her baby's sake. She put all her energy and love into the precocious little girl, and tried the best she could, to keep herself and her child out of Chet's way. It didn't always work. Over time, there were several calls to the police, which were necessary, but only served to make Chet more violent the next round.

One spring afternoon of almost perfect weather, Saundra took five-year-old Elizabeth to a small community park near the house. Saundra had made a picnic lunch of little sandwiches made with cocktail bread filled with bologna and cheese, and for dessert, chocolate pudding. The combination was Elizabeth's favorite meal. They were having a fine time playing dolls on a handmade patchwork quilt sent by Saundra's mother, spread out under a giant cottonwood tree.

"Mama, here. You be the man now." Elizabeth thrust the Ken doll into Saundra's hand.

"Okay." Saundra cleared her throat and walked Ken awkwardly towards Elizabeth's Barbie.

"Hello, miss, what's your name?" Saundra's feigned male voice made Elizabeth giggle.

"Elizabeth." The child held the doll in upright anticipation.

"How do you do?" Saundra extended Ken's hand to shake hands with Barbie.

"No, Mommy, you're not doing it right!" Elizabeth put her Barbie down on the blanket and shrugged her shoulders in disappointment.

"Yes, I am!" Saundra frowned. "I asked you your name, and now I'm waiting to shake your hand hello. What's wrong?"

"You love me, don't you Mama?" Elizabeth gave her mother her best cute face.

"More than anything, baby, why do you ask?" Saundra put down the Ken doll in front of her and leaned in to Elizabeth.

"Well, Mommy, if you love me, you're supposed to do this." Elizabeth giggled and grabbed the Ken doll, adjusting Ken's arm to make his hard plastic hand rub Barbie's breasts.

"What are you doing? What do you know about all that?" Saundra was frightfully alarmed, and jerked the Ken doll out of Elizabeth's hand and held it out of her reach.

"That's what Daddy does to me sometimes. And other stuff. He told me that's what people do who love each other." Elizabeth did not look at her mother.

Saundra felt her breathing stop for a moment and she went limp, feeling helpless. Trying not to act too shocked in front of Elizabeth until she could figure out what to do, she ended up shivering like she was freezing. How could she end up with a man who was capable of taking advantage of an innocent child? Saundra felt she must have a deep character flaw to have chosen a man like this.

After that day in the park with her daughter, Saundra was never the same. Often isolating herself in her bedroom, she wouldn't eat for long periods of time. Saundra had not protected her child from danger, and felt like a total failure as a human being. She had let a man who she didn't even particularly like dictate her entire life and wound the soul of her beautiful little daughter. Saundra began to want to die.

Being a thin woman to begin with, it didn't take much fasting before Saundra looked emaciated. Elizabeth was always after her to eat something. *I didn't protect her and now she wants to take care of me. Oh, my God, the love and trust of little children.* There were times at night, as she lay crying in an empty bed, Saundra truly believed she could hear her own heart breaking.

The days ticked by and the seasons passed and Elizabeth grew. Saundra confronted, Chet denied. The vicious cycle of fights, beatings, and remorseful make-ups continued.

One winter day, Saundra woke up and intuitively knew it was over for her. It was after ten in the morning, and she knew that Chet had already left for work, and Elizabeth to school. She had plenty of time to get ready.

As Saundra sat drinking a cup of coffee, she stared out the kitchen window admiring the Rockies, and thought of a western movie she had seen once. The Indian chief had come out of his tepee, and after studying the majestic mountains had proclaimed, "Yes, Great Spirit, it is a good day to die."

Saundra couldn't go on like this one more day. It was for real this time; she felt it down to her core. She had threatened suicide to Chet hundreds of times, just to shut him up. Even that didn't work any more. She wouldn't leave him a note and have the last laugh.

I hope it makes him drink himself to death and I wish I could be here to see it.

Elizabeth. Sweet, smart little Elizabeth. This was the hard part.

She's a tough kid, she'll be okay. Saundra knew she was lying to herself, but she just could not go on, not even for Elizabeth. She was just too weary. Her hopeful spirit, which at one time had told her there would be a way out someday, was already dead.

Saundra brought out the nice manila linen stationery she had purchased at the office supply store the week before, along with a matching envelope, and put both on the old gray formica kitchen table top. She sat for a moment, winding the music box her mother had given her when she was a girl, set it beside a white pillar candle, and gingerly opened the lid.

Inside the little maple theater was a tiny ballerina on mirrored glass, dancing to the song, *The Impossible Dream.* Saundra had memorized the words years ago, painstakingly copying the lyrics after listening to her mother's Andy Williams album over and over .

Saundra softly sang along with the tinkling accompaniment, while watching the miniature dancing figure spasmodically dance and twirl. *To dream the impossible dream...To fight the unbeatable foe...To bear with unbearable sorrow...To run, where the brave dare not go...* Saundra smiled as she sang, feeling fully in control of her life for the first time in many years.

After lighting the candle, she sat for a bit and absently stared at the flame. Saundra pinched at the fire, feeling the heat lap at her fingertips. She dipped her right index finger into the hot wax that had started to pool around the wick. It burned for a moment, then left a slick brittle shell on her skin that she cracked and peeled away.

She decided to take a shower and get dressed before writing the letter to Elizabeth. It would be the most important thing she had ever written and she wanted to do it properly. In a delicate voice, Saundra kept singing as she padded down the hall to the bathroom. *...And I know if I'll only be true to this glorious quest...That my heart will lie peaceful and calm when I'm laid to rest.*

Later, after putting on full makeup, doing her hair, and dressing in her best pink linen dress, she sat down to say goodbye to her daughter.

March 15, 1975

Dear Elizabeth—

I know you are very young now, my sweet, but maybe someday you will understand why I have to write this letter to you.

First of all, I hope you like your name. I chose it myself. My mother said she almost named me Elizabeth, but chose Saundra instead because of an aunt she was particularly fond of. I guess she did that because Elizabeth was to be your name. It fits you better.

Sarah St. Peter

I had planned my life to turn out much differently, my love. Once, I was bright and shiny like you and wanted to go out and grab the world by the tail. No one told me about the vultures that would be out there waiting for me once I got there. The world is a fierce taskmaster, darling, and you must prepare for it.

Trust no one until you are absolutely sure of their character,especially men. I am so very sorry I could not protect you from your father. He swore that if I left him, he would track us down and kill us both.I could not take that risk with your life, darling. I don't know if I did the right thing or not, but please know it haunted every breath of my existence.

I would love to tell you, my child, that the world is yours for the asking. It can be yours, Elizabeth, but you will have to do more than ask. You will have to get a college education and be twice as good at your job to compete in a man's world. You can do it, baby. You have always been smarter and stronger than me.

I would also like to be able to promise you that true love exists and that you will find it. I never found true love, Darling, but if it does exist, I wish it for you. Just never become too dependent on a man. Always have your own money, and always leave yourself a way out.

I know you will probably be mad at me for what I am about to do. I am very sorry, and beg your forgiveness, Elizabeth. I know I am weak, and please believe me when I say I see no other way out. I would never leave you unless I absolutely had to, you know that.

I love you more than I ever thought possible. You are the best thing that ever happened to me. Take care of yourself and know that I will always watch over you from heaven. Whenever you look at the stars, for the rest of your life, remember I am there, smiling back at you.

I love you,
Mama

P.S. I want you to have this music box. My mother gave it to me when I was a little girl, and it has comforted me many times. I know it's not much, but it meant a lot to me.

Saundra felt the Valium she had taken earlier kick in, making her feel free, almost happy. She wished she had enough pills left to do it that way, but there were only the two left that she took, and there were no refills available. They had been prescribed during a fairly recent trip to the emergency room, when Chet had dislocated her shoulder.

Folding the letter up and placing it carefully in the envelope, she licked the seal. She wrote the word *Elizabeth* on the front in her most loving hand, glad that she had saved that word for last. Rewinding the music box, Saundra rose from the table.

Hugging the letter to her breast, she closed her eyes and whispered a prayer of protection for her daughter. After giving it a kiss, she hung the envelope on the refrigerator under a magnet.

Saundra tenderly ran her fingers over a few of Elizabeth's drawings and paintings hanging on the refrigerator, as if she could absorb some of her daughter's energy through the textures. Saundra smiled, proud of how creative Elizabeth was. Looking back over the room, she saw signs of her beautiful daughter everywhere; her juice glass and cereal bowl in the sink, a blue sweater thrown on the back of a kitchen chair, a pink barrette lying open on the kitchen counter by the phone.

Under the television cart in the living room, hanging out of a shoe box, was a naked Barbie and Ken. They looked disheveled, thrown in with some toy cars and loose crayons. Saundra crossed the room and grabbed Ken from the box and took the plastic man back with her.

Taking a deep breath, she grasped the doorknob leading to the garage from the kitchen, and determinedly pulled it open. Saundra stepped softly into the garage, and carefully closed the door behind her.

CHAPTER 16

Elizabeth peered hard through dark sunglasses as she haphazardly jotted fake answers to the obligatory application questions for a mail drop box in the east part of town. Hard cash was the only proof of identification needed in this neighborhood anyway. It wasn't like they were going to check her references. She just needed to rent a box for as long as it took the anthrax to be mailed from her contact on the internet.

She had procured the addresses for three of these places from the classified ads, and this little grimy hole in the wall was the classiest of the lot. From the counter, she looked through the dingy storefront window to the dirty sidewalk, and thought of an alias to use.

I'll be Ginny Forester. It should at least be someone dear daddy knows. She remembered Ginny Forester, the woman Chet often had in the house while Mama was working as a teacher's aide in Elizabeth's kindergarten class. It was the only job Chet had ever permitted Saundra to have.

She remembered coming home one afternoon, many years ago with Mama, the scene still crystal clear in her mind. The two of them were carrying sacks of groceries and laughing while Mama tried to get the front door open without spilling anything. Elizabeth loved it when her mother laughed. Mama was so pretty when she smiled, but she didn't do it nearly often enough. Saundra started into the house, then she froze.

"Back up, Elizabeth. We're not going in there right now."

Before Mama nudged her back onto the porch, Elizabeth saw through Mama's arms to the couch. Daddy was naked and lying on top of a woman, pushing and grunting. When the door opened, he looked up and stopped for a moment. Then he looked straight into Mama's eyes and rammed his body into the woman over and over while his eyes bored into Mama's.

"She's giving me what you don't want to give me anymore, Saundra. And it's good." Chet thrust a few times extra hard. "Come on in here and join us, why don't ya?" His invitation was slurred, his eyes glassy.

Elizabeth had looked past the liquor bottles and glasses that were on the coffee table, and stared at the strange woman. She must have been passed out or something, because her face was turned to the back of the couch and she wasn't moving. Elizabeth wanted to bust in there and march over to the stupid woman, pull her face up by her stupid hair, and look at her stupid face. She wanted to see this woman who would come into their house when Mama wasn't home and be naked on the couch where she sat to watch television. She could never sit there again.

The seedy drop box attendant broke into her trance. "That'll be fifty bucks up front, thirty bucks a month, Miss. I only take cash, unless of course you have a better idea." He leered at her and smiled through cracked lips; a soggy, chewed cigar protruded from the corner of his mouth.

"Cash is fine. You are discreet. I mean my mail is confidential, isn't it?" She threw a hundred dollar bill on the counter.

"I got the worst memory in the world when anybody comes around asking questions about my clients. My age, you know. May even be gettin' Alzheimer's." His fat right eye winked at her. It looked like a tiny fist. "You know, if it's sexual enhancements you're looking for...you know...I mean, if that's why you're getting a drop box...I got some stuff you might want to see." The man studied her as he mouthed the half-smoked stogy. It wasn't lit, but the man still squinted as if his eyes were trained for smoke screening. "I got a little bit of everything back here." He smoothed his already slick hair and touched the tiny ponytail as if to check to make sure it was still there.

"No, thank you," Elizabeth said in her iciest voice.

"Okay. But I can get stuff for you a lot cheaper than those rip off companies you send off to."

"Please. My change." She held out her hand.

The grubby hand delivered a wilted twenty. "You know, I can develop a *really* bad memory for a twenty dollar tip."

"Thief." Elizabeth waved him the money rather than having to touch the grimy bill. She thought he looked like Jabba the Hutt from the *Star Wars* movie.

"Thank you. This confirms that I never saw you before in my life." He produced a gravelly laugh. "Rent's due the first of the month. Five dollar late charge after the fifth. Pleasure doing business with you, Ma'am."

Elizabeth rolled her eyes and smiled faintly. Despite the sleazy surroundings, she was strangely drawn to the fat man behind the counter. She stepped out into the street and was met with a man carrying an open Bible, pacing back and forth in front of the store. A raggedy man.

"Have you been saved, woman? The smoldering of sin is in your eyes. Be not deceived; God is not mocked; for whatever a man soweth, that shall he reap. Ephesians 6:7." His deep tone was accusatory and his eyes, judgmental.

Elizabeth felt anger envelope her, and she said through clenched teeth: "I tried your religion, Mister. It didn't work. Let he that is without sin among you, let him cast the first stone. John 10:7. Now, fuck off."

She turned and set a rapid pace walking back to the parking lot to get her car. She looked up at the combination XXX-rated motel and adult video store that was adjacent to the parking lot. Glancing up at a third floor window, she saw that the curtains were wide open. A bare old Hispanic man, crowned with a black cowboy hat, was masturbating full force while he watched Elizabeth through the glass.

"Jesus! It's like *Night of the Living Dead* around here. Creepy bastards," she snarled as she jerked open her car door and jumped in the driver's seat. After hurriedly starting the car, she popped it in reverse and floored it, changing gears while she was still backing up. Stomping the gas pedal again, she laid rubber as she screeched out of the parking lot, narrowly missing a unhelmeted bike rider with a red bandana tied around his neck. If he hadn't been wearing the flashy necktie, she might not have seen him in time to swerve.

Breathe. Slow down, Elizabeth. Everything's going to be all right.

Elizabeth hurried home.

CHAPTER 17

"Hello, Dad?" She nearly choked on the word. It had taken a thumbnail chewing Elizabeth nearly an hour of picking up and hanging up the phone to actually get Chet's number fully dialed.

"Hi, Honey! Glad you called. How was your business trip?" Chet's voice was enthusiastic.

Elizabeth cringed at the endearment and wondered why he couldn't just call her by her name. "Fine. Productive. I was wondering if you were busy Saturday."

"No, I'm free. What do you have in mind?"

She grinned wryly at the question. "I thought we could have lunch."

"Sure!" Chet sounded excited. "That would be great! Do you want to come here, or do you want me to come into Denver?"

Chet lived in Elk Run, a small town about fifty miles southeast of Denver, in the same house Saundra and Chet had migrated to when Elizabeth was very young. Chet had been stationed at Colorado Springs during his last hitch in the Air Force, and had been offered a job as an automobile mechanic in the tiny town after he was discharged.

"I'll come there. I want to get my car out on the road anyway. I feel like a drive. I'll pick you up about noon."

"Can you spend the day, Liz—er, Elizabeth?"

"Let's just plan on lunch this time, okay?" The idea of spending any time with him made her cringe, but she thought about her mission. About Mama.

"Sure, honey. I'll see you then. And, Elizabeth?"

"Yes?" She sincerely hoped she wasn't going to have to dodge a bunch of mush.

"Thanks for calling. Really."

"Sure." She threw down the phone and lunged for a cigarette.

❖ ❖ ❖

Saturday morning, Elizabeth had the top off the Mercedes as she zoomed eastbound on I-70, enjoying the wind blowing through her hair. She enjoyed driving this car. It had been some time since she had the car out on the open road, and made a mental note to schedule a road trip soon. The radar detector was mounted on the windshield, its red lights blinking in readiness.

Groaning at the upcoming road construction, she wished she could weave in and out of the orange cones that barred her from the fast lane. She felt her agitation build while following a big bulky, ultra slow, recreational vehicle that had bumper stickers all over the back, announcing the states its owners had visited. It reminded Elizabeth of the stickers she used to get on her papers at school. Get an A, get a sticker, see a state, get a sticker.

Attempting to fight boredom and impatience, she turned up the CD player full blast. She banged her palm on the steering wheel to the beat of Joe Cocker's, *My Love is Alive*. Once the restrictions were removed on the road, she zipped over to the fast lane and opened it up, rapidly taking the vehicle up to over ninety miles per hour. Elizabeth was pressed back into her seat by the rush of power as she accelerated, like she was piloting a plane cleared for takeoff.

As soon as she crested a hill, she saw that a highway patrolman had a red Camaro pulled over at the side of the road. Braking quickly, the Mercedes took her back down to the legal speed limit of seventy-five. She punched the steering wheel in protest. There always seemed to be obstacles in her way when she wanted to fly.

Elizabeth arrived at her father's house about a half hour late, as she had planned. Make him sweat a little bit. Make him wonder whether she was going to show up or not. The front door was open, obviously anticipating her arrival. Elizabeth pulled up in the driveway and honked.

Glancing over at the dilapidated wooden storage shed, she sighed, fondly remembering Beeper, her dog. She wondered where his bones were; she would like to give him a proper burial someday. She honked the horn again for Chet, a little longer than necessary.

Chet appeared at the front door, carrying a beige jacket. He leaned out of the open screen door and shouted to Elizabeth. "Want to come in for a minute?" He held the door open with his hand.

"No thanks," she called back. "Let's just go!"

She examined Chet with microscopic thoroughness as he walked towards the car. It had been about eight years since she had last seen him, when he showed up uninvited and drunk to her college graduation from the Master's program at the University of Colorado where she received her advanced degree in Business with honors. When she walked across the stage, Chet whooped and hollered, then fell face down in the aisle. Campus security had to remove him from the auditorium while he resisted, wriggling and yelling obscenities at the security guards the entire way.

Afterwards, they had a huge argument over Chet's big scene, and had not spoken since. He looked basically the same, just older. The same cocky gait and the same sideways smile. She felt her stomach threaten revenge for exposing it to this.

"Wow! This is a fancy car." Chet settled in and buckled his seat belt. "Bet it goes pretty fast, huh?" He smoothed his hand over the dashboard.

She seethed inside as she watched his coarse fingers fondle her beloved car. *Breathe. Calm down. Everything is going to be all right. Just get this done.*

"Where is a good place to eat around here these days? Is *Bill's Place* still open? " She tried to sound as friendly as she could.

"Nah. He went out of business years ago. Finally drank himself to death. How about we drive over to Franktown and go to Belmont's? They have good food there. Is that okay?"

"Sure." Elizabeth peeled out of the driveway, throwing gravel out of the driveway and into the street, her father clutching the sides of the passenger seat.

The restaurant was typical of the area. Casual, with an ambience of home-cooked friendliness. Each table had a well-worn but bright white linen tablecloth and silverware bundled up in matching cloth napkins. Mostly locals haunted the place, and a few people said hello to Chet as they walked through the restaurant. It was apparent that he was comfortable here, on his own turf.

"So. How have you been?" Chet asked Elizabeth with seemingly authentic interest.

She pressed her lips together and nodded her head up and down. "Fine. Good. Busy." Her eyes wandered up to a shiny ceramic rooster hanging on the wall.

Chet leaned in and grinned at her, clasping his hands in front of him on the table. "Any lucky guy yet? Any chance I will get some grandchildren someday?

She felt like leaping over the table and scratching his eyes out.

"No and no. I don't believe in marriage or having children. The world is too crazy."

Chet looked disappointed as an awkward silence followed. They both engrossed themselves in the laminated papers that served as menus, and seemed glad when the frumpy waitress appeared. Perched over a huge left breast that sagged down atop the waistband of her apron, was a name tag that read Ann.

"Hi Chet, how ya doin'? Ready to order? Special of the day is fried catfish, salad, and two side orders. Side choices are mashed potatoes, French fries, or corn. You get a dinner salad, bread, and tea or coffee with the meal. It's real good; the fish is fresh. I had some for lunch myself." Ann stood poised with the little light green order book lifted in her left hand and a pen in her right.

"That sounds good to me, Ann. Mashed potatoes and corn. French dressing on the salad. I'll have coffee, and I'll need some cream." Chet smiled. "How about you, Elizabeth?"

"Chef salad, please. Ranch on the side. Low-fat if you have it. Iced tea. Thanks."

They were again left with each other when the waitress sauntered off with their order.

"That all you eat? Salads? No wonder you're so skinny." Chet smiled.

"I like salads." She stared out the window and looked wistfully at her car. She wished she could mentally will it to pick her up and carry her far far away from here, like a magic carpet.

"Liz—Elizabeth. I wanted to talk to you about something." He nervously scratched his ear. "I'm in Alcoholics Anonymous now, trying trying to clean up my life. I wanted to tell you how deeply sorry I am for all the hell I put you through. And your mother, too."

There it was. A menagerie of flowery words followed, but Elizabeth couldn't hear them. Ribbons of meaningless drivel spewed out from Chet's guilty mouth that was immediately supposed to make everything all right. A lifetime of pain was to be corrected just because he decided to say something nice for a change. She felt her throat constrict and her jaws clench. The red screen flashed into her mind .

Remember why you're here, Elizabeth. For Mama. You can do this. Everything will be all right. Everything will be all right. Elizabeth wished it was night so she could look up at the stars right now and feel Mama smiling at her.

"Elizabeth. Are you all right?" Chet looked at her inquisitively.

"Huh? Oh, yeah. Sure. Just a little distracted is all." She took a sip of her iced tea. "I thought you would never quit drinking."

"Me either! It's a miracle. I feel better than I have in years. I just had a year anniversary away from the sauce last month." Chet beamed, obviously proud of his accomplishment.

"That's great. Really great." She faked enthusiasm as best she could. "Lunch will be my treat then. To celebrate." She lifted her glass to offer a toast.

"To you, Elizabeth. To us. To being a family again." Chet smiled as if he had won the lottery.

Their glasses clinked. Elizabeth excused herself to go to the ladies room to wash her hands. Once in the privacy of a stall, she battled a bout of anxiety and revulsion. Staring at her thumbnail, she breathed deeply and heard her mother's voice.

You can do this, Elizabeth. You were always smarter and stronger than me.

Elizabeth sat with her eyes closed, then, finally stood up, shut her eyes again, and breathed in deeply. Stepping up to the sink, she washed her shaky hands in cold water and moistened a paper towel to press on her forehead. After a few minutes, most of the feelings of distress had passed. The revulsion remained, but it only served to fuel her resolve. *Let's go get that sonofabitch,* she silently encouraged her reflection in the lavatory mirror. She felt powerful again.

CHAPTER 18

Elizabeth took two rolls of quarters into the phone booth located by a convenience store in Aurora, a Denver suburb on the east side. Not knowing a booth would be this difficult to find, she had driven around a long time before finding one. She couldn't risk anyone overhearing this conversation.

Her hand shielded with a clean tissue, she reluctantly picked up the disgusting phone receiver with her thumb and forefinger and held it near her right ear and a few inches from her mouth. A layer of scum coated the inside of the booth. It was hard to imagine the mouths that had exhaled into this mouthpiece.

Mama's voice played in her head, *Don't touch that dirty thing, Elizabeth, you don't know where it's been!* She swore she could almost feel the germs trying to jump up into her mouth. Dialing the phone number she had gotten off the internet to order the anthrax, she waited for it to ring. The number was disconnected.

"Damn!" She redialed to make sure she had the number right. The "I'm sorry, but the number you have reached is not in service," recording rejected her again. *Shit.*

Grabbing her keys from her jacket pocket, she headed back to the car. This was not something she had anticipated. While sitting in the Mercedes contemplating her options, her mind flashed back to Zipper, the guy who ran the mail drop place. What had he meant when he said, *"I've got a little bit of everything back here?"*

First things first. Elizabeth knew he could probably help get her a gun, but didn't know about the the anthrax. She supposed she was going to have to build a little rapport with him before she could spring that one on him. What a disgusting thought. She had one more idea she would try before asking Zipper for the big item on her shopping list.

❖ ❖ ❖

The next day Elizabeth got in touch with a used car rental service she had found listed in the Yellow Pages. "Tell me please, what are your requirements for renting a car?" she asked in a professional voice.

"A major credit card or five-hundred dollars cash deposit," a gruff male voice replied.

"Can I get a car this afternoon?"

"What kind do you want? We ain't got too many newer cars on hand right now."

"I don't care. I just need one that runs."

"I got an '89 Olds Cutlass. It's not bad, runs good."

"That's all that matters. Hold it for me, will you please? I'll be there by four o'clock this afternoon."

"Sure. What's your name? Just a minute. I got to get a pen that writes...all I got is crappy pens around here...okay, go ahead."

"Ginny. Ginny Forester. I'll be bringing cash."

"Fine with me. I'll see ya later. Call me if you change your mind, will you? Some people call me like this and then never show up."

"I'll be there." Elizabeth hung up the phone and smiled. She got busy returning phone messages from her clients so she could enjoy the evening with a clear conscience. Excitement was building in her stomach and for once it wasn't from panic or anxiety. She must be doing something right.

❖ ❖ ❖

At about 3:45, Elizabeth arrived at the car rental lot by taxi. The foreign cab driver had tried to start a conversation with her on the way over, but she hardly understood a word he said. It was obvious he was interested in her; she kept feeling his eyes peering at her from his rear view mirror. Staring out the side window to avoid any eye contact, she thought he might be able to look right through her even though she had sunglasses on.

She had tucked her hair up under a black turban that she had bought on a vacation in Paris several years ago. It seemed so *tres chic* at the time, but when she got back to the states, she had never worn it again. Until now. She also wore the big silver hoop earrings she had purchased once on a whim and had never worn. Today, their combination felt so right, so Bette Davis.

A black tee shirt and blazer topped the pair of snug-fitting blue jeans she wore. She had put the outfit together carefully before going to the bank this afternoon and withdrawing fifteen hundred dollars. Five hundred of it she had tucked in her blazer pocket for the rental, five hundred was tucked in her bra, and the other five was stashed in a fake book in her bookcase along with some other mad money.

At the car rental office, Ginny Forester's name adorned another bogus application, and within a few minutes, she was merrily driving out of the car lot in the Oldsmobile. It was a far cry from her Mercedes, but luxury was not an issue at this point.

Elizabeth drove back to the seedy store where she had rented the box a few days ago. She parked her car back in the same lot she had parked in on her last visit. As if by reflex, she glanced upward to the third floor window of the XXX-rated motel and was glad there was no naked man masturbating at her today. That was a definite plus. Tucking a box of expensive Havana Gold cigars under her arm, she walked across the street to have a little talk with Zipper.

A tiny bell rang as she entered the crackerbox of an office. Zipper was situated behind the counter, and a man in long dark dreadlocks turned to look at her as she entered. She walked over and peered into her mailbox, although she knew nothing would be in it.

She could see the customer at the counter out of the corner of her eye as she dialed the combination on the mailbox lock. She wondered if he ever washed his hair, or if he just wore those things until he got sick of them and then cut them off at the roots. Zipper slipped an envelope across the counter, which the man grabbed and stuck in his dingy denim jacket pocket. He left quickly. A strong whiff of body odor assaulted her nostrils as he passed by.

"How are you today, little lady?" Zipper called out to her.

Elizabeth approached the counter. "Fine. And you?"

"Better now that you're here. What's in the box?" Zipper looked curious.

"Something for you, actually. For being discreet and forgetful." She handed him the box of premium cigars.

"Wow! Havana Golds. You have good taste. They must have definitely set you back a few bucks. I can get them pretty cheap. You should have seen me first before you bought 'em."

Elizabeth tried to sound cutely sarcastic. "That would take away from the surprise of a gift, now, wouldn't it?"

"Usually when somebody brings me something, they want something back. What is it that you want, Miss Ginny?" He set the box down somewhere behind him after removing one cigar from it and putting it in his knit shirt pocket.

"I'm impressed. You remembered my name." Elizabeth moved a bit closer to the counter, where Zipper was hanging over it so far he made a huge dent in his fat middle. "I was thinking about what you said about having a little bit of everything back there."

"Uh-huh. And what might you be looking for?" He leaned on his right elbow, his chin in one hand.

"A gun." Elizabeth blurted out. "I need a gun. A single woman needs protection these days, don't you think?"

"Sure, but why don't you buy one at a sporting goods store, nice and legal-like?"

"A little problem with my record," Elizabeth lied.

"You? A record?" Zipper looked at her in disbelief. "I took you for a regular slice of American white bread."

"Nope. No white bread here. So. Can you help me or not?"

"Maybe." Zipper scrutinized her. "How do I know you're not a cop?"

"I'm not a cop, Zipper," she added in a flattering tone, "and I bet you're a pretty good judge of character. Now, can you help me or do I have to go to your competitor down the street?"

"Give me a break! I have no competitor down the street. Take off your sunglasses. I want to see your eyes." Zipper stood up straight.

Elizabeth took off her glasses and stared straight into Zipper's eyes."I am not a cop and I need a gun. Are you going to help me or not?"

Zipper studied her face for several seconds, then lifted the counter top and waved her inside. He shut the counter lid and walked across the room towards a small hallway. On his way, he pointed to the far side of the small living room. "Sit down over there. I'll be right back."

Elizabeth frowned at the couch where Zipper had told her to sit. The olive green fake velvet sofa cushions were covered with what looked like cheese curl and popcorn crumbs. The dark wooden end table held several brown beer bottles and a round black plastic ashtray full of cigarette butts. The dust on the table's veneer was so thick, she was tempted to write in it. She opted for a stark straightback oak chair next to the divan, and sat waiting, stiff as a board.

Zipper came back in the room with a black leather guitar case. He set it down on the decrepit coffee table and opened the lid. There were several handguns lying on blue felt. It was a pathetic attempt at a marketing display, but functional, she supposed.

Zipper sat down on the edge of the sofa. "So. How big you looking for? Somethin' to carry in your purse? Or bigger? I got .22s, .38s, .45s, Glocks, .44 and .357 Magnums and some bigger stuff in the back—like AK47s, Ruger automatics, Uzis, and even some grenades."

"Jeez, I just need something for my purse, I'm not planning to start a war." She quickly pulled on a pair of thin vinyl gloves she had brought along, and picked up a little .22 caliber pistol. It felt good in her hand. "How much is this one?"

"A hundred bucks. I'll even throw in a box of bullets and some dum-dums." Zipper lit up the cigar from his pocket. A sweet smokey smell filled the area around them.

"What are dum-dums?"

"Those are kick-ass bullets that mushroom out on impact. Makes it hard for cops to identify them. Plus they make a nasty, nasty, hole."

Okay. I'll take it." Elizabeth slipped the pistol in her purse and pulled off her gloves, stuffing them in the bag after the gun.

"I only take cash, of course." Zipper plopped down on the couch and reached for the ashtray.

"Of course. I have cash. Turn your head."

"What?" He parked his cigar.

"Turn your head!" She said teasingly. "The money is in my bra."

Zipper laughed. "Good thing I'm a gentleman. If I wasn't, something like that could really turn me on." Zipper kept laughing as he turned his head away towards the television. *All-Star Wrestling* was on. The sound was off, which made the characters look even more ridiculous.

Elizabeth plucked the money from the cleavage in her bra. "Okay, you can turn back around now." She grinned.

Zipper smiled. "What are you really going to do with a gun anyway, little sister? You know how to shoot?"

"Yes. Of course. Why do they call you Zipper anyway?"

Zipper rose from the sofa and pulled up his ill-fitting knit shirt to show her a long scar that started near his heart and angled down across his stomach, ending at his hip. The scar had stretched as he'd gained weight and made it look like a giant, deformed zipper.

"Nam. '67. Goddamned gook got me with a bayonet. Almost killed me. Then we come back here and get treated like shit by the fucking ungrateful American public. Didn't even get a stinkin' parade." Zipper's face reddened as he spoke.

Elizabeth knew if she didn't make her exit soon, he might either have a heart attack or she might have to suffer through a lengthy lecture on the evils of the U.S. political system. She forced herself to listen for a while, then politely interjected that she had to get going, and handed him two hundred-dollar bills. "Keep the change. It's a tip for trusting me."

Zipper folded the bills and tucked them in his front right pocket. "Thanks. Sorry I got carried away. I get so mad when I start talking about the war. You're too young to even remember it, aren't you?" Zipper walked over to the desk and and unlocked one of the drawers with a key from a ring he had pulled from his pants pocket. He took two boxes out of the drawer and handed them to Elizabeth. "Your bullets."

Elizabeth nodded and stuffed the boxes into her purse. Zipper grabbed his new cigar from the ashtray and followed her out to the counter. "Listen. You seem like a nice enough kid. Be careful, okay? I mean with the gun and all." He waved his hand with the cigar in the air, apparently trying to emphasize his point. "A gun is a big responsibility. If you don't know how to use it, someone will grab it from you and shoot you with it. Promise me you'll practice until you can load it in the dark."

"Okay, I will. Thanks, Zipper. You know that big scar you got? I got one, too, except mine's on the inside." Elizabeth pointed at her heart. Zipper shook his head empathetically. "I think I know what you mean." He paused for a second, then took a big breath. "Okay, then! If you need anything else, just holler."

"I'll do that, Zipper, I sure will. Thanks again." Elizabeth waved as she turned to leave.

Zipper leaned on the counter and watched her exit the office, cross the street and climb into the old white Oldsmobile. He mumbled to himself. "I wonder what happened to that fancy black Mercedes she was driving the other day. She's a classy little broad; probably has a rich boyfriend. Crazy eyes, though. She's out to hurt somebody. I've seen that look before." Zipper, squinting, puffed on his Havana Gold cigar and watched Elizabeth drive away.

CHAPTER 19

She pulled into a narrow strip mall near Lowry Air Force Base and parked. A sign that read Woody's hung over the blackened door leading into the dive. Elizabeth read in the newspaper some time back that a wayward GI who had planted a bomb in a warehouse at the base had been arrested while he was in this bar drinking. The article had suggested it was a hangout for skinheads, neo-nazis, and militia members.

As she peered into the rearview mirror while she put on lipstick, she reminded herself that she would have to be careful. The parking lot was not big enough to pull off what she did on her last time out. The new loaded pistol was in her purse, which hung around her neck and close to her hip.

When she opened the door of the bar, she was greeted with smoky darkness and twangy country music crying out from a jukebox. Few people were seated barside on the vinyl red and black marbled thinly-padded barstools. A middle-aged couple was making out like teenagers on the end barstool located by the restrooms. She could see that the aging Casanova's hand was up inside his plump girlfriend's skirt. A scant number of couples sat at tables talking. Four men wearing fatigues shared a table, quietly drinking beer.

Bingo. She arranged herself at the bar so that she was facing the military men. Elizabeth made a big production of pulling off her turban, and shaking her auburn hair free. She ran her fingers sensually through her hair while parting her glossy lips.

"Coors, draft," she told the attentive bartender, and laid a five dollar bill on the counter.

The bartender slid a wet rag over the area before he set the beer down in front of her. "Here you go—and your change."

"Thanks." She left the money on the bar and smoothly pulled her cigarettes and lighter out of her purse.

Her delicate, tapered fingers provocatively slipped a cigarette from its sheath. She placed it slowly between her lips, opening her mouth a little wider than necessary before clamping down on the slim cylinder. With the predictability of Pavlov's dogs, one of the uniformed men popped up, walked over, and sat down beside her.

"Can I buy you a beer?" His face was fairly attractive, although Elizabeth thought his eyes were a little too close together.

"Sure. You the leader of the pack?" She cocked her head while she looked at him, slightly smiling.

"Yeah, I guess so. The rest of 'em were too chicken to come over here and talk to you; they said you were probably a high class hooker." He had an immature goofy laugh.

Elizabeth guessed him to be twenty-one or so. "And what do you think?"

"I don't know ma'am. All I know is that you're the prettiest thing I've seen all night."

Now, there was a challenge.

Elizabeth took a long pull off her beer and wiped the foam from her lips with the back of her hand. "Do you guys always wear uniforms when you go out to a bar?"

"Naah. We just came from a meeting. We just stopped in for a beer. We ain't been here that long." He smoothed his uniform over his flat stomach.

"What kind of meeting?"

He nervously rubbed his palm over the top of his crewcut and looked towards his buddies. "Well, ma'am, I'm really not at liberty to say. It's kinda private."

This was almost too easy. "What's your name, soldier?" She leaned in closer to him.

"Ray."

Elizabeth gazed at him through hooded eyes. "Got a light, Ray?"

"Sure do." Ray deftly threw the lighter's lid open with his thumb and flicked at it until a little flame shot up. "What's your name, pretty lady?"

Elizabeth slithered her hand around his and guided it to her cigarette, while she stared in his eyes. "Ginny."

"Pretty name. Would you like to dance, Ginny?"

She managed a slightly crooked smile. "Okay, but let's have a drink first and let me smoke this cigarette. I need to relax. Would that be okay, Ray?" She crossed her legs and slid an ankle under his calf, massaging it with the top of her foot. She flashed him her big brown eyes and he was a frog in a flashlight beam, mesmerized and paralyzed.

Ray's face flushed. "Sure! Can I sit here with you while you have your drink?"

"I don't see why not. You don't bite, do you—Ray?" She giggled. As she drank her beer and smoked her cigarette, she feigned interest at his incessant chatter.

A little later, Ray excitedly led her to the dance floor, like a boy parading his prize filly in front of state fair judges. Elizabeth was sure some of the theatrics were for the benefit of his friends. She draped herself around the young man and pushed her breasts into his chest as they slowly swayed to a sad song. A somebody-left-somebody-and-their-heart-was broken-into-a-million-pieces song.

She felt through his shirt that his back was getting very hot. It was almost time for her to make her move. Maybe this wouldn't be so bad. He had a nice slender body, and was young, stupid, and controllable. Nothing like Jesse had been.

"Listen," she whispered in his ear, "do you want to go out to the car for a while?"

"Yes, I do, Ginny. In the worst way." Ray tightened his arms around her, grinding his impatient groin into hers. She was surprised he wasn't humping her leg. She had to get him away from the purse; he kept bumping into it as he tried to hold her closer.

Later, in the rented car, after kissing him until his passion turned him into a grabby octopus, she stopped him short.

"What's the matter? Don't stop, baby, please..." He groaned and tried to kiss her again.

"What kind of meeting were you at tonight, Ray?" She smiled a little and tried to look adoringly into his eyes.

Ray reluctantly took his lips off of her neck and returned her stare. "Don't ask, Ginny. You don't need to know."

"Yes, I do!" She raised her voice a little more than she intended.

Ray sighed heavily. "Okay, okay. It was a militia meeting, okay? The government is getting scary, Ginny. We have got to protect our own. The way it's going, America's own government officials are selling out our national secrets, turning us into pawns, trying to take away our rights to bear arms—"

Elizabeth interrupted his tirade. "Look, Ray. You can save the Aryan Nation mumbo jumbo for somebody that gives a shit. I'm going to make this short and sweet. I'm trying to get hold of an agent called anthrax. Can you help me?"

Ray sat up. "What? Anthrax? You want anthrax? Shit no, man! No way! I'm a bonehead, Ginny, just another frontline monkey."

I'm sure your mother is very proud.

"Don't you know somebody that can get it?"

"Hell no, Ginny! I'm scared of that shit. The Commander might be able to get it, maybe, but I can't get a hold of somethin' like that. I wouldn't even want to!" Ray began looking at her like she had actual horns growing out of her head. "What do you want that shit for? Who are you, anyway?"

"Get out of the car." Her face was stony and cold.

"What about us? What about tonight? C'mon, baby, let's go somewhere." He reached for her again.

She deliberately pulled the gun out of her purse and aimed it at Ray. "There is no us, Ray. Get out. Get out of the car! Now! I'm not kidding."

"Okay! Okay. Relax. Put down the gun. I'm going, I'm going." Ray scrambled to catch the door handle and rolled out of the car.

"Now get out of here. You should be glad I am giving you a chance to get away. The last guy who tried to push his luck with me wasn't so fortunate."

Ray slammed the car door and ran fast back into the bar while Elizabeth sped out of the parking lot as fast as the old car would go.

"Shit," she muttered under her breath. "Well, Zipper, it looks like you're it, Buddy."

CHAPTER 20

Elizabeth drove by the mailbox place to see if Zipper was still open. It was late, after 11:30, but the lights were burning and the open sign was still up. After debating on whether to stop, she decided night was a better time to do business anyway. She pulled into the familiar lot across the street.

She opened the door and heard the little bell tinkle. That thing would drive her nuts. "Hey, Zip, you around?" The murmur of the television was the only sound she heard. The place smelled like pizza.

Zipper's face appeared in the window. "Well, hello there! What brings you here? Don't you know this is a dangerous neighborhood after dark?" Zipper was chewing and wiping his hands on a paper napkin.

"Oh, Zipper, I got you to protect me." She tried to look innocent. "How's it hangin'?"

"Low and old, Babydoll." Zipper grabbed the small of his back and pushed out his stomach, stretching. "Didn't I see you once already today?"

"Yeah, I forgot something. Do you have any shoulder holsters?"

"What? A shoulder holster?" Zipper laughed as the door flew open behind them.

The annoying chime announced a short, thin, scuzzy man entering the small office. His face resembled that of a ferret, with a pointed nose and small darting black eyes. He wore a long black raincoat that hung almost to the floor.

"Go ahead, Zipper. I'll just check my mail. Catch you later." She walked over to the corner near her mailbox.

"C'mon back, Slide, " she heard Zipper say.

Zipper and the pinched-face man walked back behind the counter into the tiny attached apartment. After a few minutes, she heard their voices raise. It was hard to make out what they were saying.

The shouts continued until she heard Zipper yell, "No!"

A shot rang out and the heavy thud of a body hit the floor. Elizabeth gasped and shrank into the shadows, hoping the gunman would think she had gone. The little rodent ran past her and out the front door, his arms full of guns.

Running to the door, Elizabeth watched him as he fled down the block and jumped into an old Chrysler. It looked to be black, and bore the license tag, *CRUIZIN.*

Brilliant. Rob somebody and then use a getaway car with personalized tags. No wonder our prisons are full.

She ducked under the counter and ran to Zipper's side. He was groaning. She knelt down beside him. "Zipper! What happened? I'll call 911!"

"No! No 911," Zipper struggled to speak. "Ginny. No cops! Too much stuff in here. Cops. Just been waitin' for a chance—no cops."

Elizabeth panicked. "Zipper! I've got to do something! I can't let you just lie here and die!"

"Over there." He tried to pull his neck up and point to a small, flimsy desk across the room. "In the Rolodex. Jimmy Beach. He knows my doctor. Call him. Then get out of here, little sister, okay?" His head dropped onto the carpet and his chest rattled as he fought to breathe.

Elizabeth scrambled over to the desk, terrified, and fingered quickly through the file cards until she found the number. She snatched up the phone and punched in the number for Jimmy Beach.

"Yeah," the low male voice answered quietly.

"Hello, Jimmy? I need to talk to Jimmy Beach! Is this Jimmy?" Elizabeth asked urgently.

"Maybe...depends."

"Look. This is a friend of Zipper's. He's been shot. He needs help fast and won't let me call 911—"

"I'll be right there." The phone clicked in her ear.

She threw down the phone and rushed back to Zipper. He was mumbling something. It looked like he had lost a lot of blood.

"Fuckin' thief. Owed me money... Ginny?"

"Yeah, Zip? I'm right here." She stiffly held his huge hand in hers in an attempt to be comforting.

"Get out of here, Ginny. Now. Don't let Jimmy see you here. Go on now, I'll be all right. They'll be here soon."

Elizabeth sighed and rose up from Zipper's side. He was lying very still and appeared to have become unconscious. He couldn't be dead; his chest was still rising and falling.

As she surveyed the room, she saw that Zipper must have taken his stash out in front of the Ferret Man. There was evidence of a struggle; there was stuff pitched all over the room. The man obviously didn't have time to steal everything. There was the barrel of a handgun poking out from the edge of the couch. She retrieved it and slipped it in her purse.

Scanning the rest of the room, she saw a machine gun. The barrel was pointed towards Zipper's head, and she kicked it away. She resumed her search.

She saw two small vials that were flush against the wooden baseboard several inches in back of Zipper's head. She checked to make sure Zipper was still unconscious. She reached around him, grabbed the two vials and stuffed them into her purse, cobwebs and all.

Elizabeth had just gotten across the street and fixed into the old clunker, when she saw a long, black Lincoln Town Car pull up in the alley of Zipper's place. Three men jumped out of the car, looked up and down the road cautiously, and made their way into Zipper's back door.

She crouched down in the seat and watched from across the street. In a few minutes, two men came out carrying Zipper by his arms and legs. He looked like a doomed wild animal, tied on a stick by his limbs and carried off by savages.

The third man appeared to be locking the front door. The place went dark. They finished placing Zipper in the back seat, got in the car and sped away.

Elizabeth stared at the empty alley. *I hope he'll be okay.*

She reached in her jacket pocket and took out the two vials. She flipped on the overhead light to look at them more closely. Two small tightly-capped plastic vials lay in her hand. There were taped labels on each of them. She looked closer. The handwriting was atrocious, but she managed to read Ricin on one bottle, and Anthrax on the other .

Bingo. Thank you, Zipper. Good night, daddy dearest.

CHAPTER 21

Elizabeth lugged the awkward computer box from the apartment basement storage facility to the elevator. The doors were closing when they suddenly reopened and a handsome face appeared.

"I've got the door. Need some help with that?"

"No. It's just a big empty box. That's okay... you go ahead, I'll catch the next one."

"Nonsense! Come on in here. There's plenty of room."

She drug the box into the elevator behind her and parked it next to the gas barbecue he had.

"What floor?" He asked politely, with a smile.

"Twelve, please." She looked up at the numbers to avoid his bright blue eyes.

"You live up in the high rent district, huh?"

"It's highway robbery."

He laughed at her feeble joke and she noticed his perfectly white teeth. She wondered if they had been bonded. With his towhead and tan hard body, he looked like a surfer. "My name is Brad Richmond. I live in 704. What's your name?"

She stalled, but could do nothing but answer. This is where she lived.

"Elizabeth. Elizabeth Strong." She managed a slight smile and was suddenly acutely aware that she had no makeup on.

Time dragged on as the elevator made its way up the tower. Finally, the panel light shone seven, and it pulled to a smooth stop.

"Well, it was nice meeting you, Elizabeth. Are you going to the Spring Thing, or whatever it's called, at the apartment clubhouse Saturday? I just moved here from California and I thought I could meet some people there."

"No, I doubt it. What kind of thing is it again?"

"It was in this month's newsletter. The management company is putting on a party. They're buying the food and it's open bar. Maybe it's an attempt to help us rationalize why we spend so much money living here." They both forced a small laugh.

Elizabeth always threw the apartment newsletters away unread. She could care less what the other tenants were doing as long as they left her alone. "I have other plans, but thanks for asking."

"Some other time, then." With a boyish grin he disappeared out of the elevator, wheeling his barbecue behind him.

Elizabeth sighed. *What the hell was that?* she wondered as the door shut behind him. She punched 12 again on the number pad, and the car slowly started to rise.

She reminded herself of a worker ant as she tugged the hefty box out of the elevator, drug it down the hallway and into her apartment; it seemed she was always lugging stuff to the home pile.

Elizabeth flopped down on the couch, grabbed the phone, and dialed. She popped off her tennis shoes and wiggled her feet. While waiting for an answer, she grabbed her cigarettes off the coffee table.

The phone picked up and a male voice answered. "Hello."

"Hello, Dad. Guess what I'm doing?" She had the telephone receiver perched in the crook of her neck while she lit a cigarette.

"Hi! I have no idea, what?" Chet sounded excited to hear her voice.

"Packing up my old computer. I'm going to bring it out. You don't have one yet, do you?"

"No way. Too expensive, plus I'm not smart enough to run one of those things anyway."

"I'm going to give this one to you to use, Dad. It'll be fun! " She made a face.

"No, Elizabeth. That's too much. I don't know how—"

"Stop. Look, I can't get anything for a used computer anyway. I already have my new one set up. I'm going to bring you this old one so I can teach you how to use e-mail. I have a laptop I take on the road. So when I'm away, we can still keep in touch! Besides, it's easy. You'll learn in no time!"

"Well, when you put it that way..."

"I'll bring it out Saturday. Gotta go now. Duty calls."

"Okay."

Elizabeth hung up the phone and sneered. *What an idiot.*

CHAPTER 22

As she flew through the lobby, Elizabeth noticed a neon hot pink flyer hanging on the bulletin board by the apartment mailboxes. Spring fling, it read. That made no more sense than spring thing, as Brad had referred to it. *Seven o'clock tomorrow night... hmmm...might be a nice diversion.* She allowed herself to remember Brad's smile just for a moment.

Elizabeth exuded an air of confidence, dressed in a navy Ralph Lauren suit and matching heels. She had a lunch appointment with a client downtown at Randi's, an upscale restaurant catering to business people.

In the cab on the way to her appointment, she thought about Zipper. She hoped he was okay. She felt a little bad about stealing that stuff from him, but he would have understood, she thought.

She couldn't wait to get the luncheon meeting over with, so she could get home and put her plan into action. It was just dumb luck that Elizabeth got her hands on the anthrax so soon. She hadn't believed in luck until last night.

The taxi pulled up to the front of the restaurant. The dark-complected taxi driver was wearing a gold turban. As she paid him the fare and waited for her change, she couldn't help but wonder if his life had turned out as he'd hoped; if being in America was enough. He looked so misplaced in the bright yellow car with the dingy beige interior.

As she stepped out of the cab, she took a deep breath.

Focus.

She donned a huge smile, and went into the restaurant to secure the account of Line Interiors, Inc.

❖ ❖ ❖

"Maggie?" Elizabeth spoke cheerfully into the phone from her apartment. "I got it! Line Interiors is in the bag. We need to schedule a phone consultation with Mohr and Dawson to firm up the details."

"Will do, Ms. Str— Elizabeth. That's great! Congratulations! You're having such a great year!" Maggie's voice was bubbly.

"Thanks. I should be around home this afternoon if you have any questions. I'll bring the paperwork in on Monday." She kicked off her shoes and wiggled her toes. She couldn't wait to get her nylons off.

"Great! Do you want to talk to Mr. Mohr? Tell him the news?"

"Naah. Maggie, you do it." The last thing she wanted was to get stuck on the phone with jabberjaws Mohr on a Friday afternoon.

"Well...sure! I always like to be the bearer of good news to the boss!"

"Good. See you Monday, Maggie. I've got paperwork to do."

"Okay! Have a great weekend, and good work on Line Interiors, Elizabeth. Mr. Mohr was a little worried about it."

After washing off her makeup, Elizabeth changed into sweats, poured herself a glass of wine, and sat down in front of her new computer. The salesman had told her that the unit was a "kick-ass machine" and that it was the "next-generation Power PC." Right. The next generation would probably begin in two weeks. It was nearly impossible to keep up with technology at the speed it was progressing.

After calling up a search engine on the internet, she typed in *ricin*, the name on the other small vial she had taken from Zipper's last night. She was surprised to find it was a toxin made from castor beans, from the pulp left over from making castor oil. If it's inhaled, ricin can kill a person in one to two days from internal bleeding and major organ failure. But there's been little research done on humans. It is unclear how much it would take to kill a person. *Too risky. He might recover.*

Anthrax, on the other hand, is very predictable. It only takes a millionth of a gram to do somebody in. The victims get a low grade fever, a dry hacking cough, and weakness. They may show a small improvement during the illness, then boom. Dead. Inhalation of spores has nearly a one hundred percent mortality rate, and takes only two to three days. Good. He will have time to think about what he has done.

The only item she was missing was some sort of protective mask. She planned to get all the materials she needed this afternoon and work on her project Sunday, when she would be undisturbed. She grabbed the phone book and looked up "Military Surplus" in the Yellow Pages. She snatched up the phone and dialed.

"Ed's Surplus." The man's tone was curt, like he had been interrupted from something more important.

"Hi. I was wondering if you have those masks that protect you from inhaling chemicals?"

"Are you kidding? They are one of the hottest items I got, ma'am. What kind you looking for? Heavy duty, general purpose, or limited fielding?"

"Um... I'm not quite sure. Maybe I'll just come down and have a look. How much do they run? "

"Oh, fifteen bucks on up. It just depends on what you want."

"Okay, thanks." After hanging up, she threw on her jeans and a gray sweatshirt, and stuck her hair up under a royal blue baseball cap with Broncos embroidered on it in orange. After grabbing the cash from the fake book safe in her bookcase, she stuffed all the bills in her jeans pocket. Seizing the car keys from the kitchen counter, she was glad she still had the heap. She would return it to the rental lot tonight.

The Oldsmobile was in a parking lot a few blocks down from her apartment complex. To pay for parking, you put the appropriate amount of money in a little numbered slot corresponding to the parking space. The crude financial center was well lit and made out of solid iron. The owners came around at random times, checking the boxes. If they found someone cheating them, they towed the car away themselves, so they made a profit either way. She had stuck a twenty in the heap's matching slot last night. The old sedan was still there. It was too ugly to steal.

The military surplus store was located in a corner unit on the end of a small strip mall, not far from Zipper's. Elizabeth decided she would drive by his place after her shopping trip to see if there was any activity. She parked off to the side in front of a thrift shop, and surveyed the surplus store. This was a new experience. She didn't know what to expect, and it made her a bit nervous.

There was a mannequin dressed in full military chemical protective gear facing her as soon as she stepped in the front door. The facepiece assembly of the mask made it look like a big khaki grasshopper. There were tables of equipment, boots, and fatigues.

On the wall, over her left shoulder, was a camouflage colored two-piece outfit; a heavy coat and a pair of trousers. There was a sign hanging beside it that read: "The OG-84—Provides at least 24 hours of protection against exposure to liquid or vapor chemical agents. Its protective qualities are guaranteed to last for a minimum of 30 days."

Or what? We will cheerfully refund your money?

"Hello, I'm Ed. May I help you?" The man had to be a pin-up model for *Soldier of Fortune* magazine. She hadn't seen boots that shiny in a long time.

"Yes, I hope so. I am doing some research work in the lab at school and I will be handling some dangerous chemicals. I think I need some protection. My professor says it's no big deal, but it's my life, right?"

"Right. Absolutely. Every American should own some anyway. They just set the doomsday clock up another five minutes, did you know that?" He raised his eyebrows and gauged her face carefully for her reaction. "So. You won't be in anything heavy, right? Just working with your hands basically?" Ed walked as he talked to her over his right shoulder.

Elizabeth followed him to the rear of the store. "Right."

"Okay." He pointed to a table. "Here's the M42 Series Combat Vehicle Crewman Mask—and the AR-5. Both pretty fancy. They have microphones, filtered air...you don't need all that...hmmm...here we go... the ABC-M5 Tank CB mask." Ed pointed at the product like it was a prize on a TV game show. "It's for special fielding. It'll give you full protection and it's less bulky than the others." He handed her the heavy mask. "You'll need some chemical protective gloves, too, won't you?"

"Of course." She had no idea there was such a market for this stuff. Somebody must know something she didn't.

"Here you go, gloves—M324s. Thin enough that you can use your fingers for delicate tasks, and they provide superb protection from the agent you're working with as well."

She took the gloves he picked out for her, and followed the starched uniform to the front of the store. On the way, he stopped abruptly in front of a display of aprons.

"Oh yes. You should really get a chemical apron, too." He grabbed one and held it up for her to inspect. "Nylon with butyl rubber on both sides. See, it wraps around—has some sleeves, here—and ties in back. This would protect you from neck to boots. Or, in your case—shoes." Ed smiled and waited for her decision.

She wondered if this might be overkill, but then again, it was anthrax. "Wrap it up, Ed."

"Yes, ma'am. One M4335 Apron, toxological agents, protective." He draped the item over her arm, and whistled as he walked up to the cash register with a weighted down Elizabeth in hot pursuit.

After paying in cash, she walked out of the store with two huge bags. She threw them in the trunk of the clunker and got in, then pointed the car towards Zipper's place. On the way, she thought when she got home she would take the stairs to avoid prying eyes.

She drove by Zipper's, and craned her neck to see if there was anyone inside. Nobody. The closed sign was up in the window and there was a note hanging on the front door. She pulled over to the curb, parked sloppily, and jumped out to see what the note said.

Death in the family. Will be closed for awhile. Management. Death? Elizabeth suddenly felt very sad.

CHAPTER 23

Saturday morning, Elizabeth was running along the river on the bike path. She usually jogged early to avoid the foot traffic, especially on Saturdays, but this morning she had slept in a little. The trail was sprinkled with people walking their dogs, teenagers rollerblading, and lovers walking hand in hand. She stopped to put her foot up on a bench to tie a shoelace at the end of her run.

"Run, run, run. Wherever you go, d'ere you are," sang an ancient voice from behind her.

With a start, Elizabeth turned around to meet the gummy smile of the old red-hatted bag woman. The woman leaned possessively on a grocery cart filled with cans, a small suitcase, and a few pieces of plastic dinnerware. In the child's seat of the cart rode a stuffed pink bunny, well-worn and dirty, and the buttons that had replaced the original eyes didn't match. Nevertheless, the rabbit looked oddly alert.

"You're all over the place," was all Elizabeth could think of to say. She pulled a washcloth out of her fanny pack to mop her forehead.

"Beautiful streets of Denver is my home, Lady. Sit." The old woman plopped down on the bench and patted the space beside her. She kept a protective hand on her grocery cart.

"No, I have things to do." Elizabeth put her foot back on the ground.

"You don't have five minutes to talk to an old lady? Sit,sit,sit." The woman smiled warmly at Elizabeth. "I used to have a daughter about your age. Her name was Shelby. She was real pretty like you." She gazed off towards the mountains, hurt in her eyes.

"Was?" Elizabeth reluctantly sat down.

"Good Lord saw fit to take her when she was eighteen year old. I had a real bad spell after dat. Didn't care 'bout nothin'. Reckon that's how I got here. In dah streets, I mean. Now, it's just me and Sugar."

Elizabeth didn't tell her she was nearly twice that age at thirty-three. "Who's Sugar?"

"Dat's my rabbit, here." The old lady gave a pink furry leg a pat. "He don't say much, but dat makes him easy to get along wit'." She laughed a little.

"Sorry about your daughter. You always seem so happy when I see you." Elizabeth tapped her foot restlessly, not knowing what to say.

"Beautiful sunrise this morning and I had a nice, big, fat cinnamon roll for breakfast. Sugar liked it good, too. I reckon dat's a good enough reason as any to smile." The old woman reached out with a wrinkled, weathered hand and patted Elizabeth's. The contrast of the two skin complexions was striking.

"Are you happy, little girl?" The two dark eyes attempted to hold Elizabeth's in their gaze.

Tensing, Elizabeth pulled her hand away from the kindness. "Happy enough, I guess." Her eyes followed a teenage boy madly skateboarding down the sidewalk. She remembered as a kid, trying to make a skateboard out of a pair of dismembered roller skates hammered onto a board. It didn't work very well.

"No, you ain't. A mother can tell d'ese t'ings. What's a matter, little one? You can tell me. I don't tell nobody nothin'. Dat's how I stay alive on de street. Now tell me, what is wrong?" The old woman looked intently at Elizabeth, fully expecting an answer.

"Nothing is the matter. Everything is fine, great. Look. I've got to go." She got up to leave. The old lady suddenly looked small and vulnerable to her. "What's your name, anyway?"

"Beulah. What's yours?" Beulah gave her a big smile.

"Okay, Bye—Beulah." Elizabeth ignored the question and ran to the curb, crossing the street quickly, nearly being hit by a blue pickup that was racing down Speer Boulevard. Her heart was beating faster now than after she'd run three miles. The encounter with the bag lady had disturbed her.

CHAPTER 24

It was Saturday afternoon and Elizabeth was on the way to Chet's house for the second time in many years. The road construction seemed to have made no progress at all, that she could see. The reasonably new computer she was giving her father was nicely packed in its original box and stuffed into the back seat. Good thing she drove a convertible; she would have never got the bulky package through the car door.

Bored stiff with the forty miles per hour speed limit and trapped behind a long string of cars, she considered again her metaphor of humans imitating ants. She tried to imagine how ridiculous this long, seemingly endless vehicle caravan must look from the sky. Irritated, she pawed through the CD tote and found no promise of music that suited her mood. As a last resort, she snapped on the radio. She pushed one of her preset buttons and Chris Isaak's haunting voice filled the car singing *Wicked Game.*

"Strange what desire will make foolish people do."

The phrase caught her attention, and she began to sing along.

"What a wicked game you played, to make me feel this way."

She smiled smugly and listened to the words. She understood irony these days.

The neon orange road sign announced that the construction had ended and she darted to the fast lane. Her foot pressed on the accelerator. The row of cars that had previously stood in her way soon looked very small in her rearview mirror.

She watched the speedometer needle climb...*65, 80, 90.* She clicked by several cars. Her stomach churned with excitement as she gripped the steering wheel...*100, 110.*

I could just jump that median and hit that semi or smash into that bridge up there and all this shit would all be over with. Mama's face came in her mind, beautiful and fragile. The thought of being with her again made her smile. She squinted her eyes, clenched her jaw and floored it, determined and excited.

I want to fly too, Mama. I want to see what freedom feels like.

The comforting vision dissolved instantly at the shrill alarm of the radar detector. The red screen in her head went away and came back to black. She braked quickly and pulled over into the slower lane. Ahead, she could see where a state trooper had an eighteen-wheeler pulled over and was walking around the monstrosity with a clipboard in his hand.

❖ ❖ ❖

Chet watched Elizabeth as she skillfully pushed metal cord ends into mysterious sockets.

"You don't need no manuals or anything to set that up?" Chet seemed genuinely impressed. He crossed his arms as he sat on her old bed and watched her set up the computer.

"No. It's not as hard as it looks, especially after you've done it a thousand times." It wasn't long until the machine was ready. The computer's eye blinked awake after she hit the power button.

"Okay. Sit up here in this chair in front of the computer." She hovered over Chet's right shoulder, careful not to touch him, and pointed at a paper. "I've written down all the instructions, step-by-step, including how to turn the machine on. I'll go through the basic stuff with you today, then you practice during this coming week. I'll come back next Saturday to teach you how to send e-mail and access the internet, okay?"

Chet looked at the monitor, bewildered. "Are you sure I'll be able to do this?"

"I'm positive. It's not that hard, I promise." She smiled with encouragement.

"Well, okay. If you're sure. Oh, look, a little smiley face." Chet pointed at the screen, grinning and interested.

They spent the next hour or so going through the simple written steps Elizabeth had prepared for his initial training. Before long, Chet was confident enough with his technological performance to promise that he would practice during the week.

"Well, I have to go. I have some stuff to do." She reached out and retrieved her windbreaker from the back of the chair she had been sitting in. She slipped it on.

"Oh,no!" Chet's face fell. "I thought we could go have some dinner together or something after awhile. Maybe go catch a movie?"

"No, I can't. I have a date tonight." She grabbed her purse.

"Really?" Chet tone was playful. "Who's the lucky guy?"

She continued moving towards the front door. "Nobody. It's just a picnic."

"Can I at least have a hug?" Chet held out his arms.

Her tone was even and cool as her gaze. "No, I don't think so. It's too soon."

Chet let his arms drop to his sides. "I understand, honey. See you next Saturday, then?"

"Sure. Same time." She leaned on the front screen door, longing to make her escape.

"Okay. That'll be great. Thanks for the use of the computer. I think I'm really starting to get the hang of it." Chet moved toward the kitchen.

She glanced through the kitchen, and heard a dark laugh bouncing around the inside of her head. *The hang of it. Very funny, you bastard.*

"Yes, I'm sure you will. I have got to go now. See ya."

Chet beamed at her from the kitchen counter. "You be careful on that date tonight. There's a lot of crazies out there in the city."

Elizabeth bit the inside of her lip. "I will. See ya." She left the house hurriedly, relieved to get to her car.

I'll show you crazy. You're a dead man.

CHAPTER 25

Elizabeth sat sipping brandy on the veranda, smoking a cigarette and listening to her mother's music box which she had brought out and placed on the patio table. She was trying to decide whether to go to the spring fling or not.

Already dressed for the event, she wore a comfortable light-weight black cotton jumpsuit, topped with a teal, ivory, and black batik vest. A wide black belt hugged her waist and she wore comfortable low-heeled black sandals. She knew the outfit flattered her.

She contemplated why she had ever even *considered* going to this event. It was stupid. She lit a fresh cigarette from the smoldering end of the one that was already going. Flinging the still lit butt over the railing, she thought of how hard it was to admit to herself she had felt a flutter in her stomach when she met Brad in the elevator the other day.

Her practical nature scolded her. *That would be dumb to start something up with this guy. He lives in your building. What if he starts bugging you?*

Elizabeth knew the answer was simple enough, but there was a tiny part of her that did get lonely. A part that longed for a kind word or a hug now and then. The voice reminded her how ludicrous these yearnings were.

You have a terrible track record with men. Why would you do this to yourself? Why bother?

Staring up at the stars, she remembered the words from the letter Mama had left her long ago.

I never found true love darling, but if it does exist, I wish it for you.

Elizabeth stood and tipped up her glass to finish off the brandy. It wouldn't hurt to go for a little while. She took a last deep drag off the cigarette and tossed it off the balcony, watching it spiral and float to the concrete.

❖ ❖ ❖

Elizabeth looked through a thick glass pane of the door leading to the courtyard from the hall of the elevator, and assessed the situation. The party was going full blast by the time she got there. Food and beverages were set up in the clubhouse and people had spilled out into the courtyard, away from the loud music and disk jockey, talking.

Her eyes settled on a beautiful, leggy blonde woman. Wearing short shorts and a flip tee top, the vamp displayed a tan flat stomach that sported a pierced bellybutton with a small silver hoop. The siren looked to be talking a mile a minute in front of three guys that were clustered closely around her. They might as well of hung their tongues out and drooled, they were as subtle. It was obvious the confident flirt enjoyed the men's agog attention. She made it look so easy.

Breathe. Focus. You can do this. Go get a drink.

She shuffled into the clubhouse and got a beer from the bar, then stood alone sipping, pretending to read flyers on a bulletin board.

This is stupid. You don't belong here. I told you it would be stupid. Get out of here. This inner dialogue had just convinced her to go home, when she heard a deep male voice behind her.

"I was just about to give up on you."

She turned with a start. "I was just leaving."

"You just got here!" Brad objected, frowning.

"I just stopped by for a beer. I never intended to stay." She took a sip from her glass.

"Did you get some food?" Brad pointed over to the buffet table. It was stocked with nachos, several type of cold cuts, assorted cheeses, crackers, potato chips, and cookies.

"No, I'm not hungry. Besides, the stuff they have out to eat—you might as well shoot up with lard."

Brad laughed. "Hey, this party is a drag anyway. What do you say we go downtown for coffee and dessert?" Brad had such a pitiful look on his face. It looked well practiced.

She couldn't help but smile at his overdone expression. "Sorry, no. Really, I can't. I have a big day tomorrow. But thanks anyway. Maybe another time."

"Well, how about you at least drop by my place for a drink on the way up to your apartment? I am a freelance photographer. Maybe you would like to see some of my photographs.."

Come see my etchings? Priceless. This guy is a jerk. Get out of here, Elizabeth. Now.

It was as if Brad read her thoughts. He laughed. "Boy, that sounded stupid. I'm kinda nervous, I guess. I just wanted to talk to you alone for a little while.

Sure, what's it going to be next? "Come here, just lay down on the bed beside me. We'll just talk. You can leave your shoes on."

The words spilled out of her mouth against her better judgement. "Well, all right. But not for very long, okay?"

"Sure. Of course. That's fine." Brad smiled, and flashed those bright teeth that fascinated her so much.

The two tossed their beer cups in the trash and walked toward the elevator together. Partygoers poured out as the door opened. Walking behind her, Brad lightly touched her back in a gentlemanly fashion as they filed in past the crowd. His touch sent a burst of energy crackling up her spine.

As the elevator rose, Elizabeth looked up at the numbers again, as if the car wouldn't move unless she monitored its progress. She could feel Brad's eyes watching her face.

"I'm glad you showed up tonight." Brad crossed his arms and leaned against the wall casually.

"Thanks," was all she could come up with. She managed to briefly glance at him and grin. Her hands were clasped in front of her, to keep them from shaking. She felt very nervous and confused.

His apartment was beautifully done. The tasteful tints of the carpet, drapes, and walls were in neutral beiges; the accessories were in gorgeous, deep and vivid burgundies, forest greens, and accenting teals. There was a large white leather couch situated in the middle of the room, with exquisite tapestry throw pillows, in front of a staggered row of silk ficus and faux palm trees. The room had an inviting openness.

"Sit down." Brad waved to the sofa. "Can I fix you a drink?" He moved behind a massive oak wet bar and began checking bottle labels.

She sat stiffly on one end of the divan. "Sure. Do you have any brandy?" She furtively inspected Brad's computer equipment off to her right. It was set up on a beautiful oak desk with built-in speakers. Very impressive.

"Of course. What self-respecting host wouldn't?"

Breathe. Calm down. Relax. Everything is going to be all right.

Her shoulder blades were drawn up so tight they felt like they were meeting in the middle. She consciously released her shoulders and took a deep breath. Her eyes went to the wall on her left, to a framed photograph of a bald eagle in full wingspread, gliding high over a misty valley towards a nest. It was an awesome shot . She got up to take a closer look.

That has to be what freedom looks like.

"Did you take this?" Although she had already seen his name in the corner of the print, it gave her something to say.

Brad walked up beside her. "Yes, I did. That one was taken in Baja. I used to live in California. I'm hoping to photograph some eagles here in the Rockies. They like to sit in the tall pine trees, you know. It makes it easier for them to spot prey."

"It's nice. I really like it." She moved to the next picture hanging beside the eagle. "This is great, too. Is this a lioness?" She studied the lovely cat stretched out on the trunk of a fallen tree.

"No, actually that's a Florida Panther. The coloring is similar, though. That one was taken in their Everglades habitat, which itself is threatened, so the panthers are having a rough go of it. There are fewer than fifty of them left in the wild. " Brad gazed thoughtfully at the photo. "I sold that one to National Geographic. It's one of my favorites. Well, shall we sit down and have our drink?" Brad led the way back to the couch.

She took the place on the leather couch where she had sat before. Brad sprawled out on the other end. He appeared to be completely relaxed.

"So, how about you, Elizabeth? What do you do?" He asked, then took a sip of what looked to be a martini. It had an olive in it anyway.

"I'm in software. Selling systems and training." She looked down to see herself gripping the armrest of the sofa so hard her knuckles were turning white.

"Do you enjoy it?" Brad's eyes sparkled. It was apparent he was a few drinks ahead of her.

"Yes. Most of the time." She drank a gulp of her brandy.

"Are you always this nervous?" Brad spoke in a low voice and smoothly moved to the center of the couch.

She popped up like a fishing bobber, set her drink on the end table, and walked toward the door. She turned to face him. "Look, Brad. It's not you. I've been under a lot of stress lately. I just don't have room for this sort of thing in my life right now."

"What sort of thing? We're just having a drink. What did I do?" Brad widened his eyes and shrugged his shoulders.

"Nothing,really. It's me. I have to go; thanks for the drink." She reached for the doorknob. "I'll let myself out."

"Whatever." Brad didn't get up, just sat dumbly holding his drink, watching her go.

"Stupid, stupid, stupid." Elizabeth hit her head repeatedly with the heel of her right hand on the way back to the elevator, muttering to herself. She held and rocked against the safety rails in the elevator.

The dark voice soothed her. *Forget about it! He's a prick, just like all the others. He didn't even walk you to the door.*

CHAPTER 26

Elizabeth did not go through her usual Sunday morning ritual, leisurely drinking coffee while reading the newspaper in bed. Instead, she rose early, eager to begin. After quickly dressing in her running gear, she brushed her hair back in a ponytail, and set out for her morning jog. It was early, she should have the bike path mostly to herself.

After her run, Elizabeth showered and dressed, and ate a bowl of shredded wheat. She cleared the breakfast dishes and removed the dried flower centerpiece from the dining room table. She brought out craft wire, packages of new diskettes, diskette mailers, baggies, an eye dropper, scissors, and a tube of glue.

Before working with the real thing, she was planning a trial run. Going into her bedroom, she grabbed a small bottle of Calvin Klein's Obsession perfume from the vanity and brought it back to the worktable. She picked up a pair of scissors and began working.

She carefully snipped off a corner of a baggie in the shape of a square, which left her a tiny vessel with two open sides and two closed ones. She then placed a drop of perfume inside, at the bottom of the small square. She glued each of the two open sides shut with a drop of glue, but left an opening where the two open edges met at the corner. She cut a short strand of craft wire off the roll.

After putting a tiny drop of glue down first, she set the small bag in a corner of the open disk. She put another spot of glue on the end of the wire and tacked it inside, along the top front of the bag, through the opening. She glued the other end of the wire to the magnetic disk.

When the diskette was put back together and in the disk drive, the magnetic circle would spin and jerk the wire out, thus turning the sack mostly inside out, or tearing it open. Either was acceptable. Whatever was on the inside of the little bag would be dispensed into the room by the tiny fans that blew air over the computer circuitry and out the vents in the rear of the hard drive tower.

Elizabeth snapped the disk back together and decided to air the compelling fragrance out of the room before she began the test. She poured herself a cup of coffee and went to the balcony. She left the patio door standing open behind her.

As she sat in her balcony chair and sipped hazelnut coffee, she looked across the street to the river bike path. The sunny scene seemed to have filled up with couples since her morning run. Couples with children, couples without children, couples sitting together, holding hands, looking at each other the way lovers do. She turned away to the mountains, and painfully remembered the humiliating scene at Brad's apartment last night.

Shaking her head in disgust with herself, she felt very alone and inadequate. After standing, she paused for a moment to look over the side of the railing all the way down to the concrete drive and wondered what a fall like that would do to a human body.

She went back inside to complete her experiment. She pushed the disk into the drive and waited for its image to appear on the computer monitor. As the computer read the newly inserted disk, a hard snap sounded from within the drive. It was only seconds before a fresh wave of Obsession filled her nostrils. It was the sweet smell of victory.

She clicked away the Defective Disk error message and selected Eject Disk from the Special Menu. She retrieved and inspected the disk carefully to see how it had held up on its maiden voyage. It looked just like the many other diskettes she owned, it just smelled better.

CHAPTER 27

She drug the heavy sacks out of her closet, sat down on the carpet, and studied the protective chemical warfare gear lying in her own bedroom.

Elizabeth hoisted the heavy vinyl apron and positioned herself in front of the dressing mirror. She put her arms through the sleeves, and reached around to tie the ties of the apron behind her. Weighted down, she awkwardly bent over and grabbed the protective mask.

She put her head through the vinyl seals of the opening and attempted to rest the mask on her shoulders comfortably. Maybe these masks aren't supposed to be comfortable, she thought, to better keep the soldier wearing it in a constant state of readiness.

The reflection she saw in the mirror made her start laughing. Plus, the way the mouthpiece protruded, it made her look like an anteater. She laughed until she fell wearily back on her bed, gas mask and all.

Tears fell from her eyes, down the sides of her face and over her temples. She heard herself breathing inside of the mask. This must be what it feels like to be inside one of those shells that you can hear the ocean in. Her ears strained to listen. She was almost sure she heard sounds of the sea, the gentle ocean breezes. Then she dozed off.

Elizabeth dreamed of the time she and Mama had walked in on her father and that Ginny woman on the couch. Only this time, she was armored with chemical safety attire, and bravely edged past her mother to the inside to face the evil viruses alone.

Elizabeth walked into her old living room in full protective gear, carrying a can with a hose connected to it. She marched up to the sofa to the venal germs, her father and that Ginny Forester, and sprayed them with the contents of the can she was carrying.

As she hosed them down with the deadly mist, they curled up like she had seen ants do when they were dying after Mama sprayed them. After the two faces of human bacteria crinkled and gnarled for a few minutes, they disappeared into thin air. Elizabeth was very happy she had exterminated them, and turned to Mama who was peering through the screen door. She told her to come on in, that everything was okay now. Mama smiled and happily hurried through the door to give Elizabeth a big hug.

She woke with a start when she heard the phone ring. She pulled off the clunky mask, and struggled with the apron. She decided not to answer it; she was still shaken from the vivid dream. The phone rang four times before the answering machine clicked on.

"Hello? Elizabeth? Are you there, Honey?" She flinched at the stupid question and the "H" word.

Chet's voice was perky. "I just wanted to say Hi, and let you know that I am doing real good with my lessons on the computer. It's fun. Call me when you get a chance."

"Fat chance," she laughed darkly, as she pulled on protective chemical gloves.

Elizabeth spent the rest of the afternoon preparing poison computer disks. She was determined to go through this production only once, so she decided to finish the box of diskettes she had on hand. Ten times she went through the painstaking process of making the little sacks, tapping a bit of anthrax into each one, and securing them and the wires into the disks.

She replaced each disk into its protective plastic jacket first, then placed each of the tampered disks directly into a mailer and sealed it with its attached adhesive strip. She then placed each diskette mailer into a baggie and sealed that, then repeated the process with another plastic bag. She put all the filled mailers into a shoe box and placed it in her bedroom closet on the floor at the back. After enclosing the vial containing the remaining anthrax in a small plastic bag, she put the bag into the library book safe and replaced it in the bookcase.

She put everything left over into a plastic trash bag that she would take out on a run and drop into a litter basket somewhere along the way. She vacuumed the entire apartment, still wearing the chemical protective gear, and placed the disposable vacuum bag in another plastic trash bag; she'd drop it in a different waste bin. She scrubbed her work surface with a mixture of chlorine bleach and water; the internet article said this would kill anthrax spores.

The heavy protective gear was packed into two extra-strength trash bags. She threw the little .22 she had bought at Zipper's in one of the bags so she would have an emergency gun off-premises. She used wide plastic mailing tape to seal up the tops, then wiped them off with the chlorine mixture. She threw her sweats in the washing machine, added a generous shot of bleach to the hot rushing water, then walked naked to the shower.

She dressed in casual jeans and a sloppy tee shirt, quickly ran a comb threw her wet hair, and went down to the lobby. She grabbed a rolling luggage rack from the closet beside the concierge station. It was after ten o'clock, William was long gone, and the atrium was empty .

It was Sunday night, and traffic on the elevator was sparse. She only saw one person on the way back up, and it wasn't Brad. She sighed heavily.

After loading the trash bags of protective gear onto the cart, she got the load down to the basement storage area without seeing anyone. Grunting, she scooted the bags under a large, dark green canvas tarp.

She put a new heavy-duty combination lock on the hasp which, without notification, was a management policy tabu. Tenants were bound by their lease agreement to furnish management with the combinations or spare keys to the locks on their storage areas in case of an emergency. She didn't care what management wanted; she didn't want people she didn't know to have access to her things. Especially these things.

CHAPTER 28

During the Monday morning staff meeting, Elizabeth was informed that she would be leaving for Line Interiors' headquarters in Dallas the following week. Mr. Mohr had given her raving accolades for the acquisition of the tough account in front of everyone in attendance. She didn't like the attention Mohr gave her, she just wanted to do her job, take the money, and run.

"Hey, Queen Elizabeth, thanks for another week of making us look bad. What's your secret, besides having great legs?" Doug Weller, a fellow sales executive, teased her as they filed out of the meeting. She liked Weller all right. He'd always treated her like "one of the guys." Most of the other men seemed intimidated by her sales record and steered clear of her, which was fine with her.

"It helps if you get out of bed before noon once in a while, Weller." She good naturedly teased back. Doug's starched pudginess was endearing. He looked like a teddy bear with a suit on. They fell into step as they trudged back toward their offices.

"Oh, gee. I never thought of that. Mohr was really shining on you today, wasn't he?"

Elizabeth rolled her eyes. "He can say what he wants, as long as he keeps signing the checks."

Doug laughed. "Hey, some of us are going to lunch at Penguin's today, want to join us?" Doug loosened his tie.

"No thanks, but I'll take a rain check. I got an appointment."

"Out stealing my leads again, or got a hot lunch date?"

"Yeah, right, like I'd tell you." She smiled as she turned off into her corner office. "See ya later, Doug. Have a good lunch."

After taking a short detour by her apartment, she changed from her business suit to a pair of jeans and a tee shirt. She washed her makeup off, put her hair up in a ponytail, donned a baseball cap, and hurried downstairs to catch the cab she had asked William to call for her. Today she was going to a different used car rental place, a business that carried the classy name, Rent-A-Heap-Cheap.

She struck up the same deal as she had with the other car rental lot; a five-hundred dollar deposit allowed her to drive off the lot with an '82 Buick Le Sabre. She had seen a lot of these models around, still being driven. They must be the year of the Buick that wouldn't die. It reminded her of a bad drive-in movie title.

She drove by Zipper's and found the open sign up. She caught herself smiling at the thought of seeing Zipper again, glad that he was alive. She pulled into the parking lot adjacent to the XXX-rated motel. She was beginning to feel like a regular.

No naked man in the third floor window again this time. Good news, although she did see a potbellied trucker type in his underwear admitting a gaudy woman wearing fishnet hose and stiletto heels into his ground floor motel room.

She hurried across the street and pushed her way into the office, eager to see Zipper and see how he was doing. Maybe the bullet wound had looked worse than it really was. The annoying bell rang as she entered.

"Help ya?" A skinny, gristly man appeared in the counter window. His face looked as pasty as biscuit dough, and his dark hair was greasy and slicked back.

"Where's Zipper?" She leaned slightly over the counter trying to peer into the little apartment.

The man moved to block her view. "He won't be back."

"Why not?"

"You writing a book? Leave that chapter out. What can I help you with?" His rudeness was only exceeded by his ugliness.

"Nothing. Just wondered. Never mind, I'm just checking my mail."

With a grunt, the tactless man disappeared again, and she walked over to peer into her mailbox. There was actually something in there. She wondered if drop boxes got junk mail and hurried up in turning the combination to its lock. She jerked open the tiny door and pulled out an envelope that had *Ginny* printed on it.

She slipped it in her jeans pocket, flew out the front door, and ran back across the street to her car. The bible-thumping Ichabod Crane-ish looking vagrant glared at her from his pacing in front of the adult book and video store. He did not approach her again.

She locked the door, ripped open the envelope and pulled out the note.

> *Dear Ginny—Thanks for saving my life. I owe you a shoulder holster. I won't be back to this place. I am staying at a friend's for now til I get better. I would really like to say thank you in person. Call me at 892-3938 if you would. Hope you are okay, Zipper*

She felt a surge of relief. Zipper had grown on her in a strange way, and she was glad he was alive. She pulled up to a drive-up pay phone at a convenience store, put in her coins, and dialed the number Zipper had given her.

A deep male voice answered. "Yeah."

"Hello. I was looking for Zipper."

"Who wants him?"

"Ginny. My name is Ginny Forester."

"Just a minute."

She heard a hand cover the receiver and two muffled male voices speak to each other. After a minute or so, she was greeted with Zipper's voice.

"Well, hello, little sister, how are you?" The voice was weak but cheerful.

"The question is, how are you? What happened? Are you okay?"

"Lesson number one. Never discuss intimate details over the phone. Can you come and visit me?"

She pondered the request for a moment. "Yeah, sure, why not?"

Zipper gave her a Lodo address, an elite area in lower downtown where warehouses had been renovated into expensive lofts.

"It will have to be tonight, Zip. I have to work this afternoon."

"Tonight's better anyway. How about nineish? Do you mind bringing some Chinese Food? I can't get nothing fit to eat around here. I've had soup until it's running out of my ears. Can you bring some Kung Pao chicken? I've been dreaming about it."

"Sure, Zipper. See you tonight."

CHAPTER 29

After her call to Zipper, she went home to complete the other tasks she had planned to get done that afternoon. She stopped the rental car in the back row of the basement loading garage instead of in her usual place on the third floor. Mostly staff, security vehicles, and a few boats on trailers were parked down on this level.

It was the middle of the day and a good time to move the gas mask and other things she had stored in her basement storage area. Most of the apartment residents were youngish upscale professionals, so most would still be at work now. She heaved the heavy bags into the elevator by using the luggage cart again. The elevator door reopened at the loading entrance.

She had cleared the elevator doors when she saw Brad walking in loaded down with photography equipment. At his side, carrying a camera tripod and a small black leather purse, was a vivacious blonde woman. If she ever felt more stupid, she couldn't remember when. She silently blessed the person who invented sunglasses.

"Hello, Elizabeth. How are you?" Brad smiled, although his demeanor was stilted.

"Fine, Brad. And you?" She managed a stiff smile as well.

"Great. This is my friend Kyla. She's a policewoman." Brad patted Kyla's arm as he introduced her. "Kyla Gillespie, Elizabeth Strong. Elizabeth, Kyla."

"Detective, not policewoman, Brad. There's a difference." Kyla said, and turned attentively to Elizabeth. "Hi, Elizabeth. Nice to meet you. Do you need some help with those bags? Brad, let's give her a hand." Kyla stepped towards Elizabeth.

"It seems like every time I see you, Elizabeth, you're lugging something around." Brad said a bit sarcastically, while walking towards her.

"No! I can get this, I'm a big ant! " Elizabeth bellowed. The couple stopped their advance. "Joke. Get it, ant? Carrying heavy stuff around?" She felt her face get hot. "Anyway, no. I don't need any help, it's not that heavy. I'm just taking some stuff down to Goodwill. Thanks, anyway." She produced a small smile. "Nice to meet you, Kyla." She wanted to be anywhere else but here.

Brad seemed relieved Elizabeth had refused the help and hurried Kyla off to the elevator. As soon as they disappeared, Elizabeth sat down beside the bags on the luggage cart and deflated.

Shit, shit, shit. What're the odds? That must be his new girlfriend. Elizabeth suddenly felt the crushing weight of rejection. She felt so very alone, except for the company of the merciless critic in her head.

Why shouldn't he be with another woman? You blew it! You had your chance. If you weren't so stupid...

She drooped even lower at the thought of Brad with Kyla. She sighed. The other voice, the dark voice, came to her rescue. *Forget about it. He doesn't deserve us anyway. You saw how he treated you, Elizabeth, he couldn't wait to get that blonde cop upstairs. He's just like all the others. Maybe you'll have to teach him a lesson.*

Elizabeth didn't allow the voices to continue spinning in her head. She snapped to and again focused on getting the bulky cart through the double exit doors and out to the rental car. She was thankful Brad and his girlfriend hadn't shown up any later or they would have seen the pathetic car she was driving. She struggled to get the trash bags into the Buick's deep trunk.

She jumped into the old car and fired out of the parking garage as fast as its bald tires would take her. As soon as she got into downtown traffic, she lit a cigarette, and began to feel a little better. Her thoughts turned back to the mission at hand.

Her plan was to rent a storage unit somewhere in the low rent district and dump the chemical protection suit and the gun. It was perfect. She could get at the stuff if she needed to, if not, she could just stop paying the rent. The worst that could happen was that Ginny Forester would have incurred a bad credit reference.

Arriving at the address she had gotten from the Yellow Pages, she pulled into the driveway of an independently owned, somewhat run-down, mini-storage business. It was in the same part of town that she had been frequenting lately, so she wasn't expecting much in the way of amenities.

Elizabeth got out of the car and went into the small red brick building. Stale fried onions or boiled cabbage, smoke, and other unidentifiable smells ambushed her nose as she approached the front desk. Its white formica top had a gold pattern running through it that reminded her of pictures of neurons.

She looked over the counter through an open door to a living room where an older man sat in a threadbare green and white plaid, slightly stuffed armchair. He sat transfixed in front of a portable television screen, a cigarette burning between his fingers. On the snack tray set up next to him was a *TV Guide*, a can of mixed nuts, a bottle of whiskey, and a shot glass. Elizabeth rang a small bell stationed by a little sign that read Ring for Service.

"Louise! Get out here! Somebody's here! " The rummy turned back to watching Jerry Springer after taking another swig of the amber liquid.

Elizabeth smiled as she looked around the odd decor in the front office. All kinds of photocopied dirty jokes hung on the walls, with and without illustrations. A flyswatter lay on the counter with squashed black globs stuck in its mesh. She winced.

To the right of the apartment door was an enormous moose head. The unfortunate mammal practically took up the whole wall behind the cash register. She had to laugh out loud at the sight, although she did so quietly.

A thinnish woman with a cigarette hanging out of her mouth made her way to the counter, pulling off a large pair of yellow rubber gloves. A pine scent followed her into the room. "Help you?" The smoke gathered around the woman's face, and she squinted as she threw the gloves under the counter.

"Hi. Yes. I'm looking for a small storage unit. The smallest you have will probably be big enough." She could see the woman's scalp through her brown-grayish hair.

The woman looked at Elizabeth intently for a moment. "Ain't for drugs is it? You got to sign a paper saying you ain't storing drugs in here. The cops bring their dogs around ever so often and have them sniff the place out. Nothing we can do about it. "

She was a little curt. "I'm not storing any drugs, Ma'am."

"Sorry. We just tell that to everybody right up front. That way there's no misunderstandings and no hassles. We don't want to piss the cops off no how. Being in this part a town, we need all the protection we can get. "

"Ma'am, I'm just storing some things I don't have room for in my apartment."

"Yep, okay. Sign here, then." She made an X by the signature line on the agreement and slid the paper and pen at Elizabeth. "That's thirty a month cash, thirty dollars deposit. We give two weeks grace period for late payments, then we cut the lock, take the stuff out and put it in our storage for thirty days, then we sell it. I hope you brought your own lock. We don't furnish locks. That's number 13-A, right around the first building at the left there."

"Thirteen. Is that the only number you have left?"

"Yep. Of the smallest ones. Next size I have is nine by twelve. You don't believe in that stuff anyway, do you?" The woman snickered and lit another cigarette, although the butt of her old one was still smoldering beside her on the counter in a black plastic ashtray.

"No, of course not." Elizabeth pushed the signed paper, a fifty and a ten dollar bill across the counter. The smoking woman grabbed up the currency with the speed of a pickpocket.

After getting her receipt, Elizabeth backed up in front of the small storage module. She slid on a pair of thin vinyl gloves, peeled back the plastic cover from the cardboard, and extracted the new lock she'd bought on the way over. Taking a deep breath, she jumped out of the car to get rid of the evidence.

CHAPTER 30

Elizabeth walked cautiously into the renovated warehouse and took the lift up to the fourth floor, as Zipper had instructed; the wooden cage rattled and shook all the way up. A white, grease-spotted sack of Chinese food hung in her hand.

There looked to be only two units on the fourth floor. One had clear glass doors; the other had a tinted plate glass window in its wooden door. She wondered if it might be a one-way mirror, so that the apartment occupants could identify visitors and watch the people behind the transparent door across the hall.

In the large open room, five attractive young women sat in office modules, each equipped with a computer screen and a telephone headset. There was no clear indication of what they were doing. She knocked on the other door, where a brass number seven was mounted. The anticipation reminded her of that old game show, *Let's Make a Deal,* where the contestants sometimes chose the wrong numbered door and were greeted with billy goats or other farm animals.

A huge bear of a man answered the door. Not exactly your typical barnyard beast. She was certain of one thing, though. The monstrous man answering the door with his sports jacket tucked behind his shoulder holster wasn't smiling. Adrenalin sent the fight or flight question up her spine.

As Elizabeth turned to escape, she heard Zipper call out from somewhere behind the massive man. "Ginny? Is that you?"

"Yes, Zipper, it's me." She smiled, relieved, and took a deep breath. She never took her eyes off the big man, though.

"Want me to check out her sack for you, Boss?" The huge man started to reach toward her with his endless arms. He reminded her of Frankenstein.

Zipper was lying on the couch. "Keep your damn snout out of my Kung Pao Chicken, Hendrix. Come on in, Ginny. Don't be afraid of Hendrix. He's usually quite docile."

Zipper clapped his left hand to his chest and smiled when he saw her walking towards him. "Well, well, well, how's my nubile little friend?"

"Nubile!" Elizabeth laughed. "Where did you learn a word like that?"

"Nubile. A six-letter word for a sexually attractive young woman. All I do all day is work crossword puzzles, watch television, and dream of the days when my tallywhacker worked. "

"Thanks for sharing." Elizabeth grinned.

"Anytime. I do hope you are getting your share of fooling around, little sister, that beautiful face won't last forever in today's marketplace. The glitter of youth disappears before you know it."

"Can we discuss something besides my sex life, thank you very much?" She set the sack down on the coffee table. "Here's the food you whined for. How are you anyway?"

"The doctor said I'll be as good as new in a few weeks. I took a pretty good hit in the shoulder, but thank the Lord it missed the ole ticker. Guess that's the last time I'll be going out to get the feel of the streets."

"I told you so, Boss." Hendrix interjected during a brief pause from poking on his Gameboy. "I told you it was a bad idea."

"Thanks, Hendrix. An I-told-you-so is always music to my ears." Zipper rolled his eyes and waved Hendrix away. "Now, go play with yourself somewhere else."

Elizabeth suddenly understood Zipper's improved diction and absence of a coarse accent tonight. He had been playing the part of a two-bit street hustler the times she had seen him before. Actually, it looked like Zipper might be more the brains of the place. That would also explain why there was such a quick response when she had called Jimmy Beach the night he was shot.

"You sure, Boss? You know her good enough?" Hendrix wore a concerned look on his face.

"Did I stutter? Go on, now. It's not often I get some intelligent conversation around here, and I don't want you around screwing it up. She's fine. Now, vamoose! Sit down, Ginny, please." Zipper struggled up and began tearing into the little white cardboard food cartons like he was starving. "Want some?" He asked, but the offer sounded hollow. He quickly picked up his two chopsticks and dug in.

Hendrix skulked off towards the kitchen, his Gameboy encased by huge meaty fingers hanging at the end of his right arm. She suspected Hendrix probably had hair on his back.

"No thanks, I already ate." She sat down in a wooden chair across from Zipper.

"Did you have any trouble finding the place?" Zipper dropped some rice grains in his lap. He pinched them up and popped them into his mouth.

"No, I drove right to it. You gave good directions. What's that place across the hall?" She nodded towards the door. "Is that yours, too?

"Oh, that. It's nothing much, just a little sports book I run for an outfit out of Vegas. Gives me a little pin money. A detail I would prefer you keep to yourself."

"No problem." Like she was going to say anything else.

Zipper wiped his mouth with a paper napkin and cleared his throat. He dropped his shoulders, folded his hands in his lap, and looked at Elizabeth in earnest.

"The reason I asked you over was to thank you for saving my life. Where I come from, that means I owe you a favor. Anytime, anywhere, anyplace, for any reason." Zipper locked her eyes with his as he spoke.

The effect of Zipper's promise was powerful. She gulped. "That's not necessary, Zipper. I would have done it for anyone." She looked at her feet.

"Anytime—anywhere—anyplace—for any reason," Zipper repeated as he strained with his left arm to reach behind the couch. Her eyes widened. Zipper's hand soon came back into view, holding a box. It was tackily packaged in red, white, and blue birthday paper, topped with a big red bow. The haphazard wrapping and excessive tape made it appear almost comical.

She exhaled.

"That goofball Hendrix wrapped it for me and he did a terrible job. Look at this paper he used! I know it's probably not your birthday. I would have wrapped it myself, but I can't move my right arm right now, thanks to Slide, that fuckin' bastard. Wish I could find that little weasel." Zipper's eyes turned cold and dark when he spoke. "When I do—"

"So," she interrupted, "is that present for me? I feel bad. I didn't bring you a get well gift." She felt a little guilty.

Zipper smiled. "Yeah. That'd be good. Open this." He handed her the package. "Ginny, you did too bring me something. You brought me some terrific Kung Pao Chicken. That was a great gift; it was just what I wanted." Zipper smiled, burped, and laid back down. He looked tired.

She tore the wrapping paper from the package and flipped the lid off the box. A huge grin spread across her face. It was a beautiful black leather shoulder holster, complete with its own gun. She hadn't been this happy with a gift since she had opened her Chatty Cathy for Christmas when she was five. She wondered if this gun was used. The mystery of it just made her more intrigued with it.

"What kind is it?" She looked wide-eyed at Zipper.

"A Bulldog Tracker, a .357 Magnum with a four-inch barrel. If you're going to shoot somebody, use something that will make a dent. Don't dick around with those little pansy guns. You nail somebody, say, the size of Hendrix with a measly .22, and he's likely to catch and chew up the speeding bullets, eat the gun for dessert, and then get really pissed off."

She stared at the handgun, fascinated that it was actually hers. It made her feel powerful and safe. "Thanks, Zipper," she said.

CHAPTER 31

After thanking him for the gift several more times and saying her goodbyes, Elizabeth left Zipper's. He had wanted her to stay longer, but a nurse showed up about an hour after she got there to change his bandages and give him his meds. She barely escaped, Zipper not happy with her leaving until she promised a return visit soon. It was obvious he enjoyed her company. But, it had been a big day, and she was ready to go home and go to bed.

She drove on north Larimer Street on the way home, a stretch that most cautious people avoided at night. With her new gun under her jacket tucked into its trim holster, she felt prepared to deal with any situation that might arise. It gave her a rush to be among the hardened people who crawled the Denver streets at night.

The route was littered with dingy neighborhood bars and crummy cafes. While she waited at one stoplight, she glanced over to see an old black man looking down, trying hard not to topple over. In a moment it became clear that he was trying to urinate on a fire hydrant. She continued her tour. Parked in front of a club called the Dew Drop Inn, a name she imagined dubbed by a drunk punster, she saw it. In the tavern's parking lot, as big as you please, was the black Chrysler with the personalized license plates that read CRUIZIN. Imagine that. And her with her brand new gun. She turned the next corner to circle the block, glad she still had the rental car.

There was a dark alley running next to the club that she parked at the end of, and got out of the rental. Approaching the CRUIZIN car, but keeping close to the building, she strained to see inside of it. It appeared no one was sitting in the car. She skittered up and paused at its side. She pulled on the vinyl gloves that were still in her jacket pocket from the afternoon trip to the storage lot and reached for the car door handle. The screen door to the club slammed. She squatted down beside the car and froze.

An obviously inebriated, wrinkled old man came out of the club and paused near the entrance, as if he couldn't decide which way to go. She rose a little to peek through the car windows at him. He finally wandered off in the opposite direction.

Elizabeth pulled on the car handle. It was unlocked. Opening the car door as little as necessary, she pulled the seat forward and crept inside to the back, sliding down in the seat to wait. She could smell the grease from fast food and maybe hair pomade. Paper and plastic crinkled under her feet and she tried not to think about what all might be down there.

It was twelve-forty-three before Slide stepped outside of the bar. She knew the exact time because she had been checking her watch every two minutes for the last hour. She drew her new gun.

There he was, the ferret, Zipper's weasel. Slide ambled drunkenly over to the car and fumbled in his pockets for the keys. Finally fishing them out, he held the keys up in the air and grumbled, sorting through them. He opened the door and clumsily tumbled into the driver's seat. She held her breath. Slide made a big production of finding the keyhole somewhere down near the steering column.

"Don't you know you're not supposed to drink and drive, Slide?" She said in her deepest, throatiest voice. Slide jerked up hard and swiveled back toward her. He squinted, as if trying to make her out.

"Whoozat? Scared the shit outta me!" He belched and rested his head heavily on the steering wheel for a moment. Suddenly, in an angry voice, Slide turned back to her and yelled, "Hey! Who the hell are you, anyway? Whaddya want? Get out of my car!" It was obvious the bartenders didn't cut people off for one too many at this bar. The air swam with vile vapors.

"Hey, scumbag, don't you know you're not supposed to take stuff that's not yours from my friends?" She stuck the tip of the gun hard in Slide's temple.

"What? I didn't do anything." Slide ceased moving.

"And a liar, too. Shut up! Now, where was I? Oh, yeah... and then on top of that, after you robbed him, you had the balls to shoot my friend? That's not nice, Slide. I'm very angry with you. I should shoot you."

"Nooo..." Slide whined. "It waddn't personal, lady. He was just so easy...c'mon."

Elizabeth thought that remark confirmed what Hendrix thought of his boss's trial run back out in the trenches. Zipper had lost the necessary street-fighting edge, because he had gotten too fat and spoiled. It made him an easy target. Best he stay up in the ivory tower and call the shots from there.

"So, that's your excuse? That it was easy? You stole stuff from Zipper because it was easy? Then had the nerve to shoot him?" She grumbled in his ear as she increased the pressure on his temple with the piece. "You're pathetic."

She shoved his head up fast and bounced it off the steering wheel while she jumped out of the car from the passenger side. Through the open door, she stooped to take one more look inside the car when Slide suddenly took on a striking resemblance to her father. The screen in her head went red and she went into a trancelike state. She calmly raised the pistol, aiming at Slide's head.

"Boom," she said in a monotone, and pulled the trigger.

The window behind him looked like one of those paint-spinning pictures kids used to make at the state fair for a couple of bucks. This one was done all in deep red. She shook her head. "Ick. What a mess." She replaced the gun in its holster and looked around. There was no one reacting to the gunshot. Nobody running out to defend this putrid specimen of a human being.

Another virus exterminated, she thought smugly.

Elizabeth walked calmly to the car at the end of the alley. If anyone had seen her with Slide they wouldn't talk, and even if they did, what could they say? She sat for a few minutes to compose herself, then drove the car back to the closed rental place, parked it, and placed the keys through the slot in the door. Using the window cleaner and paper towel she had initially brought with her to clean the inside of the windshield, she wiped down everything in and out of the car she could think of.

After checking the door locks, she left the car to walk the few miles home. Being alone in the night didn't frighten her; besides, she had the gun. As she walked home, she followed her established routine of disposing of evidence. A glove and a paper towel in a trash can here, the other glove in a dumpster there, and she tossed the window cleaner in the back of an old truck loaded with old tires.

Order having been restored, she began to enjoy her walk home. The gun lent a pleasant pressure to her rib cage, reminding her of the powerful sentinel she now had at her side. She toyed with Zipper's offer of a favor; it might be a way to get Chet taken care of. She brightened for a moment at the thought, when the dark voice reminded her: *No way, Elizabeth. We are doing this ourselves. It's personal.* Elizabeth looked up to the stars and smiled, hoping that Mama was smiling back.

CHAPTER 32

When she got home, there had been a message on the answering machine from Chet blabbing about how much fun he had practicing on the computer during the week. Elizabeth wasn't looking forward to going to his house again. It was just something she had to do.

On the way to give Chet his internet and e-mail lesson, she called Zipper from a gas station pay phone. After she got through Hendrix's clumsy screening process, Zipper's voice came on the phone.

"Hi, Ginny! I'm so glad you called! I really enjoyed our visit last night. Guess what? I got a call this morning; it seems Slide met with an unfortunate demise last night. He lost his head, so to speak." Zipper cackled happily into the receiver.

"Oh, really?"

"Now that's the way to kick off a weekend." Zipper's laughter was making him wheeze and snort. "Ooh-boy... sorry...I can't quit laughing."

"You're sick, Zipper," she chuckled a little. "I just called to thank you again for the gift. It works real well."

There was instant silence on the other end of the line.

"And, of course, to see how you're doing. I'm glad to hear you're enjoying your get well gift."

"You? I—"

"Gotta git. Got an appointment. Take care of yourself. Bye!" She hung up and smiled to herself, proud that she had made Zipper happy.

❖ ❖ ❖

The trip out to her father's house was painfully redundant. Boredom at the road construction, then a fast flight into Elk Run from the end of it. Elizabeth hoped this was the last time she would have to make the trip.

She arrived a little earlier than expected. She figured the sooner she got there, the sooner she could get out. Chet opened the door, happy and freshly shaven, greeting her with open arms. She held up a shielding hand in front of her, and smiled weakly.

"I'm glad you came early," Chet said. "I am so anxious to learn some more about this thing." He looked at her with bright, clear eyes, although her rebuff had dulled his cheerful expression a little.

She scooted by him and he followed her to the makeshift computer table in the bedroom that used to be hers. Except for an accumulation of clutter, the basic furnishings of her old room were the same, down to the thin pink chenille bedspread and cheap cotton curtains. A vacuum, a set of barbells, free weights, and various-sized brown boxes sitting around disturbed the still girlish decor. The disarray reminded her of a fungus that looked like it would eventually swallow up the whole room.

So much for making your room a shrine, Elizabeth, the dark voice tattled to her.

"I brought in an extra seat so we could both sit down," Chet said.

"Good," she replied, and sat in the folding chair in front of the computer. She began logging on to the web browser. "So you had fun working with the word processing program this week?"

Chet puffed up with pride. "Oh yeah! I've even been writing letters to people! Ron hooked it up to an old printer his wife had and told me I could use it till I got one of my own. I been printing out stuff left and right. My typing sucks, but it's still fun!"

They spent a good part of the afternoon getting acquainted with the Internet, how to use search engines, how to send e-mail. Chet was attentive all the way through and seemed to be picking up the information quickly. It was obvious he had found a new hobby and was eager to learn how to start enjoying it. She broke his technology daze.

"Well, I have got to get going. You know everything you need to get started, plus you have written instructions in case you forget."

"Can't you stay for supper?" Chet looked pained.

"No, not tonight." It was the last thing Elizabeth wanted to do, to be alone in this house with Chet after dark.

"One more thing before you go then, Elizabeth. There's a guy on the painting crew that was talking about chat rooms on the net. Do you know anything about those?"

"Ready for chat rooms already, huh? You are a quick study," she remarked and silently translated to herself. *Good. That means I won't have to deal with you as long as I had expected to. Yes!*

"Well, I am your old man. You had to get your smarts from somewhere." Chet smiled at her.

"Yeah, I guess." Her stomach threatened to surface. She stepped back to the computer and, after sitting down, did a few searches for chat rooms for older singles. She chose a couple that didn't look too raunchy. She bookmarked them and thought she would go ahead and get him a password for the chat rooms while she was there. That part could be a little complicated for a beginner.

"What do you want to go by?" Elizabeth asked.

Chet's eyebrows went up. "What do you mean?"

"What name do you want to use for yourself in the chat rooms?" Elizabeth felt a little bothered at having to repeat herself.

Chet still looked puzzled. "What's wrong with Chet?"

"Most people like use a nickname to be more anonymous." She clicked her fingernails on the mouse pad.

"People couldn't get my last name could they?"

"Not usually. Not unless you piss off some hacker, then they might. But they don't usually waste their time unless they can get some money or sex somehow."

"Not a chance there, the money part at least." Chet laughed. "Let's just use Chet, then. That way I won't forget it. I just won't fight with nobody; anyway, I'm a lover, not a fighter." Chet laughed again, but the joke hung in the air.

Elizabeth didn't laugh. In fact, she wanted in the worst way to get up, go out, get the Magnum from under the seat and blow his stupid fucking brains out. Instead, she determinedly typed his name and password into each of the requesting sign-in screens of the chat rooms.

The typing helped her regain her composure. "When it asks for your password, just type in Chet again, got that?"

"Okay. I should be able to remember that!" Chet jotted down the information on the side of the paper anyway.

Elizabeth rose to leave. "Well, that wraps it up. I've really got to go now. I need a cigarette."

Chet looked surprised. "I didn't know you smoked, Elizabeth."

"I don't." She kept walking out of the house, across the porch, and out to her car. She never looked back.

CHAPTER 33

"Another Saturday night and I ain't got nobody, I got some money 'cause I just got paid. How I wish I had someone to talk to—I'm in an awful state..."

Elizabeth rolled her eyes and snapped the radio off, stopping the song in midstream. She didn't need some masochistic disk jockey reminding her how lonely her life was. Wrestling with the music case in the passenger seat, she finally found the Bonnie Raitt CD she was looking for.

Suddenly, an icy fear gripped her heart. Her throat felt like a thick rope was tightly winding around it. She dropped the CD into the passenger seat and quickly lifted her foot off the gas pedal. She pulled over to the shoulder of the road and stopped, terrified. This is what her former therapist had called "an episode." She called it "feeling like dying."

She stared at her thumb and mumbled, "I can do all things through Christ who strengthens me. I can do all things through Christ who strengthens me," over and over again like a mantra, even though the words stuck in her taut throat. It seemed odd to Elizabeth that every time she felt like this, she prayed. When she felt okay, the thought of praying rarely occurred to her. She'd think more about that later when she didn't feel like something was trying to pinch off her head at the neck.

After sitting calmly for several minutes, the frantic feeling subsided considerably, and she steered the car back out onto the highway. Hyper-alert to the way she felt, Elizabeth monitored her body's progress back to normalcy as she resumed the speed limit westbound. She picked up the CD off the passenger seat and popped it into the stereo player.

She forced herself to sing along with Bonnie Raitt's *Fundamental Things* in an attempt to get her mind off her distress. It wasn't working very well. Her index finger was keeping fair time with the music on the steering wheel, when a second attack hit her.

Panic and rage boiled up from her legs as she felt white heat inch its way up her body, igniting her senses along the way. Flashes of the faces of Jesse and Slide twitched through her mind, as well as some of her mother, Chet, and Zipper. Elizabeth hurriedly pulled the car over to the shoulder and stopped for the second time. She had never experienced two attacks so close together before.

She grabbed her stomach and started to growl and grunt while her face turned crimson. Screaming and crying, she beat on the steering wheel with her hands. Fleeing the car, she ran down the ditch and up the other side. She straddled the barbed wire fence, and started running through the open field. She ran until she was out of breath, over thin grass and sinkholes, then finally stopped and bent slightly to clutch her knees.

She straightened up and looked around the barren field. There was a small herd of Holstein cows staring at her inquisitively from a safe distance. She turned to see how far she had come. Although she couldn't see her car anymore, she could see snatches of tractor-trailer rigs periodically zooming by over the horizon. She figured the highway to be a couple of miles away. Spotting a large limestone rock, she went to sit down and catch her breath.

The run had calmed her nerves some and, after getting her bearings, she walked back to her vehicle at a relaxed pace. By the time she got back to her car, it was dusk. As she was putting her seat belt on, a man pulled up behind her in a red four-wheel drive utility vehicle and hopped out. Elizabeth checked her rearview mirror. He was alone.

A handsome male face appeared in her side window. "Need some help?"

She touched the power button and her window went down about six inches. "No, I don't think so."

His bright green eyes peered at her. "You sure? You sick? You're pretty pale. Sure you don't need a ride somewhere to call someone?"

The dark voice inside heckled her. *Call someone. Very funny. Who would you call, Elizabeth?*

"I'm fine, really. Thanks for stopping, but it's best if you go now. Thanks again."

The dark voice mocked her. *Aw...Elizabeth...going to let this golden opportunity pass you by? He would be so easy... and that new gun works so well. C'mon, take a load off your chest and put it into his.*

Afraid, Elizabeth quickly started the Mercedes and sped off, leaving a very puzzled looking Good Samaritan in the dust. "Sorry I didn't say goodbye, Buddy, but I was looking out for your health," she guaranteed the shrinking figure in the rearview mirror.

CHAPTER 34

Chet sat his fried chicken TV dinner next to the keyboard and settled down in front of the computer. It was really nice of Lizzie to set him up with this rig. She must be doing pretty well for herself to be giving away high priced pieces of equipment like this.

Their father-daughter reunion wasn't going as well as he had hoped. Lizzie was as cold as a frozen fish. She was polite and everything, but she was like a robot when they were together. She wouldn't loosen up no matter what he said. He had been sober a whole year; Chet couldn't see what her problem was.

And what was the big deal about her name, anyway? He had always called her Lizzie. Now she's all high and mighty, driving a Mercedes, and wanting to be called Elizabeth. He never did like that name anyway, but Saundra had insisted, and he'd agreed on it in a weak moment. He had wanted a boy and hadn't given any thought to girl names.

AA slogans ran through his mind: *Stinkin' thinkin'. One day at a time. First things first. Keep it simple, stupid.*

Bud, his AA sponsor, had told him repeatedly during their talks that he would have to learn to be accepting of his daughter as she was now. To let her warm up to him at her own pace; to give her some time. As difficult as it had proved to be, he continued to try to be patient with her. He was hopeful that her idea of getting to know each other again by e-mail would give him a chance to show her how he'd changed.

Playing with the Internet search engines for a while, he looked up different topics that interested him. He wondered if there was any way to look up some of his old Air Force buddies on the net. He would have to ask her about that.

Chet looked up "sex," and a few other choice words, and couldn't believe the wealth of information that was returned to him. He stumbled onto some sex sites, but left when they asked for credit card numbers. He was mesmerized.

Chet remembered the bookmarks for the chat rooms she had set up for him. He followed the steps carefully and found himself thrust into a chat room where there were eight other people talking. The screen was easy to read, with each person choosing a different color to communicate in. Chet chose red.

"Chet enters the room," the screen read.

Remus: Hi Chet!

Zooboy: Howdy-doddy, Chet

Zooboy: oops doddy=doody

Chet: Hi everyone!

Chet spent a couple of hours chatting with his new friends and never moved from the chair. Although his typing speed improved from one finger to two during the evening, his spelling and spacing still suffered. He was having a lot of fun, but he did have to take a break and get something to drink.

This was great. Being in a chat room was sort of like being at a bar, with fewer complications. Maybe if he would have had a computer before, he wouldn't have been so bored and wouldn't have drank so much. Chet dismissed the bar images as best he could, and grabbed the iced tea out of the refrigerator. He should probably call Bud about Lizzie's visit today, but it could wait. After making a pit stop in the bathroom, he settled back before the computer screen.

All typed conversation in the chat room stayed on the screen until it scrolled off, so when Chet returned to the screen, he noticed that a new person had entered the chat room while he was gone. Since he had tired of the others, he decided to greet her.

Chet: Hi Rosie!

Rosie: Hi Chet! You new? I haven't seen you in here before.

Chet:	Yep. I am. You been coming in here al ong time?
Rosie:	About six months, I guess. What's your status?
Chet:	Male. 56. Widowd. You?
Rosie:	Female. 43. Divorced.
Chet:	You're just a pup! I like younger women thoguh
Rosie:	A pup! LOL!
Chet:	What's LOL mean/
Rosie:	Laugh Out Loud!

The conversation went on for a couple of hours. They talked about their interests, relationships, dreams, all the personal stuff people talk about on first dates. Finally, Chet felt like he was going to fall asleep at the mouse, and had to sign off. They made arrangements to talk the next evening.

CHAPTER 35

Elizabeth finally made it home Saturday evening after the second panic attack. She was notably frightened of the frequency and intensity of the anxiety and the insistence of the dark voice. In the past, it had spoken to her only occasionally, mostly in the form of sarcastic remarks about people when she couldn't say them out loud. Lately, it came and went more often, and had become more demanding.

She thought a few times in the past few days about calling Dr. Arnold to make an appointment, but couldn't bring herself to do it. Having learned to bring the anxiety under control consistently using relaxation techniques, she had quit visiting the therapist several months ago. Throughout her therapy, she never mentioned the voice to Dr. Arnold. Neither had she told the doctor about her chaotic childhood. She had gone to therapy strictly to learn how to control the panic attacks. When the concerned doctor had tried to probe into her past, Elizabeth put her off. Now, it seemed too late for all that anyway.

Exhausted, she hit the couch practically the minute she walked in the door. After dozing for about an hour, she woke up with renewed nervous energy. She threw her suitcase open on the bed and started packing for her trip to Dallas the next day.

She was due at Line Interiors' executive offices early Monday morning for the kickoff presentation of their new software system.

Management wanted her to give them a preview of what was involved so they could better prepare their employees for the upcoming changes.

She quickly bored with the tedium of packing for the trip, poured herself a brandy, and wandered over to the computer. She logged on to the TechChat room and bantered with Chip a little while, but soon the conversation went flat, and she said her goodbyes. She was not in the mood for unproductive small talk.

She thought it might be a bit too soon to expect Chet in one of the chat rooms, but she decided to check it out anyway. It was possible; he was learning very fast. The screens leading into the room were cluttered with bawdy ads, marketers promising possibilities of true love, and links to other hot singles pages. Obviously, there must be a lot of lonely people out there. That made her feel a little better somehow.

The first singles chat room she entered using her screen name, mouse, was empty. But he was in the second one she tried. She didn't join in the conversation, but just sat and watched to see how he interacted with the other chatters in the room. After several minutes, she logged out of the room. She waited a bit, then she logged back into the room with a new handle, Rosie, as a nickname.

As Rosie, she flirted with and praised Chet's starving male ego. She laughed at his dumb jokes and typing mistakes. He seemed fascinated with her and one time even suggested they meet. She told him that she was from Dallas to keep him at bay, but figured it still sounded close enough to keep him on the line.

She imagined conversing with her father through the eyes of her mother, when her mother first met Chet. He could be so charming, and she understood how Mama had been hooked by the lure of this deadly flesh fisherman.

CHAPTER 36

Elizabeth took off her shoes and stretched out on the king-sized bed in her hotel room, feeling spent after her flight from Denver to Dallas on Sunday. Although the flight was smooth, the airports of both cities seemed more like amusement parks than airline terminals. She loved to fly, but didn't love all the hassles at airports.

She tuned in the radio beside her bed to a classical music station and listened closely for a moment: Mozart's *Overture to the Magic Flute.* She settled back down on the bed and let her mind wander freely. She loved Mozart's music and the stories of his brilliance—ever since she'd selected him as a research paper topic for a music appreciation class in college.

She tried to relax, but disturbing images began to flash through her mind. Airports as amusement parks triggered the recall of an occasion where Chet had taken her to the state fair once after Mama died. She must have been about nine or ten years old. He begrudgingly paid her admission to get in the gate, gave her five dollars, and told her to go have some fun. He hadn't allowed her to bring a friend, and he had spent the entire afternoon in the beer tent. She had roamed about the fairgrounds trying to amuse herself with rides and games, but she felt so horribly alone and just wanted to go home. High in the air on the ferris wheel that day, Elizabeth remembered promising herself that she would get away from Chet as soon as possible, like she had promised Mama she would.

Several years later, Mrs. Brummitt, her seventh grade creative writing teacher, assigned the students in her class to write a poem expressing a painful memory. Elizabeth had written about that awful day at the carnival. The theatrical Mrs. Brummitt raved to the class about her poetry, claiming Elizabeth's poem was clearly a metaphor. A lone tormented and tortured soul wandering around a carnival was compared to man's futile and desperate attempts to connect to an inherently cold and economically driven society. Elizabeth thought she had just written about a little girl's sad day at the fair.

Mrs. Brummitt made sure the poem was printed in the school paper. The praise she received for writing the poem renewed her confidence and determination. She threw herself even harder into her studies, determined to get a college scholarship so she could leave home the instant she graduated from high school. If he didn't have to pay for it, Chet couldn't stop her.

She dozed off for a short nap, but woke with a start and looked at her watch. Good. She still had two hours before she had to meet Chet in the chat room at ten. She climbed wearily off the bed and went to shower, then put on a comfortable cotton nightshirt.

She was more relaxed after her water ritual. She munched on a chef salad she had ordered from room service, and removed her laptop computer from its case and set it up. First, she checked her e-mail messages and returned the ones that were work related. Finally, she opened the e-mail that Chet had sent her that afternoon.

To: *Estrong@gomail.com*
From: *Chet@parkernews.com*
Subject: *Hi there*

Hi, Elizabeth. How was your trip? I am getting pretty good at typing, I am up to using two fingers now! I'm not very fast and I don't spell two goood (ha ha), but I'm having fun. I really like this computer business. I am meeting some new people in the chat rooms you fixed me up on. Thanks again for the use of the machine.

I got some work starting tomorrow that will last about a week. Ron got us a job painting some new fast food place.

Hope you have a good day!
Love,
Dad

Love, Dad? Ick. Elizabeth stared at the two words. This is the first time she could remember her father writing her a personal note. After staring at the memo for some time, she deleted the correspondence, uncomfortable with Chet's words displayed on her screen, and shut off the computer. She reached for the phone and dialed out.

"Hi, Hendrix, is Zipper there?" She played with the phone cord, wrapping the beige plastic coated coils around her index finger.

"Who is this?"

"Ginny Forester. Remember me?"

"Oh, yeah. How can I forget? Boss talks about you all the time. Just a minute, I'll get him."

There was a pause and a murmur of voices in the background. She heard someone blow their nose, and then the phone was picked up.

"Hi, Ginny! Where are you?" Zipper's voice was upbeat and friendly.

"Out of town on business—Dallas. How are you?" She wasn't sure why she called, but knew that Zipper's voice was like a soothing balm to her frazzled nerves.

"Getting stronger every day. When will you be home?"

"In a few days. I thought I might come visit you when I get back."

She looked down and picked at the bedspread, which was burgundy with yellow and pink flowers on it.

"Great! You're always welcome here. I need to talk to you anyway."

"What about?" She asked suspiciously.

"Oh, nothing important. I just want to see you."

"Okay. I'll call you when I get back and we'll go from there, okay?" She smiled into the phone.

"Sure. Oh, and Ginny?"

"Yeah, Zip?"

"Take care of yourself."

"You, too. Bye." Elizabeth hung up the phone, feeling better having called.

CHAPTER 37

Chet stewed and paced at not being able to get the computer to work. Every time he turned it on, it gave him some bomb picture and the screen froze up. He called Ron for help, but Ron had another kind of computer and couldn't help him with the problem.

It was Thursday evening and he had chatted with Rosie every night since they had met last Saturday evening. He looked forward to talking to her every day. They got along so well, it seemed like he had known her for years. They had made a date to meet again tonight, and he couldn't figure out a way to get word to her. He didn't even have her e-mail address so he could go to Ron's and send her a note from there.

Chet called Elizabeth in a dither. He left a message on her machine. He wasn't even sure when she was coming home, she didn't say in her short e-mail. According to the Yellow Pages, the closest computer store that fixed Apple computers was in Parker, a town about thirty miles away. He called the service department at the store and discovered he couldn't afford a service call anyway. He ate a light supper of a tuna fish sandwich and potato chips and channel surfed the television in an attempt to forget about the computer and Rosie for awhile.

Chet tried to relax and attempted to put the situation in a more reasonable perspectives. *As Bud would say, I'm obsessing again. Hell, I haven't even had this thing a month. You get addicted to anything that makes you feel better, don't you, you old bastard?* The question accompanied a thought that just maybe he should call his sponsor, Bud, and vent a little frustration. He squelched the thought. *Good God, give the poor man a rest. You've already driven him crazy lately with this Lizzie situation*. He considered going to an AA meeting, but didn't want to be gone in the event that she tried to call.

The phone rang. He jumped for it, thinking it might be Lizzie.

"Hello!"

"Hi, Chet, this is Greta." The little voice of one of Chet's AA friends was weak and shaky.

"Hi, Greta. Is it possible I could call you back later? I am sorta expecting a call." He shifted from one foot to the other.

"Chet, I need help." Greta's voice seemed sincere.

"What's wrong?" Chet heard her crying.

She talked through choked sobs. "I drank after two years in the program. Two years, Chet! I feel so damn bad. I even started smoking again and I've been off cigarettes for over a year!" Greta's sobs subsided a little, then she questioned him: "How come we never went out, Chet? I called you, and you never called me back. What's wrong with me? Wait...wait a minute."

Chet heard a cap unscrew and liquid pouring. "Greta? You still drinking? You're not still drinking are you? You need some help?"

"Hey, Chet. Never mind, I gotta go."

The receiver clicked in his ear. Chet sat for a minute, staring at the phone.

Should I go over there? Bud said a man wasn't supposed to go out on a call to a drinking woman's house alone and vice-versa. What if I miss Lizzie's call? But aren't we supposed to help other AA members when they call for help?

The confused debate raged on in his head. Chet picked up the phone and dialed Bud's number. The phone rang seventeen long, empty times. Obviously, no Bud and no answering machine.

Chet grabbed his jacket and left for Greta's.

When he arrived at the tidy white house, he saw it was shut up tight. There was no indication that anyone was home. He stepped up onto the small cement porch and rapped on the screen door. A friendly golden retriever ran around to the front of the house, letting loose a few token barks, wagging its tail the whole time. He came up on the porch and stood beside Chet watching the door, like he was interested in where the heck Greta was, too.

Chet knocked again and called out. "Greta! Are you in there?" He listened closely for any response while obliging the dog's demands for attention by absentmindedly patting it on the head. "C'mon, Greta, let me in! It's Chet! I want to help you!"

A narrow crack sliced the inside door opening. A sad face barely peered out. Mascara had run rivulets straight down Greta's cheeks, making her look like a mime gone bad.

"What do you want, Chet? When I was sober and pretty, you didn't gimme the time a day. Now that I'm a drunk ugly mess, here you are!" The door shut in Chet's face.

"C'mon, Greta, let me in. I'll make us some coffee. We can talk." Chet opened the screen door and rapped hard on the inside door. "C'mon, Greta! Open up!"

The door opened again and Greta retreated back into the dark interior of the house. Chet cautiously followed, careful to leave the dog outside. As soon as he stepped into the small living room, he saw that Greta was buck naked. She was sitting, legs crossed in a smallish stuffed chair covered with a light pink sheet. There was a red plastic ashtray perched on one armrest, filled with cigarette butts. A fifth of Jack Daniels was nestled down by her feet.

"Sit down, Chet." She flicked her fine brunette hair to one side, and motioned to the slick blue and white flowered sofa directly across the small room. "You know what, Chet?" Picking her cigarette up from the ashtray, she left it burning between her long slender fingers on her left hand. Her right hand was wrapped around a plastic cartooned tumbler, the kind purchased at convenience stores usually filled with soda. Lately, judging from Greta's condition, the glass obviously had been holding generous portions of bourbon.

Greta looked at the television. The sound was off, but the picture on the screen seemed to captivate her for a moment, then she turned back to Chet. "I lost my job the other day. Downsized, they said. I had been commuting to Denver for over a year—a year, mind ya—for those sonsabitches and this, this, is what I get." Greta clumsily took a puff off her cigarette and intertwined her muscular legs.

Chet stared shamelessly, hypnotized by her two dark nipples staring at him like eyes. It had been so long since he'd had a woman. He felt the denim over the crotch of his jeans grow taut.

"Want a drink, Chet? I know you do. You're like me, Chet. You hate being sober. Reality sucks, don't it?" Greta laughed darkly and glanced at him sideways through partially closed eyelids, but didn't make a move to share her bottle. Instead, she stood up carefully and moved across the room, landing on the sofa cushion beside Chet.

Chet figured her to be a well-kept early forties. Her body was mostly firm and plenty inviting. Her face, in Chet's opinion up to now, had been rather plain, but tonight she looked like Sophia Loren.

Blood ran hot in his veins. The old feelings of burning passion and intoxicating power coursed through his body. From that moment, he wanted to possess her, pound her with his desire into the couch until she begged for mercy.

You can't fall into a bucket of paint without getting some on you. You can't walk into a barber shop without getting a haircut. Chet heard Bud's hackneyed pearls of wisdom rattle around in his head. It wasn't the head he was using for thinking at the moment.

"Am I desirable to you, Chet?" Her voice sounded hopeful, but her bedroom eyes looked vacant.

"Of course you are, Greta. It's just that I'm trying to stay clean."

"I'm clean, Chet. See for yourself." She picked up his hand and placed it directly between her legs.

Chet groaned, pinned her head to the back of the couch, and kissed her hungrily, exploring greedily with his hand at her insistence. Both were ravenous in attacking their longing. After a time, he broke away, breathless.

"Greta."

"Wha—?" She didn't stop moving against him, lost in her lust.

"I believe I will have that drink now."

CHAPTER 38

Elizabeth had corresponded with Chet as Rosie every night until she left Dallas to go home that Thursday afternoon. He was taking the bait, hook, line, and sinker. The presentations and training with management at Line Interiors had gone well. The trip had been a welcome diversion, but she was ready to be home.

After traversing the busy city streets, airline terminals, and surviving plane and taxi rides, she finally arrived at her apartment late that evening. The answering machine held a dire plea from Chet.

"Elizabeth, there's something wrong with the computer. All I get is this bomb exploding, then the screen freezes up and I have to turn it off. Can you call and tell me how to fix it or something? I've met this woman in the chat room that I really hit it off with and it's pretty important I get it fixed right away. I don't have any way to get hold of her. I don't want her to think I dumped her. Can you call me back as soon as you get home? Thanks. Bye."

She rolled her eyes at Chet's clamor. There was no way she could guide a novice through the sophisticated process of running system checks and hard drive repair programs over the phone. *Damnit. I never wanted to set foot in that stinking house again.* Remembering the difficult time she had on the way home last weekend, she groaned at the thought of repeating the trip.

She went straight to bed. She was beat and wanted to get to the office early the next morning. The trip had generated a pile of paperwork that needed to be completed before she returned to Dallas next week. She liked to write reports while the information was fresh in her mind.

Friday morning, she returned Chet's call from her office during a break. The phone rang about four times, when an answering machine picked up. "Hello. This is Chet Strong. I'm not in right now. Please leave your message at the beep."

She sipped her coffee as she listened to the short recorded message, and then spoke in a professional manner after the tone. "Chet, this is Elizabeth. I got your call about the computer. I can't make it out there until tomorrow about the same time as usual. I have to work all day at the office today, and there's no way I can explain how to fix a computer over the phone. I'll see you then."

She punched a clear line out and dialed *67 to block the number to her office phone in case Zipper had caller ID. She poked the rest of the number into the desk phone and swiveled to look out at the mountains while it rang. Hendrix was actually pleasant to her this time when he answered. Zipper was delighted to hear from her, and they made plans for her to visit that evening.

The cuisine request for tonight was for Schezuan beef, extra spicy. She had the feeling Zipper was probably using her as an accomplice to avoid doctor's orders of no hot foods or something. She didn't mind. She figured it would take more than cayenne pepper to take Zipper out, the tough old boot.

CHAPTER 39

In addition to Zipper's request, she picked herself up an order of veggie lo mein, and added an extra entree of Schezuan beef for Hendrix. She hoped the three of them might even be able sit at a table and have a meal together, like normal people do. Grinning at the comical memory of Zipper dragging food out of a white paper carton with his chopsticks last time, she checked to make sure the PuPu container in her sack remained level.

She thought it might be fun to share the different appetizers held in her sack. There was crab Rangoon, teriyaki chicken strips, spring rolls, shrimp tempura, and some stuff she'd never heard of before. A PuPu platter may not look so hot served in Styrofoam, but she figured it was the thought that counted. She was almost up to the door of Zipper's building when she met Beulah coming out.

Her grin straightened to a thin line across her face. "What are you doing here?" She asked incredulously.

"Hello, Elizabeth!" Beulah flashed her that big ridiculous smile.

Elizabeth quickly scanned her memory for a time she may have told Beulah her real name. She did not come up with one. "How do you know my name?"

"The Boss. I find out t'ings for him sometimes. I knowed him a long time. He's a good boy." Beulah looked longingly at the sacks she was carrying. It did smell good.

"You know Zipper?"

"Oh, yeah!" Beulah put one her hand on her hip and waved the other at Elizabeth. "Kid, everybody knows Zipper. He's always done right by me. He knows; he used to be on the streets hisself long time ago. He makes sure me and Sugar gets enough to eat and a warm place to sleep in the wintertime. All I gotta do is run a few errands for him once in a while. He's a good boy. Yep, a good man." Beulah kept staring hungrily at the food sacks.

She cocked her head at the old woman. "Been a while since you've had Chinese food, Beulah?"

"Sure has. And it sure smells good." Beulah held her hands clasped up close to her chest.

She put down one of her sacks on the sidewalk and pulled a ten dollar bill and a couple of ones out of the back pocket of her jeans.

"Here ya go, Beulah. It's Friday night. Live it up. Take this and go get you some Chinese food." She handed Beulah the bills.

"T'anks, lady—Elizabeth. Pretty name, Elizabeth. Bye, girl. Have a nice dinner, now." Beulah hurried away with her meal tickets.

Her entrance into Zipper's condo went a little smoother this time, especially after Hendrix learned that she had brought him something to eat. After she set out the silverware and transferred the food into glass bowls and onto plates, they all sat down at the kitchen table. Zipper squealed and whined about Hendrix sitting with them.

"Oh, let him stay, Zipper. He needs his energy to put up with you!" She laughed, then bit into the gooey part of a crab Rangoon.

"Oh? He don't do anything except play with that Gameboy all day long, isn't that right, Hendrix?" Zipper forked a big bite of beef into his mouth. "Mmmm..."

"Sure Boss, that's all I do." Hendrix chewed and smiled at his boss. It was apparent that Hendrix and Zipper shared a private joke.

"So, Ginny — if that is your real name—how was your week?" Zipper looked at her expectantly.

She wiped her mouth with a paper napkin. "Very funny. I met Beulah in front when I was coming in. She told me you know my real name. How?"

"Please don't be offended, Elizabeth. We make it a habit to check out anyone that does any business with us. The first time you came into the drop front, you were driving a Mercedes. I had a friend run your tag. A leased Mercedes in the name of Cleardrive, Inc. is what came back." Zipper paused for a sip of water. "So, then I had my buddy Hendrix here call Cleardrive, and they never heard of Ginny Forester. We showed Beulah a picture of you and sent her over there. By the way, she told me she already knew you but didn't know your name."

Elizabeth broke in. "A picture of me? Where did you get a picture of me?" She dropped her fork on her plate.

"We got a couple cameras set up at different angles in a few of the empty mailboxes over at the drop. It may look like a dump, but we run a boatload of cash through there. The security system in there is fairly high tech."

"Man, you can't even rely on finding an authentic slum to do business in anymore. Everything is something else and everybody is somebody else." Elizabeth sulked, pushing her food around on the plate.

"Not everybody, Elizabeth. I am who I am. So, anyway, like I said, I sent Beulah over to Cleardrive to scout it out. She pointed to you and asked someone who you were when you were leaving work one day." He snapped off a bite of spring roll.

"I never saw her at my office building," she said, feeling violated.

Zipper kept talking with his mouth partially full. "Beulah, she's a sly one; she can be pretty invisible when she wants to be. Don't worry, she just told them she was looking for her sister's kid, and that wasn't the name she was looking for. But it was your name, little sister. What gives?"

She looked irritated. "Can we just eat dinner first?"

"But, how come you been going around as somebody else? How come you took it upon yourself to take care of my little weasel problem? And records show that you have a damn good job and make plenty of money. Why would you do all that? It doesn't make any sense. " Zipper cut of piece of beef with his knife and fork and stuffed it in his mouth.

"I'm not even going to ask you how you found out about my income. One more word about me, and I'll get up and leave right now. We can discuss it after dinner, okay? Would you pass the fried rice, please?"

"Yes. But don't think for a moment I don't know you're stalling." Zipper passed the bowl to her.

"Thank you." She dumped rice out of the serving bowl with a spoon onto her plate.

Hendrix looked on, seemingly dumbfounded at the argument.

After dinner, they moved back into the living room so that Zipper could lie down for a little while. Hendrix sat off in the corner watching television without the sound on, and soon dozed off. She sat in a wooden chair that she had placed so Zipper could see her without having to strain his neck. He seemed a little better than when she saw him last time, but he still seemed to tire easily.

Zipper grinned toward Hendrix. "Just like a big ole dog. Gets his stomach full and has to take a nap. Just as loyal, too." Zipper sighed. "We been through a lot together—hey! This getting shot bullshit has made me all maudlin and mushy. Sorry. Must be the pain pills. I'm more worried about you, Elizabeth. You seem so alone."

"Don't be. I'm fine. This name thing is real personal. I really can't talk about it right now, okay?" She looked down, her eyes tearing up, and tapped her foot nervously.

Zipper studied her face. "Okay. No pressure tonight. I'll tell you a little bit about me instead, okay?"

"Okay." She felt relieved and wiped away the moistness from her eyes.

Zipper told her about being a fresh faced, idealistic kid sent over to Viet Nam in 1967, and of the time when his company was ordered to take Hill 881. He described the horror that followed.

"Then my M-16 jammed, and a Viet Cong rushed me with a bayonet and left me for dead—and I almost did die. I laid on the ground for several hours before I received any medical attention. My best friend got killed taking me out of there." Zipper stopped for a moment and swallowed hard. "I couldn't understand why God had left me alive in that hellhole and took my buddy when he had a wife and kid waiting for him at home. I came back to the States as soon as I could travel, and wandered the streets here for a couple of years, drinking hard and being pissed off at God and the world that I was alive. I had nightmares every night. I saw them over and over again, the terrified expressions on the faces of my friends as they fell, one by one. All the booze in the world couldn't erase their memories from my mind, and Lord knows I tried." Zipper stopped for a moment, obviously choking back tears.

"Here." Elizabeth handed Zipper a tissue from the end table.

"Thanks." He blotted his eyes and blew his nose. "That's how I met Beulah. She was already on the streets back then. I would pass out wherever and she would stick around and make sure no one bothered me, whether I was unconscious in an alley or under a bridge. Most times, she'd be there smiling at me when I woke up."

Elizabeth smiled. "So how did you get here?"

"I got in a fight one night in a bar and kicked the shit out of some wise guy's bodyguard over a woman. I ended up answering to the big kahuna, who as it turned out, was a Viet Nam vet, too. We had some drinks, reminisced, cried, grieved, had a few laughs, and then he offered me a little piece of some Vegas action. He gave me a chance to clean up my act and make something of myself. I couldn't go back to the same world I came from before I went to Nam. It just wasn't possible."

Tears leaked out of Elizabeth's eyes as she felt emotions that she couldn't quite identify.

"I'm sorry, Zip. I'm really sorry." She went to Zipper's side, knelt down beside the couch, reached for his hand and held it. Neither of them said another word to each other that night. She tenderly held Zipper's hand until he fell asleep.

She went to let herself out but, as soon as she turned the doorknob, Hendrix was right behind her, breathing down her neck. She jerked, startled. "Jesus, Hendrix, you don't have to scare me to death."

"Sorry; it's my job. Goodnight, Elizabeth. Thanks for the food." He held the door open for her.

"You're welcome, Hendrix, goodnight. Tell Zipper I'll call him soon. Bye."

"Okay." Hendrix shut the door quietly behind her. She heard the dead bolts click into place. The girls across the hall were busily talking into their mouthpieces and punching madly on their computer keyboards.

Little piece of the action. Pin money, I bet. She grinned as she climbed into the lift, and headed for home.

CHAPTER 40

Saturday morning, Elizabeth drove the long, banal route to Chet's house once again, and was not in a good mood about it. To reward herself for getting through the road construction once more without going stark raving berserk, she took the Mercedes up to 110 miles an hour. She allowed her mind to think of nothing but the sweet serenade of the engine singing down the road.

She was thoroughly enjoying the rush of speed whizzing past her ears when she came upon a bulky half of a double wide trailer being transported, trespassing on her side of the white line. With razor sharp reflexes and a mouth full of cuss words, she slowed quickly and hugged the far left side of the road, easily slipping by the mobile home without incident.

When she finally turned into the familiar gravel driveway on the outskirts of Elk Run, she saw her father's truck parked, not in the garage, but beneath the huge cottonwood tree she loved to climb as a girl. Her antennae went up. That used to be the spot where Chet parked his vehicle when he came home drunk and wasn't able to aim it into the garage.

She had sat high in that majestic old tree, watching her father drunkenly weave and sputter around on the ground, unaware he was being watched. Elizabeth loved that tree. It was one of the few things that made sense to her as a child growing up in a house full of confusion. It was always there, waiting to take her in its strong, faithful arms, to hold her far above the dangerous monster. She looked to it now for inner strength.

She rapped on the front door. No answer. There was no way she was coming all the way out here and not fix the damn computer. Elizabeth did not want to make this trip again. The screen door leaning against her back, she tried the doorknob to the inside door and found it unlocked. She cautiously made her way into the house.

Chet was asleep on the couch. She stood at the entrance for a moment, assessing the situation and listening to his loud snoring. A long snort, then silence, like he had stopped breathing altogether for a moment; then a sharp intake of air and the cycle was repeated.

A couple of liquor bottles sat on the coffee table. One was drained, the other about half empty of a clear liquid, probably vodka or gin. A paper plate of half-eaten eggs and a piece of soggy bacon bathed in yellow egg yolk, sat beside the booze. A piece of toast lay under the table on the light green shag carpet.

Well, well, well. An old tiger never changes his stripes. You're making this so easy, you sonofabitch.

Elizabeth crept silently into her old bedroom, to the computer. With any luck, she could fix it, leave a note, and get the hell out of there before he woke up.

Turning on the computer with the First Aid disk, she willed it to hurry through its startup routine. It gave her the creeps to be in here when Chet was drunk. Tense, she took a deep breath and willed her shoulders to relax. Not wanting to look at her old bed, she stared straight ahead. She quickly reinstalled the system software and relaunched the internet software as well, just for good measure.

Elizabeth had just finished testing her repairs and had written the note, when she heard the toilet flush across the hall. Grabbing her jean jacket, she was making her way out of the bedroom when Chet came out of the bathroom, putting the two in the hallway at the same time.

"Lizzie! I didn't know you were here. I didn't hear you come in. I musta been asleep." He slurred his words and held his eyebrows up in an attempt to appear alert. His face was mottled, matching his bloodshot eyes.

"I saw. And once again, my name is Elizabeth. I fixed the computer. I have to go now." She avoided looking at him.

"What's the deal with this name thing? I've always called you Lizzie." Chet stretched both his arms out, holding a palm up against each wall, blocking her path.

"And I have always hated it. Could you let me by, please?" Elizabeth tried hard to keep her cool.

"Wait a minute. Can we talk?" Chet asked her, bleary-eyed.

"No. Not while you're drunk. Now, if you would excuse me." She waited for him to take his arms down from the hallway, to unblock her getaway.

"Shit, Lizzie. You don't talk to me when I'm sober either! What's the difference?" Chet showed no intention of moving.

"Just get out of my way." Elizabeth pronounced each word slowly and deliberately.

"No. Come on, let's sit down and have a talk. Can't you understand we need to talk?" Chet squinted, like he was having trouble focusing on her.

"I have no desire to talk to you. Now, move!" Elizabeth ducked under one of his arms and was running through the hall toward the door when he lunged for the back of her denim jacket, and caught the tail of it.

She spun around, hatred in her eyes, and pointed an index finger as she spoke. "Don't you ever, ever, touch me again, you slimy piece of shit!" She slapped him hard in the face and ran to the front door.

Chet grabbed his cheek. "Why, you little bitch." Chet lurched after her as she fled, but she was too fast and he was too drunk.

The screen in her head was bathed in red, as if she were standing in the middle of Hell's broiling fires. Elizabeth sprinted out to the car, jerked open the car door, and reached under the driver's seat. The cool metal of the Magnum slipped easily into her hand, like a waiting comrade. The contact seemed to restore her composure, and she walked determinedly back up to the house, the gun hanging ready by her right side, her focus a laser beam on the front door. Turning the doorknob, she found it had been locked behind her.

"You cowardly bastard! Open this door!" She ferociously kicked the bottom of the wooden screen door repeatedly. "Open up, you fuckin' bully! I am ready to talk now! C'mon! Let's have our talk, you worthless fuckin' loser!" Elizabeth resisted the urge to shoot the lock off the damn door.

There was no answer to Elizabeth's screaming fury. She frantically paced the porch, and considered breaking the living room picture window to go in after the bastard. The curtains were open and she could see that he had passed out on the couch again. She envied Chet's oblivion for a moment, but soon was left to her rage and indecision.

Don't do it! the dark Voice ordered. *He wouldn't even feel it. It would be too easy... too merciful. The sonofabitch has to suffer the way he has made us suffer. Stick to the plan, Elizabeth, stick to the plan.*

CHAPTER 41

On the way back to Denver from the fiasco at Chet's, Elizabeth bubbled over with rage; growling, pulling her hair, and beating on the steering wheel with her right hand. It was as if all the cells in her body were battling to crawl out of her skin in opposite directions. She kept checking the odometer, watching the tenths of a mile click away, assuring herself of her progress. As she neared the small town of Bennett, she saw a lone hitchhiker by the side of the road sitting under a viaduct holding a cardboard sign that said, Denver.

How convenient, the Voice mused. *Look at it as stress management, Elizabeth. He's probably just trash anyway; stop and give him ride, won't you?*

A wry smile crossed her face. Elizabeth slowed, and pulled over to the shoulder of the road. She leaned down to touch the Magnum for reassurance as she approached, and saw that the supposed vagabond was a clean-cut young man. Certainly no throwaway. He rose to his feet and clearly smiled at the prospect of a ride.

Elizabeth stopped about fifty feet before she got to him. Her eyes registered his every move as he walked toward her car. When he reached the Mercedes, she pressed the control button to let the passenger side window down a little, but left the doors locked.

She shut her eyes and took a deep breath while the Voice nagged her. *Well, what are you waiting for? Open the door!*

"Hi! Thanks for stopping." His smiling fresh face peered in at her, looking like a happy teenage boy's "after" picture in an acne cream commercial.

"What part of Denver you headed for?" Elizabeth inquired, while gauging his wholesomeness.

"Arvada, it's on the northwest side. Well, Boulder, really. I go to CU. But if I can get to Denver, I can call my parents to come and get me. How far you going?"

Elizabeth stared straight ahead, unmoving. "All the way."

"Can I get a ride then?" He looked at her blank face expectantly.

Elizabeth didn't answer.

"Ma'am? You okay?" His concern seemed genuine.

She slowly turned towards him, and in his face saw two loving parents, a basketball hoop in the driveway, and hot nutritious dinners with his family every night. She gazed at him, knowing that he was somebody's little boy. People would miss someone like this.

"Hey, kid. Don't you know it's dangerous to hitchhike? Don't you know there are sickos out there? Someone could pick you up, blow you away, and your parents would be picking you up all right, in a body bag! Don't you ever hitchhike again! You hear me? Promise me!" Her voice had raised to a fever pitch. "Promise me!"

College boy looked at her perplexed. "Uh, sure, okay. Whatever you say," he agreed quickly. "You going to unlock this door?"

She stared at him in disbelief. "Jesus Christ! You didn't hear a fuckin' word I said, did you?" She revved the engine, threw the car into gear and sped out, narrowly missing an ancient automobile decked out with four gawking old people pushing the lower speed limit.

The young man looked after her with a bewildered expression, arms up in question, and athletic bag at his feet. He quickly disappeared from her rearview mirror.

She roared down the highway the short distance to the Bennett exit, found a phone at the first gas station she came to, and dialed Zipper's number.

"Hendrix. Let me talk to Zipper, please!" Her voice came out more anxious than she'd intended.

"Elizabeth?" Hendrix's questioning voice was calm.

"Yes, Hendrix. This is Elizabeth. Please, is Zipper there?" Her voice was urgent. If he wasn't there, she didn't know what she would do. She crossed her fingers and shut her eyes tight.

"Sure, just a minute, I'll get him." The phone was obviously put down in the vicinity of a television playing cartoons. She heard Foghorn Leghorn's voice in the background.

"Hello, Elizabeth! How nice to hear from you!" Zipper's tone was enthusiastic.

"Can I come over?" She realized she had forgotten to say hello.

"Well, sure! Is everything okay?"

Elizabeth appreciated the concerned sound of Zipper's voice. "Okay enough to get there. I'll see you in about thirty minutes, okay?" She sighed in relief.

"Okay, then. See you soon."

Elizabeth hung up and settled back into her car, calmed knowing she had a safe place to go where someone was expecting her, and maybe even cared about her a little. It was enough to keep her from making any more stops along the way.

CHAPTER 42

Elizabeth felt a little guilty arriving at Zipper's empty handed, but she was certain she wouldn't have enough patience to wait for carryout at the Chinese place. Zipper answered her knock at the door.

"Elizabeth! Good Lord, girl, you look like death warmed over!"

"Nice to see you, too." Elizabeth stood in the hallway, looking at him expectantly.

Zipper waved her into the apartment. "Get yourself on in here!"

She managed a smile and sauntered through the door, over to the couch, and sat down. She felt bone tired. "Where's Hendrix?"

"I sent him out for a couple of hours. His mother lives out somewhere on the south side of town. He likes to go see her when he can. She loves to cook for him. Are you hungry?"

"No, thanks, but I would take a little brandy if you have it."

"Sure thing." Zipper hurried off to the dining room and rattled around in a cabinet. He called back to her. "Are you okay?"

She sighed and rested her head on the back of the sofa, staring at the ceiling. It was different than her ceiling. It had white bumps instead of swirls.

Zipper came back into the room with their drinks. He handed her a large snifter full of topaz colored liquid, and settled down beside her on the sofa, sympathetically studying her face. "Now, tell old Zipper what's up."

"I almost shot my father today, Zip." She took a big gulp from the snifter.

"Your father? Why?"

"Because he needs to be dead. He's pond scum." She returned her head to the back of the couch, and resumed staring at the ceiling.

"Tell me more."

Elizabeth sat silently for a long time, slightly rocking from her waist and occasionally sipping her brandy. Then, as if a door had been burst open, the words began to tumble out. She recounted the events of the day, the past weeks, her life. Chet's abuse. Saundra's suicide. Beeper. Jesse. Slide. The anthrax. All of it. She had never shared her story with anyone before, and it poured out of her until there wasn't one more word left inside. She had wrung her saturated psyche out like a dishrag, and every last drop of her secret truths lay pooled at Zipper's feet.

It was a long time before Zipper spoke. "I am so sorry you had to go through all that, Elizabeth. A little kid doesn't deserve stuff like that to happen to them. I'm so very sorry." Tears welled in his eyes.

Elizabeth started to cry. What started with a few tears soon turned into racking sobs that boiled up from great chasms of grief and pain. Zipper carefully put an arm around her and drew her to him, gently rocking both of them from the waist.

At first, she stiffly put her head on his shoulder. It wasn't long until her face was buried in his chest and she was weeping uncontrollably. Zipper patted her back reassuringly and offered her spare words of comfort, and let her cry.

She bawled until there wasn't a bead of moisture left in her eyes. Finally, leaving the comfort of Zipper's supportive arms, she shifted to lie down, her legs drawn up. Shutting her eyes, she tucked her hands up tightly beneath her neck. Zipper slipped a pillow under her head and took a blue woven throw from the back of the sofa and covered her with it, tucking the soft edges around her like she was a treasured baby.

When she woke up several hours later, Zipper still sat like a sentinel at the end of the couch, reading a newspaper. He quickly put it aside when he saw that she had opened her eyes. The way Zipper rested his wrists on his knees, together with the swell of his round belly, stamped a skewed impression of a statue of Buddha in her mind. She smiled at him weakly.

"How about a peanut butter and jelly sandwich?" Zipper smiled, with obviously forced enthusiasm.

"Sure, I am kinda hungry." Elizabeth rubbed her eyes and stretched. "What time is it?"

Zipper looked at his watch. "Nine. Gotta be somewhere tonight?"

"Nope." She followed Zipper into the kitchen. "I'm impressed. You're using your right arm already."

"Working on it. The doctor says I'm in pretty good shape for the shape I'm in." Zipper pulled a loaf of white bread from a wooden bread box and tossed it on the counter. "I'm getting better ever day."

She worked on opening the loaf's twist tie to get to the sandwich slices. "I am really glad to hear you're doing well, Zip. I'm so glad you didn't die on me."

Zipper glanced back and grinned at her as he pulled a couple of table knives from the silverware drawer. The whole counter was soon filled with jars and sacks of food. They giggled and crunched on potato chips as they hovered over bread slices, arguing over sandwich-making mechanics. He slid the jar of peanut butter over to her across the counter.

Elizabeth caught it, picked it up to look at it, and made a face at its label. "Don't you have any crunchy peanut butter?"

"Wouldn't have it in the house. Creamy rules." Zipper grabbed the jar from her hands and opened the lid.

"I suppose you don't have any grape jelly, either."

"As a matter of fact I do, although, everyone knows strawberry preserves is better with peanut butter." Zipper turned and soon retrieved the jars of preserves and jelly from the refrigerator.

"You're nuts. I suppose you like bananas on your peanut butter sandwiches, too. Maybe you're really Elvis, incognito," she snickered.

"Don't laugh. Maybe I am." Zipper spread a ridiculously thick layer of peanut butter on his bread.

They ended up putting one half grape jelly and one half strawberry preserves on each sandwich and challenged each other to a taste test. At the kitchen table, they sat devouring their creations in silence, washing them down with a glass of milk.

"Why don't you just let me take care of it for you?" Zipper frowned and stared at the filling in his sandwich.

"It?" She wiped her milk moustache off with a paper towel.

"Your father." Zipper stopped chewing and soberly looked to her.

Elizabeth laid her sandwich down and picked at the crust. She smiled warmly at her benefactor. "No thanks, Zipper. I appreciate it, but this is personal. It's something I have to do myself."

"I understand. Just be careful, Elizabeth, and if you need me, I'll be right here."

CHAPTER 43

Sunday morning, Elizabeth felt better than she had in a long time. It had felt good getting all that stuff off her chest at Zipper's yesterday. She felt lighter and more energetic, like she'd had some sort of a psychic enema.

It was about ten o'clock on a sunny, beautiful day, and the running path had started to fill up with folks enjoying the gorgeous weather. After her workout, she stretched and did some cool down exercises against a silver maple tree on a grassy berm, then sat down on a bench to people-watch. She cursed her revived cigarette habit for stealing her wind, and vowed again to quit.

A handsome young couple, deeply engrossed in each other, paraded by in front of her, holding hands. She felt deeply envious. Never had a man looked at her the way this man was looking at this woman; like she was the most precious being alive on the planet. Elizabeth sighed and turned to the river where a drake mallard was rapidly approaching to see if Elizabeth had his breakfast. She wished she had brought some bread along in her fanny pack.

She thought of Brad. She looked down the path; the pair stopped under the viaduct and kissed each other sweetly. No groping or pulling, just the tender meeting of the lips of lovers in love.

As Elizabeth crossed the street, she glanced to her right and saw Brad about a block away walking towards their apartment building with a white sack in his hand. He was probably coming from the grocery store located nearby. Her heart sped up. Maybe there was such thing as fate after all.

She arrived in the lobby earlier than he did, and kept a furtive eye on his approach. Timing it so she caught the elevator door for him after he entered the lobby, she smiled and welcomed him, acting like it was a chance meeting. As he entered the elevator, Elizabeth noticed his thick blonde hair wasn't as neatly combed as it usually was. That made her feel better about being in her sweaty running gear.

"Good morning," she said with a smile and searched his eyes for an indication of his mood.

"Good morning. How are you?" Brad avoided her gaze and stiffly shifted his bakery bag from one hand to the other.

"Fine. And you?" She felt corny.

"Good." He wagged his head up and down evenly, like those fake loose-necked dogs she had seen through the back windshields of cars.

She stared up at the numerals. Dead silence ensued. She ventured out of her comfort zone once again. "How's Kyla, the detective? She seemed nice." She crossed her fingers that were hidden behind the security railing as she held on to the smooth steel bar.

"Oh, Kyla? Great. We're just good friends. She's really helped me learn my way around town and introduced me to a lot of people."

Just good friends. There you go, ask him! This elevator ride isn't going to last forever, you know. Elizabeth braced herself and took a deep breath. Her grip tightened on the railing.

"Brad, I was wondering. What do you think about us having that coffee and dessert sometime? I'm leaving town today on business for a few days, but—"

Brad broke in. "I can't go out with you now; I'm seeing someone and it's pretty serious." He held the bakery bag up towards her face and raised his eyebrows. "Tracy's upstairs waiting for me now. I think she could be the one." He smiled smugly. "See, Liz? You snooze, you lose."

Elizabeth was shocked. She felt so stupid, she couldn't think of anything but getting off the elevator. Her face flushed, and she was sure she was shrinking right in front of his icy blue eyes. Looking up, she thought about action movies where sometimes people busted through the tops of elevator cars and rode bare wire cables towards safety in the dark.

The car stopped at the fifth floor and opened up to a plump couple baring their teeth while smiling at her. Elizabeth pushed by them without a word, chin quivering but determined not to cry in front of anyone. She jerked open the door to the stairwell and climbed the stairs to the twelfth floor like a robotron, thinking of nothing but getting to the safety of her apartment.

Finally inside the familiar confines of her home, Elizabeth collapsed on the couch. She couldn't figure out why she felt this way. It wasn't like her to get upset over a man. Nevertheless, her head was buried in a pillow, and she was crying like a baby.

Stupid, stupid, stupid. I can't believe you even asked him that, Elizabeth. You are so stupid. She pounded on the couch with her fist.

The Voice came back with a vengeance. *You snooze, you lose? My God, Elizabeth, how infantile. I told you so. He's just like the rest of them. When will you listen to me when I tell you something? He's a prick. Forget about it—just send two diskettes instead of just one tomorrow. That'll fix his arrogant ass.*

Elizabeth quit crying and fell asleep.

She woke at noon and looked at her watch. Her flight was at four this afternoon. After having a few mugs of coffee and several cigarettes on the balcony, she called the airline and postponed her flight to Dallas until the next morning. She didn't have to give her presentation at Line Interiors until Monday afternoon, anyway. Lying back down on the couch, she slept the afternoon away.

That evening, feeling stronger after her long rest, she slipped on a pair of vinyl gloves and knelt on the floor, peering to the rear of her bedroom closet. There was the shoe box. She reached out and drew it to her. She pulled off the lid, carefully extracted two diskette mailers, replaced the lid tightly, and slid the box back to its corner.

The two plastic bags hung from her thumb and forefinger like she was carrying live mice by their tails. She gingerly laid the bags on the dining room table and stared at the diskette mailers, a little afraid to touch them. Visions of anthrax spores being like little supermen, savagely ripping through the baggie and leaping down her lungs, filled her head.

After carefully addressing each mailer in block letters with her left hand, one each to Chet and Brad, she affixed four self-adhesive postage stamps on each one, and replaced them in their respective baggies. She had put *Rosie* on the return address for Chet's disk and

National Geographic Field Station for Brad's, both completed with bogus Dallas addresses.

Elizabeth put both of those bags in a manila envelope, sealed the flap and slipped it into her suitcase. She wiped the marble table top down with bleach and water, threw the gloves and the pen in the trash, and went to take a shower. She planned to look for Chet later this evening in the chat rooms. Surely the vermin had sobered up by now.

CHAPTER 44

Chet woke up slowly, his aching eyes feeling like they had been on the wrong end of a power sander. Clad only in a sagging pair of white briefs, he struggled to a sitting position on the couch and took stock of his situation. He ran tired fingers through his thin, tousled hair. His mouth was dry as a desert, so he grabbed a glass of whatever from the coffee table and drained it. Noticing the empty liquor bottles, he panicked.

Oh, shit no, and it's Sunday. Oh, man.

Chet rose, unsteadily, and tramped to the kitchen. He ran himself a glass of water from the tap and gulped down the whole thing. He threw the plastic tumbler in the sink and began jerking open cabinet doors, checking the refrigerator and counter drawers, trying to remember if he had stashed a bottle anywhere. When he repeatedly came up empty handed, his searching became frantic.

Shit! Nothing. Not a fuckin' thing in the house to drink. Beer was the most he could hope for today, if he couldn't scrounge up anything better. He hadn't wanted to go to the liquor store in Elk Run yesterday. And he sure didn't want to sit in any bars around here today. It wouldn't be five minutes before everyone in town knew that Chet was drinking again, and oh, my, wasn't it a shame? Those people from Alcoholics Anonymous would be calling and coming by, tracking him down like a pack of wild dingoes after a fat baby.

He thought of Glen, a guy he used to drink with. Glen was the only guy Chet knew who was a worse drunk than he was. Maybe he would have some extra sunshine on hand, Chet had bought it there before. Of course, his prices were outrageous, old Glen knew how to work a buck. Oh well, it's the price you pay for being a booze junkie.

Chet fumbled with the phone book and tried to remember Glen's last name. *Let's see, Buckener... Buckley... Buckner, Glen...* He kept his finger pointed at the number while he looked around for a pen.

The phone rang four times before Glen answered.

"Hello, Glen? Chet Strong. Long time no see. Hey buddy, how you been doin'?"

Chet waited not so patiently while Glen droned on—something about having had to quit drinking because he had an operation or some shit. Chet forced himself to exchange a few pleasantries and hung up. But not before Glen had given him the name of someone else he could try to call.

"Hello, Beaver?" Glen had assured Chet that it was the name the guy went by all the time.

"Yeah. Whoziss?" The gravelly voice wasn't particularly friendly.

Chet explained his dilemma to Beaver.

"I'm low. We had a big birthday party last night. All I got left is a case of cold duck, a couple bottles of pink champagne, and a fifth of tequila.

Cold duck? Blech. That's the worst thing he could think of to drink besides Listerine. Life was full of little emergencies.

"I'll be after the tequila, definitely. And maybe I'll try one of those pink champagnes. You know, for dinner or somethin'." That should hold him until he could drive to a liquor store in Parker Monday morning. No one knew him there.

❖ ❖ ❖

Sunday evening, Chet took his tumbler of wine and a toaster pastry and sat down at the keyboard. There was a note tucked under its side.

Computer's fixed, was all that it said.

Chet flinched, wadded up the note and threw it away. He didn't want to be reminded of what little he remembered of the bad scene with Lizzie. He turned back toward the computer monitor.

Rosie was probably angry with him. He tried to remember how long it had been since he talked to her. Anyway... too long.

Chet got out the paper instructions that Lizzie had written out for him and and logged on to the Internet.

Chet enters the room. *Finally!*

Chet: Hi everyone!

Zooboy: Long time no see.

Dimples: Hi Chet! How are you tonight?

Chet: anyone seen Rosie?

Rosie: Surprise! Here I am!

Chet took a big swig of his champagne. He was so happy to see her, that he asked her to go to a private chat room right away. She agreed.

Chet cooed over Rosie, telling her how much he had missed her. His typing skills had not improved. They had chatted back and forth for only about an hour when Chet felt the cold sting of reality. Rosie said she had to log out soon because she had to get up early in the morning. This was the bad part about these chat rooms. When you flip the switch, you're totally alone again.

Rosie: I have an idea!

Chet: What?Wat?

Rosie: I could send you a picture of me. Would you like that?

Chet: Yes! yes! That wouldbe great!

Rosie: The only good one I have, is a shot of me they took for a brochure at work. I could scan it and send it to you on a disk, since I don't have an extra hard copy. I could put some other stuff on there too, like some poetry and short stories I've written, if you're interested. As a matter of fact, one of the poems is about you...

Chet: Really? Cool! Id like that vry much. Please send it soon! I'll look for a picture ofm e to send too,okay?

Rosie: That would be great! Goodnight, Chet! I'll be thinking of you...

Chet: Goodnight, Rosie! I will have sweet dreams of you, too!

CHAPTER 45

"You did what?" Zipper's raised voice held an incredulous tone as he paced. "I could see why you would want to waste your old man, but why the guy in your building? Please tell me you are kidding me, Elizabeth." He continued while she sat there like a stone. "You can't go around killing people for not going out with you, especially when they live in your own damn building!" Zipper stopped in front of her. "Jeez. I can't believe you would put yourself at risk like this." He began pacing back and forth again, running his right hand through his meager hair, making his tiny ponytail bob up and down.

"He's the only guy I've ever asked out in my whole life. He didn't have to be such such a jerk about it." She looked down and picked at a string on the side seam of her jeans. "I'm not sorry, really." She hadn't felt much of anything since she had mailed the diskettes. No regrets, no sadness, just numbness.

"When did you mail the disks?" Zipper asked, looking totally exasperated.

"Monday morning. From the Dallas airport." Elizabeth bit the inside of her lip.

"Let's see. Today's Thursday. They both probably got the disks yesterday, or will today. How long is the incubation period on this stuff?"

"I read it's less than seven days, but usually about three, maybe even less. It depends on the person. Then it takes a couple of days for them to die." She resumed picking at the string on her jeans.

"Good God, girl, I hope you never get mad at me. Damn, Elizabeth, how did a pretty little head like yours think of something so damn gruesome?" Zipper shook his head while walking, then stopped suddenly. A light went on in his eyes and he clapped his hands. "Okay. Here's what we're gonna do. I am going to arrange for you to win a free trip to Vegas, courtesy of a casino on the strip. And, you will go. You hear me? You'll draw less suspicion if you're out of town when they croak. The only catch to the prize will be you have to go this weekend. You got any vacation days coming?"

"Tons. I never go anywhere. I finished the job in Dallas this week. It would be a good time take a few days off, actually. I don't have anything pressing coming up."

"Do it then. You'll leave tomorrow for seven fun-filled days and nights in sunny Las Vegas. I'll arrange everything. I'll have one of our friendly operators tape the winning call for proof in case we need it later. It's all on the up and up, I just have to call and make sure you're on the randomly-chosen winner's list." Zipper chuckled, obviously proud of his idea.

She winced. "Las Vegas? I've never been to Vegas. What am I supposed to do in Las Vegas?"

"Gamble, eat, play; whatever you want. You'll have an open account at the hotel. Maybe you could actually have some fun for a change. I can meet you out there in a couple of days. I need to make a trip out there and do a little business anyway." Zipper sat down on the sofa and smiled. "I'll give you the guided tour, Zipper style. We'll go to some shows and have a few laughs. How does that sound?"

"Great, I guess. But if you make me watch Elvis impersonators, I warn you, I will leave town." She grinned back at him.

"Hey! Watch your mouth, girlfriend. There are some pretty good Elvises out there." Zipper waved her towards the door. "Now scoot on home so you can get that winning call. Call your boss, then pack a bag and come back. You'll stay here tonight. I have a guest room you can stay in. Hendrix can take you to the airport in the morning."

Elizabeth rolled her eyes. "I don't need to come back here tonight, Zipper. I'm a big girl."

"Did I stutter?" Zipper's face softened. "You don't need to be sitting home, up there by yourself, wondering what's going on downstairs with your boyfriend's insides minute by minute."

"Zipper, I don't need you to protect me." She held her hands on her hips.

"Look, Elizabeth. I am acting in your best interest, which is more than I can say for you lately. Now, go. And bring some Chinese food back with you." Zipper waved her towards the door.

"That's the real reason you want me to come back, isn't it?"

"Oh yeah, sure. That's the only reason." Zipper smiled warmly at her. "Oh—and bring the rest of the disks back with you, too. We'll lock them up in the safe."

CHAPTER 46

Chet had laid off the booze for a couple of days, but was back drinking by Wednesday. He tried to keep his drinking in a maintenance pattern so he could at least function a little. He called Ron and told him he wouldn't be working this week, that he'd be available next Monday. If Ron knew Chet had been drinking, he didn't let on.

Chet sauntered out to check the mail before *Jerry Springer* started. He brightened when he saw the diskette mailer in among the electric bill and some junk mail. Smiling, he softly ran his index finger over the inked word, Rosie, in the return address. She was real. Here was proof.

Barefooted, he hurried back into the house, flinching and cussing along the way at the sharp gravel. He swore for the millionth time to start wearing shoes out to the mailbox. Among other things, he'd been saying that for years.

Sitting down at his computer desk, he flipped on the unit and pulled the perforated strip allowing him access to the diskette. He anxiously fished it out and stuck it into the disk drive. He ran to the kitchen to fix himself a drink while he waited for the computer to go through all its opening gyrations.

When he came back into the room, he snapped on the white plastic radio that sat on Lizzie's old dresser and adjusted the dial to his favorite country station. Country music was very meaningful to him when he was in love. He settled back down in front of the computer.

Chet excitedly clicked the disk icon on the screen. He couldn't wait to see what his beloved Rosie looked like. Instead, he was met with an error message. Something about the disk being unreadable and did he want to initialize it. Not having a clue of what to do and no one to ask, he clicked on *OK*.

Chet heard a distinct popping noise and the disk ejected itself. The screen said it was a defective disk. He pushed it back in. The machine popped it right back out at him, like the tongue of a petulant child. He sat there for a few minutes, staring at the screen and cursing his misfortune.

Damnit! That's just my luck, she sends me a bum disk. Damn!

He hoisted up his glass and took a big gulp of his whiskey. His newfound elation punctured, he turned off the computer, turned off the radio, and ambled back into the living room to watch television.

CHAPTER 47

Elizabeth lazily returned to the Vegas hotel suite after her swim; her sandals slapped her heels as she traipsed down the plush hall of the hotel in her white terry robe and wet hair. She had stopped in the concession room for a bucket of ice and a soda on her way. Setting the ice down on the dresser, she tossed her damp beach towel on the floor.

She stood outside the shower, testing the water's temperature before she stepped in. Humming to herself as she bathed, she was thankful to be having lots more fun than she thought she would in this strange, imposed exile. She didn't know what to expect before she came to Vegas, but she would have never guessed she would like it here as much as she did.

Las Vegas was like a magical storybook land, making her forget all the troubles she had left behind in Colorado. Day was night and night was day. The neon lights were outrageous, each massive marquee trying to outdo the next, flashing more lights, making promises of *more* fun, and definitely touting *more* jackpots. Most of the people she observed were either quite friendly and smiling, or looked desperate and afraid. There didn't seem to be a lot of middle ground.

The Tropicana Hotel had the most amazing pool she had ever seen. It had a five acre tropical swimming complex that ran through mysterious, dark grottoes with gorgeous waterfalls pouring down in front of craggy entrances. Magnificent stone fountains were plentiful, and it even had a swim-up blackjack table. She had never seen anything like it.

When she wasn't gambling or sleeping or eating, she wandered the sidewalks, watching all the different kinds of people milling about. There were young and old, fat and skinny, and most ethnic groups were represented. She imagined the bulk of the people were either tourists dreaming of hitting the big jackpot, or shrewd locals scoring a fast buck off the visitors. It was amazing to watch commerce in action at different levels, money changing hands at the speed of light.

Elizabeth was in good mood when Zipper arrived Saturday afternoon. She sat on his bed while he unpacked, filling him in on what she had been doing. He seemed anxious to start showing her around.

"Hey, Elizabeth. Would you come see Wayne Newton with me tonight? He always heckles me about not having a date. For once, I would like to show up with a good looking woman hanging on my arm."

He looked pitiful. What a mug. "You don't know Wayne Newton! You're messing with my head."

"I most certainly do. I have played poker with him a million times. And, I have beat the pants off him several of those times, I might add."

Elizabeth couldn't tell if he was lying or not. Deciding to give him the benefit of the doubt, she finally agreed, but not until he promised to go with her to the Comedy Stop the next night.

For the next several days, they concentrated on having fun. Nothing was mentioned about what might be going on back home. Zipper gave her tips on beating the house playing Blackjack and how to spot the hot slots. She got a kick out of watching old women guard their slot machines like irritated pit bulls. She stood by his side sometimes as he played craps. Whenever he got a good run going on the table, he told her she was his good luck charm. Even Hendrix appeared to be enjoying himself, especially at the cheap buffets.

It felt delicious to be out of sync with the world. She established a routine of staying up all night and sleeping until the middle of the afternoon. After waking up, she would go swimming for a few hours, sipping margaritas by the pool, and then take a short nap.

She developed a penchant for Blackjack. Something about the hope of the next card being "the one" sucked her in. When the right card flipped up, it was such a rush. It was one of the games she stayed up all night to play.

There were no clocks in any of the casinos, and Zipper told her the hotels pumped oxygen into the betting areas to keep people awake and spending money. It was the perfect nonreality. The lights were always on, keeping the darkness at bay. It felt like being at the fair, except this time, with a friend. She wished she could stay here forever.

CHAPTER 48

Detective Kyla Gillespie stood in Brad's apartment, looking around, trying to find something that signaled her intuition to investigate further. She had stopped over, with the permission of the family, to pick up some photographs Brad had developed for her last week. She saw them and the negatives lying in his out basket by the door.

Kyla felt strange, being in this room now with Brad gone. She sat down on the white leather couch and spun one of the tapestry pillows around in her hands, thinking and looking around. Brad's sudden death just didn't make sense to her. Here was a strong, virile, young man, and according to his mother, had no past history of heart problems. He was athletic and, to her knowledge, not a drug user. Brad shouldn't have had a massive heart attack and died from a common cold. She would know soon enough. Brad's parents, wealthy grape farmers from Napa Valley in California, were staying in town until the results of the autopsy came back. It was scheduled for tomorrow.

Kyla thought about Brad. He had hit on her during their first meeting several months ago, but she had made it clear from the start she wasn't interested in that way. Brad seemed the type that needed an adoring woman around, and Kyla didn't have the time, nor the inclination, for games. Brad had been a friend, though. He was funny and easy to talk to, and made a damn good lasagna. She would miss him.

Kyla jumped when she heard a faint knock at the door, and she turned to see Tracy, Brad's most recent girlfriend, peeking her head in the apartment. She was a tiny blonde and without makeup, looked almost like an adolescent.

"Hello? Is anyone here?" Tracy's voice was cautious.

"Over here, Tracy. It's Kyla." Kyla waved to her from the couch.

"Hi, Kyla. I just came by to get my things. I left a few clothes and some CDs here." Tracy's eyes were red-rimmed and swollen.

"How are you holding up?"

"Okay, I guess. You know, Kyla, Brad and I had only been dating a little while, but it seems like I knew him forever. I'd never met anyone like him...and now...now...he's gone." Tracy blew her nose through tears.

"I'm sorry, Tracy. Come and sit down." Kyla patted the seat next to her. "When was the last time you talked to him?"

Tracy sat demurely on the edge of the sofa cushions. "Friday night. We were supposed to go out, but he said he had a bad cold and a high fever. I heard him hacking. He sounded awful. I offered to bring him some chicken soup and keep him company, but he said he just wanted to go to bed and sleep, and that he would call me Saturday." Tracy took a sharp intake of air and her bottom lip started to quiver. "I tried calling him a few times off and on during the weekend, but I figured he had turned off the phone to get some rest. When he didn't call by Sunday night, and didn't answer the phone, that's when I got worried and called you."

"You did the right thing, Tracy. When did you talk to him last, before Friday?"

"Wednesday. Brad came over to my place for dinner. He was in a real good mood because he'd received a disk assignment from *National Geographic*. He was going to review it that night after he got home, so he went home early. That's the last time I ever saw him." Tracy began sobbing.

Kyla gathered Tracy into her arms and gave her a hug, patting her back. "There, there...I'm sorry, Tracy, but I can't allow anything to be moved from the apartment right now. I will also need to take your key. Make a list of your things for me and I'll bring you the stuff later."

Tracy dropped Brad's apartment key into Kyla's hand. "He was so healthy, it doesn't make sense, does it? What happened?"

"I don't know, Tracy, we have to wait for the results of the autopsy."

"Okay," Tracy said weakly, still sniffling.

Tracy jotted down the items she was looking for on Kyla's note pad. The list was short; a few CDs, a white negligee, a pair of black panties, and a toothbrush. "I know it doesn't seem like a lot to worry about, but I feel weird leaving them here, his parents being in town and all. They are so nice."

"That's the last thing on their minds right now, Tracy, I promise. I'll get them back to you when this is over, okay? That it? Ready to go?"

Tracy nodded, got up, and slowly followed Kyla across the room to the door. Kyla grabbed the photographs from the out basket, and locked the door behind them. The nagging feeling that something was wrong wouldn't go away.

CHAPTER 49

Bedraggled, Elizabeth entered her apartment Thursday night and wearily dropped her bags in the foyer. She sighed deeply. Not wanting to have left Las Vegas, she sauntered over to the living room couch, plopped down, and sulked. Since the plane touched down, she had felt an overwhelming dark depression swallowing her up and dropping her into the belly of a swirling black emotional abyss.

The air felt syrup heavy, and it was a struggle to put one foot in front of the other. Zipper had urged her to stay at his place again, but she refused, finally convincing him that she had to come home sometime. This was supposed to be her home, but it didn't feel like it anymore. Instead, it felt like a tomb, sealed up with its occupant still alive.

When she saw the message light blinking on the answering machine, she averted her eyes. Glancing through her bills and catalogs, she realized how little personal mail she got. She couldn't ignore the blinking red bulb. The tiny red dot soon became a huge flashing beacon, clanging in her brain. She poured herself a brandy, grabbed her cigarettes, and escaped to the patio.

Elizabeth sat and smoked and looked over the lights of the city, feeling tiny and insignificant. She looked up to the night sky. It was overcast, so she couldn't see any stars. When she couldn't see the stars, she couldn't feel her mother around her, and that bothered her quite a lot. Zeroing in on a lit window in her favorite skyscraper, she wondered what peoples' lives were like that worked in that office, making up theoretical realities for them. It was a game she played with herself when she was particularly stressed.

She knew she was stalling, but didn't want to admit to herself she was simply afraid to play the messages from the answering machine. She knew what was stored on its cruel memory chip; proof that reality had not magically disappeared since she had been gone. Proof that Las Vegas wasn't the land of enchantment, although it was the closest Elizabeth had ever come to it. Her stay there had been the most fun she had ever had in her life.

It took two hours, three brandies, and five cigarettes for her to work up the nerve to finally push the play button on the answering machine. She flopped on the couch, hung over the arm, and stared raptly at the black box. The beep sounded, then Elizabeth heard Chet's voice.

He sounded faint and vague, and she heard him gasping for air and hacking. "Lizzie, I'm real sick. My head is burning up and I can't catch my breath. I wondered if you could come out and help me. I don't have any insurance and I'm really sick. It's not the booze, either; this is different. I'm scared. Help me, Lizzie. Please." The message stopped with a click, then another beep sounded, and the electronic voice announced the next message that came in a day later. It was Chet again. The raspy voice was barely more than a whisper.

"Lizzie...help me...can't breathe...I think I'm dying...I mean it...please come...help me." Then, she heard a few feeble coughs and a phone dropping to the floor, some fumbling, and a disconnect.

There was one more call from Chet a few minutes later.

Elizabeth could barely hear him. "Lizzie—" then the phone went silent. She did not hear a hangup. There was no sound until her machine had shut off automatically.

There it was. He was dead. Dead. No last words of eternal love for his daughter, just dead. *Ding dong, the witch is dead.* She heard the munchkins from *The Wizard of Oz* singing in her head. At least the munchkins had each other to celebrate with. Elizabeth felt as alone as she'd ever felt, even emptier than the feeling of being alone on holidays. But this was a different shade of lonely. Deeper and more intense. Scarier. It was as if her world were a living canvas, and the red hues of her pulsing pain and raw fear were the only colors randomly smeared on its surface. She remembered suddenly to breathe, took in a sharp wedge of air, and rested her head on the back of the couch. Closing her eyes, she waited for the spinning to pass.

Lizzie...help me. Chet's voice infested her head. *I'm dying.* She put her hands over her ears. *La la lalala la...I can't hear you.* Too much information, too much everything. Elizabeth didn't know how she felt or what was happening. Her heart pounding, she was afraid she would die, but was more afraid that she wouldn't.

What to do...what to do...everything is going to be okay...no... no...it's not okay...NO! It will never be okay for you, Lizzie... Be-e-eper...come home...probably just humping the neighbor dog... lalala...I can't hear you...My name is... Elizabeth... I am, Elizabeth... I am. I am. Oh, my God, Oh, my God... It's not working. Mama, it's not working anymore.

She felt a breath away from madness, maybe even a bit closer. Elizabeth tightly hung on to the sofa. Finally, after her muscles ached and ticked from tension, a calm washed over her, leaving her spent on the couch. Her hair was soaked with perspiration and was sticking to her head.

Elizabeth's Voice crisply spoke to Chet with disdain. *"I told you never to call me Lizzie, you bastard. My name is Elizabeth. You signed your own death warrant. Now you know what it's like to be really afraid—gut level afraid—how does it feel, Daddy? Burn in hell, you evil sonofabitch. Burn in the bowels of hell!"*

Elizabeth, surprised, looked around the room like she had heard a voice other than her own speak to her out loud. She buried her sweating face in the crack of the couch as far as she could and waited, although she didn't know what for. Hearing her own labored breathing, she prayed and struggled to settle down.

The phone rang and her shoulders jerked hard in fear. Her heart was beating wildly against her chest when she heard an unfamiliar voice speak from the answering machine.

"Miss Strong, this is Sergeant Mattingly from the Denver Police Department. We have been trying to reach you for several days. Please call 640-2011 when you get in. This is an emergency. I repeat, this is an emergency."

Oh my God. I am going to have to talk to the people. Oh, my God, the people. Mama, I don't know if I can do it. Help me, Mama, help me. She buried her face even deeper into the crack of the couch, and cried herself to sleep.

CHAPTER 50

The next morning, Elizabeth had dialed the phone all the way up to the last number about ten times, until she finally punched the final digit that would connect her to the Denver police station. As the phone rang in her ear, her heart skittered in her chest. Elizabeth took a deep breath, focused on her thumbnail, and tried to conjure up a shred of courage. It gave her a little jolt when someone answered her call.

"Denver Police Department. How may I direct your call?" The voice was pleasant and businesslike.

"Sergeant Mattingly, please."

"May I ask who's calling?"

She paused a second before answering, still considering an escape. "Elizabeth Strong."

"Thank you. One moment, I will see if he is in." The phone went on hold and some dim elevator music started playing.

She drummed her fingers on her knee and, again, considered hanging up. After a few minutes, a pleasant male voice came on the line.

"Sergeant Mattingly. May I help you?"

"Hello, this is Elizabeth Strong. I got several messages that you called while I was on vacation." Elizabeth coiled the phone cord in her fingers.

"Hello, Miss Strong! I'm so glad you called. I've been trying to reach you since Tuesday. I talked to your secretary...let's see...Maggie, I believe it is, at your work and all she knew is that you were in Las Vegas. She didn't know what hotel you were staying in."

"I didn't think it was necessary I tell her, after all, it was a vacation. May I ask what you are calling about, Officer Mattingly?" She suddenly felt very impatient.

"I have something urgent to tell you. I can be there within thirty minutes."

"Officer, what is it?" She came across a bit strong. "I'd rather not have company today. I'm very tired from the trip. I got in very late last night. Can't you just tell me whatever it is you need to tell me over the phone?"

"Ma'am, it is normal procedure that I or another officer deliver this information in person." Sergeant Mattingly cleared his throat.

She paused for a moment. *Normal procedure. Ding dong, the witch is dead.* She didn't want to draw too much suspicion by being difficult. Calling up all the pleasantness she could find, she replied nicely,"Yes, of course. Come on by, I'll be here."

"I will see you momentarily, Miss Strong."

The Voice scolded her. *Smooth, Elizabeth. You got the police coming over here now. Why didn't you volunteer to go down there? They are going to be in here! Inside your house! What were you thinking? Stupid. You are so very very stupid.*

She tried to pull herself together. Parts of her seemed to be going off in directions she could not understand or control. Struggling to be rational, she looked at the facts. There is nothing out in plain sight in this place that looks questionable.

Chill out, Elizabeth. They are not coming over here with a search warrant, they're just coming over here to tell you that Chet's kicked the bucket. No need to get in an uproar.

She hadn't unpacked yet, but the clutter would serve to support her story of the Las Vegas trip to the officer. She plodded to the bathroom, washed her face, brushed her teeth and put her hair back in a ponytail. She slipped a clean tee shirt on over her jeans. Then she went back to sit on the couch and wait. She wound the music box, placed it back on the coffee table and hummed along with its song.

She was deep in thought, considering how the officer would expect her to act upon hearing the terrible news, when the doorbell rang. She jerked even though she had been anticipating it. Her stomach was churning.

Focus...focus. Focus! You can do this, you can do this. Everything is going to be all right. As she was taking some deep breaths, the doorbell chimed again. She stood and made her way to the door, opening it after checking the peephole.

"Hello. Are you Sergeant Mattingly?" She asked, although she had already read the silver name tag on his uniform. A young female officer was hanging back behind him a few steps. She read her name tag also.

"Yes, Miss Strong, and this is my partner, Officer Payne." He had a notably formal air about him. "May we please come in?"

"Sure. Please, have a seat." She waved them in. As they walked toward the couch, she saw them glancing around her apartment. Elizabeth wondered if they were looking for something, or just curious. It felt as if her guilt was scrawled in huge red letters on the walls.

Focus. Focus. She followed them into the living room, and sat down in a leather swivel armchair, facing them.

"What is it, Officer? What's the emergency?" Her tone was inquisitive, and she tried hard to make her face a blank slate.

"Miss Strong. I am sorry to have to tell you this, but your father, Chet Strong, was found dead this Tuesday afternoon in his home in Elk Run. The county coroner ruled the cause of death myocardial infarction. That's a heart attack." The officer held his knees as he spoke.

She tried to look stunned. "Who found him?"

"Ron Wagner," Sergeant Mattingly glanced at some notes he held in his right hand. "Apparently your father was supposed to do some work for him this week, but he didn't show up Monday morning. He got worried when Mr. Strong didn't show up or call by Tuesday morning, so Mr. Wagner stopped by his house during his lunch hour. He found your father on the living room floor."

"Had he been drinking again?" Elizabeth had been staring intently at the officer, causing her eyes to tear. She squeezed her eyes tight and a few drops of water ran down her face.

"Yes, Ma'am, he had. His blood alcohol level was point eighteen. Looks like his heart just gave out on him. Here is the name and number of the funeral home where his body is being held pending your instructions. Do you want to call someone? We can stay with you until they get here. I am very sorry for your loss, Miss Strong."

"No, no. Thanks. I just want to be alone for a little bit. This comes as quite a shock. I just saw him the other day, and he was fine." She tried on a very sad face.

"Are you sure you'll be okay? We would be glad to stay for a little while, if you want us to." Sergeant Mattingly sounded very sympathetic, and his partner looked it.

"Yes, I'm sure. I just need to be alone. I'll call some friends after a while, I promise." She pulled a tissue from a box on an end table and blew her nose.

"Okay, then. We'll show ourselves out." The male officer stood, and the female followed suit. "Please, don't hesitate to call us if you need anything."

"I will, thank you, Officer." She watched the two as they filed out, shut the door quietly behind them, and quickly locked the dead bolt. Leaning on the back of the door and sighing in relief, she looked at the name and phone number on the card Sergeant Mattingly had given her. She walked across the room and picked up the phone.

A somber voice greeted her call. "Forest Pines. May I help you please?"

"My name is Elizabeth Strong. I understand you are holding my father, Chet Strong, at your facility. I need to make some arrangements for the cremation of the body."

"One moment, please." Some baroque classical music came over the line. She winced.

A Jean somebody finally came on the line and talked with her at length, offering far too much detail about cremation procedures and how they were handled at Forest Pines.

Jean probed Elizabeth for more information. "Did you need to arrange a memorial service as well?"

"No." Elizabeth was nonchalant. "It is possible you could just ship me the ashes in the mail?"

There was a pause at the other end of the phone. "That is highly irregular, Ma'am, but the answer would be yes. We could send your father's cremated remains to you via Federal Express. Would you like to come out this afternoon and sign the papers?"

"I'll be there."

CHAPTER 51

"After two weeks with no rent, we clean out people's storage units and put the stuff in our warehouse. That way, if they come back after it, we can get our money up front. You wait too long and they sneak back, take their stuff, and bail out on you. We sell the stuff after thirty days. It's all in the rental agreement they sign. That's what we did on this Ginny Forester deal. We tried to call the phone number she put on her application, but it was bogus, so we went on in. That's when we found it," Louise, the owner of the mini-storage lot reported to Detective Gillespie, then lit a cigarette.

"Go on," Kyla scratched notes on a small notepad.

"Well, when we got in here, there was just these two sacks. We opened one up and saw the gun and the gas mask and all that and called you. We didn't touch the other sack." Louise kept the burning cigarette up close to her mouth, her eyes squinted in defense.

"Can you describe this Ginny Forester?"

"Well, I can do you one better. I'll show you what she looks like." Louise looked self-confident.

"How?" Kyla was surprised.

"Follow me." She locked up the unit, led Kyla back inside the office and pointed to the wall over the cash register. "See this moose?"

"It's hard to miss." Kyla smiled.

"There's a camera in there. It turns on whenever the front door opens, then I can turn it off and on with this button here on the floor," Louise pointed. "I get a shot of all our new customers that way."

"Pretty fancy rig for an operation this size." Kyla crossed her arms.

"I shot that moose!" Red called from his chair as he poured himself a drink. "In the wild." He laughed.

"Oh, you did not, you old fool! It was here when we bought this place." Then Louise beamed. "Our son Tony rigged it up for us one time when he was here on house arrest. He is so smart—he could of done something with hisself, but no—that boy—he's never going to learn." Her face fell. "Got picked up for burglary again two months ago. Now he's back in the clink. I told him once, I told him a thousand times." Louise paused and puffed on her cigarette. "Anyhow, we been robbed a couple a times and he thought this might help us out."

Kyla peered closely at the moose's large black eyes. Sure enough, there was an outline of a small camera lens in the right eye.

"This is too much," Kyla grinned. "So you have a tape of her?"

"Sure do, right this way." Louise puffed on her cigarette then walked through the smoke. Kyla coughed. They were following Red; the moment they entered the meager living room, he jumped in his drab green armchair in front of the television.

Louise dug through a pile of videotapes stacked on a card table on the side of the room. "Here it is." She popped it into the VCR and fast forwarded it to the date she was looking for, and pushed play.

The face of a very pretty woman was looking directly into the camera, smiling at the moose. The date and time were displayed on the bottom left hand side of the screen. It matched the date on the application.

I know this woman, Kyla thought. *But from where?* She watched the woman talking to the lot owner in the video. *Sure. At Brad's apartment building. Elizabeth something. In fact, she was taking these sacks out when I saw her. Elizabeth Strong, that's it.*

"Amazing. Can I borrow this tape?" Kyla asked.

"Sure, if it gets us our money." Louise replaced the videotape in its box and handed it to Kyla.

"I'll give it my best shot. Don't touch anything. It could be involved in a homicide investigation. Thanks for this." Kyla held up the video.

"Hell, no, we won't touch nothing." Louise puffed on her cigarette. "People are crazy."

Kyla walked out the front door, wondering if the moose was taking a picture of her behind as she was leaving. She got in her car, locked the tape in the glove box, and headed downtown.

Kyla parked in front in a visitor's space, entered Brad's apartment complex lobby, and approached the concierge station. The service window was open, but there was no one to be seen. Kyla turned the doorknob, crept in, and looked at the key board to the right of the window. Per usual, security breaches were blatant in apartment buildings. She scanned the board and saw the key for 1201. Kyla had just pocketed it and turned to go when William, the concierge, came through the door.

He frowned when he saw Kyla invading his domain. "Excuse me, may I help you with something?" His tone was a little sarcastic.

"I'm Detective Kyla Gillespie, Denver P.D." She reached into her blazer pocket and pulled out her badge, flipping the holder open for him to inspect. "I was just looking for Brad Richmond's key. I am authorized by the parents to get into his apartment." Kyla's heart was beating fast.

William wasn't impressed with her fast improvisation. "Please, if you'll step to the outside of the counter, Ma'am, I will check." He held the door open for her, waited until she passed through, and locked it behind her. He ran his eyes up and down some paper attached to a clipboard. "Kyla Gillespie, Denver P.D. Here you are." He reached to the board and took a key from 704. He pushed the clipboard and a pen at her.

"Please sign here stating you took the key and sign it back in at your departure. If you fail to return it, the Denver Police Department will receive a bill for fifty dollars."

Kyla scrawled her name on the form and scooted it back to him. "I will, thanks. Have a nice day." Kyla took the key and punched seven on the elevator keypad. At the seventh floor, she got out and took the stairs up to twelve.

It was a Friday, so Kyla hoped Elizabeth would be at work. She rang the doorbell twice, waiting a few minutes after each ring. Not hearing a response, she put the key in the lock.

Walking into the foyer, she was taken with the starkness of the interior of the apartment. It was well thought out and tastefully done in a modern eclectic motif, but there was little in it to tell her anything personal about its resident. No photographs were displayed. There didn't seem to be any pets. The place felt very stiff, like a model home; everything matched and it was clutter free.

The background colors were various shades of beiges, with a few strong pieces of furniture placed throughout the space. A large mahogany credenza, a huge marble-topped dining room table, a long tan leather couch. The place was immaculate.

Kyla went into the master bedroom, studying the sterile surroundings. Nearly everything in the space was white or off white. It looked more like a hospital ward than a bedroom. The bedroom was the place most people hid their secrets. It was a good place to start looking for something, she just wished she knew what. She pulled a pair of vinyl gloves from her pocket, slipped them on, and began her search.

In the back of a closet, behind the clothes, hung a shoulder holster nestling a .357 Magnum with a tidy four-inch barrel. Next, Kyla carefully pawed through Elizabeth's underwear drawer. A .38-caliber five-shot snubby was snuggled into the back corner. This woman was well armed.

Kyla went into the bathroom off the bedroom, and opened the medicine cabinet. Dental floss, cough syrup, aspirin, nothing unusual. Then, a small topaz vial on the top shelf of the medicine cabinet caught her eye. Kyla brought it down and read the label, *Ricin*. Not recognizing the name, she peered into the bottle from the side and saw it was half-full of a fine powder. She jotted the label name in her notebook and replaced it on the shelf.

CHAPTER 52

"You can't just have them mail you the ashes! Jeezus! Why don't you just hire a skywriter to announce to the world that you hated your old man? Zipper turned alternately to scold Elizabeth and watch the road. "Or are you just trying to draw attention to yourself on purpose?"

She forced her speech through clenched teeth. "I'm going to flush his ashes down the toilet. That's where he belongs, down in the sewer with the other pieces of shit." Her fist balled up and dug into her thigh.

"I don't give a damn if you sprinkle him on your dinner salad like croutons later, but right now, you got to look like a good daughter, and that means you at least have to have a memorial service for the poor bastard!" Zipper shook his head in disbelief. "I worry about you, Elizabeth, I really do."

Zipper drove and Elizabeth rode up front in the passenger seat of the Mercedes. Hendrix had stuffed himself in the back, although he had to drape his legs over the entire length of the back seat to do it. It was a good thing she had the top off the car or Hendrix's head would have been bumping along on the roof all the way.

Elizabeth had gone straight to Zipper's place after the cops left. After thinking it over, she decided she couldn't go to the funeral home alone. She just couldn't. Not knowing what constituted order anymore, her brain felt like an off balance load in the spin cycle of a washer, clanging and banging against the sides of her head.

"Take the next exit. Forest Pines should be up here about three miles on the east side of the road." She folded her arms defensively in front of her.

"Elizabeth, I wasn't trying to be hard on you , I was just trying to get you to think. I only want to protect you." Zipper looked at her kindly.

"Me, too." A huge paw from the back seat reached over and patted her left shoulder. Surprised, she jumped at Hendrix's touch.

"Thanks, guys. I know." She stared out the window on her side of the car until they pulled up in front of Forest Pines. There was a fountain in the courtyard with a large white dove as its centerpiece. The water shot up, then bounced and dribbled off tiers that were attached to the core of the fountain. The effect reminded her of Jesse's blood dripping off his face that night. "Blecch," she complained as she got out of the car and slammed the door behind her, catching Hendrix's leg as he started to wriggle out of the car. "Oops, sorry Hendrix. I'm a little nervous."

"It's okay." Hendrix grunted bravely, pulled down his sock and examined his ankle.

Zipper quickly came around the car and held out his arm. "May I escort you inside, Madame?"

Elizabeth looped her arm through his. "Thanks, Zipper. You know, I would rather have a red hot poker shoved through my right eye than go in there and plan that service." She felt her mind and heart starting to race and she pulled back, stopping their advance toward the door.

"Look, Elizabeth. I will be right beside you the whole time. So will Hendrix. We'll all get through this together. I promise." Zipper looked sincerely into her eyes. "Remember? Anytime, anywhere, anyplace? This is one of those times. You were there for me when I needed you. Now, let me be there for you; let me help you. C'mon. Let's go do this thing." He patted her hand.

Elizabeth took a deep breath and strengthened her grip on Zipper's arm. They entered the lobby of the funeral home and Zipper left her a few steps back and approached the dark marble counter alone. A young brunette receptionist asked for the name.

After a few minutes, an attractive older woman with salt and pepper hair and wearing a conservative gray suit walked out of an office. "Miss Strong, it is so nice to meet you." Her hand thrust out in welcome. Elizabeth gave her a limp fish handshake. "My name is Jean. Please, let's go to a conference room where we can talk privately."

"My friends are coming with me," Elizabeth said.

"Yes, of course. This way, please." Jean glided to a room and held the door open for the rest of the party. With her right hand, Jean flipped a discreet sign on the door to Occupied. It reminded Elizabeth of a sign on the door of an airline commode. Maybe this was kind of like joining the Mile High Club, but instead, it was the Six-Feet Deep Club. She heard dark laughter bounce around the walls of her head.

"Please, everyone, have a seat. Make yourselves comfortable. May I get anyone coffee or tea? Soft drink?" Jean motioned for them to take a seat around a beautiful dark oak table. They all declined beverages. The chairs were plush black velvet and Elizabeth noticed crystal coasters sitting by her elbow. A single, live red rose was the only colorful decoration in the room, placed in a silver bud vase in the center of the table.

"So, Elizabeth, we spoke on the phone earlier today, right?" Jean looked concerned.

Before she could answer, Zipper piped up. "Yes, she did, Ma'am. Elizabeth told me what she said about you mailing her father's ashes to her. Please, Ma'am, forgive her, she's still in shock. She just can't believe he's gone. She loved him very much." Zipper gently covered Elizabeth's hand with his.

Elizabeth glared at Zipper and frowned. Zipper squeezed her hand tightly, probably as a sign for her to keep quiet.

"I understand." Jean looked sympathetically towards Elizabeth and smiled sweetly. "We all have different ways of handling our grief."

What grief? Just torch him and let's get on our way.

Zipper increased the pressure of his hand on hers. "Show us your nicest memorial service, Jean."

"Yes, Sir." Jean replied enthusiastically.

Zipper made all the necessary arrangements with Jean while Elizabeth chewed on her thumbnail. Now that people thought she was in extreme grief, she figured she could get by without paying any attention at all. The only effort she made was to sign documents where Zipper pointed.

When they were finished with the paperwork, Jean slowly turned to Elizabeth, with a kind, concerned look on her face. "Miss Strong, would you like to view the body? Do you need to say goodbye to your father, perhaps to have some closure?" Jean spoke in a low soothing voice.

View him? Ick. No. Well, maybe...No! We don't need to see that. As a matter of fact, we need to get the hell out of here. She got up from the table, ran out of the room through the lobby and out to the car. Zipper and Hendrix soon followed.

Zipper stepped into her comfort zone. "You okay? Really, Elizabeth, I think you might need to see a doctor or something. I don't think you're okay with this." He went to put his arm around her.

Bothered by the intimacy, she bolted. "No, I just need to get the hell out of this place." She jumped into the passenger seat and crossed her arms.

"Okay, but you're staying with me tonight. And I will not take no for an answer. I'll have Hendrix sit on you if you try to leave."

"Yeah, and I'm heavy, too," Hendrix offered in a baritone voice.

"Oh, okay." She was secretly relieved. She felt safe with these two odd men she'd come to depend on.

CHAPTER 53

Dr. Ming was a Denver County deputy medical examiner and was known to be very cooperative with law enforcement in homicide cases. He was excellent at his job and took it very seriously. He ignored the insensitive jokes many squeamish police personnel felt they had to make when they visited his place of business. It seemed he didn't have a sense of humor.

On his behalf, Kyla thought that perhaps forensic pathology wasn't very humorous, especially working with cadavers every day. She thought the job would certainly lend itself to a constant awareness of matters of one's own mortality. Perhaps that's why Kyla chose to call instead of visit Dr. Ming in person. He soon came on the line when she called for him at the city morgue.

"How may I help you, Detective Gillespie?" His voice carried a slight Asian accent.

"Hi, Dr. Ming. I was wondering if you had any results to report on Brad Richmond's autopsy yet."

"No, not yet. A very unusual case, Mr. Richmond. I had to send some tissue specimens and blood samples to the National Center for Infectious Diseases, or NCID in Atlanta. I found cyanosis consistent with myocardial infarction, but there was also systemic hemorrhagic pathology, and I was uncertain of the cause. Their report could take some time."

"Do you have any educated guesses, Doctor?"

"Not that I would care to share right now. I can tell you the pathology was similar to a few autopsies I assisted with on casualties from the Gulf War."

"Are you talking bacterial agents here?" Kyla asked anxiously.

After a short pause, the doctor answered. "Perhaps."

"Doctor, do you know what ricin is?"

"Yes. It is a protein toxin produced from the castor bean plant. Ricin kills by destroying an important component of the protein synthesizing machinery of cells, the ribosome. It works as a slow poison, eventually causing a total body collapse as necessary proteins are not replaced."

"Could ricin be the cause of death in this case?"

"Maybe, but I'm not sure ricin would cause this much hemorrhaging. It would tend to be more paralytic. This is something more insidious, more deadly. But I can't be sure until we get the results back from NCID."

"Does this stuff die? Is it safe to be around after a certain amount of time?" Kyla thought about being inside Brad's apartment after his death.

"No, it doesn't die. Many bacterial agents can be produced and stored in dry form for decades. A military chemical protective mask is effective against inhalation, but a person is well advised to make sure skin does not get in contact with it either. If the spores enter through cuts or abrasions, it can also put a person at risk."

"Would there be any signs of exposure on the outside of the body?"

"Not usually with inhalation."

"Thanks, Dr. Ming. You have been most helpful. I appreciate your counsel."

"Any time, Detective Gillespie. I will let you know when I get the results back from Atlanta. I am most curious myself."

CHAPTER 54

Elizabeth sat in the front pew of the intimate memorial room at Forest Pines, and longed to be somewhere else. She chewed at the cuticle of her thumbnail.

The organ music that played as people sprinkled in was creepy, but the flamboyant older woman producing the eerie chords was even creepier. Elizabeth wondered if the aging organ player secretly dreamed of being a star.

Elizabeth marveled at the beautiful cut flower arrangements placed around the light oak podium and stage. There were stunning sprays of brilliant gladiolus, pots of luscious greenery, and gorgeous rose bouquets. A live ficus tree stood on the side of the speaker's stand. Next to the lectern, an ornate gold-colored urn containing Chet's ashes sat in the middle of a portable oak stage. The surface under the urn was covered with a blue velvet throw that had glamorous gold tassels dangling at its ends. The effect was quite flashy.

"Did you pick out that urn?" She whispered to Zipper as she scrutinized the scene.

"Yep. It's a beauty, isn't it?"

"It's really gaudy. You sent all those flowers, too, didn't you?"

Zipper leaned in to answer her question. "Sshhh, not all of them. He must have had at least a couple of friends."

"I doubt it." Elizabeth peeked over her shoulder at the smattering of mourners sitting randomly in the benches behind her. On the end of an usher's tucked arm, she thought she recognized the buxom waitress from Belmont's, the restaurant she and Chet had eaten in recently. That lunch date seemed like it had happened eons ago.

A man with her father's facial features sat in the second row at the end of the pew. He was sitting with an older woman that also resembled Chet. Elizabeth decided they must be Chet's brother Chuck and his sister Helen. She hadn't seen her aunt and uncle since she was a little girl, and didn't know them at all. They seemed genuinely upset.

And there was that woman who, before they were seated, had introduced herself as Greta, an old friend of Chet's. She had grabbed Elizabeth's hand, delivering profuse and mushy apologies to the perceived grieving daughter of the deceased. Elizabeth smelled minty mouthwash masking liquor on the woman's breath, and could just imagine what kind of friends Chet and Greta had been. She was repulsed by the woman's touch.

Elizabeth gave her attention back to the smallish urn. A whole, big man's body was in there. A once living, breathing, human being was reduced to powder on the inside of a paltry pot. Elizabeth wondered if she rubbed the bottle if a Chet genie would pop out. She grinned a little.

A stately, robed Jean, entered from a darkly draped door on the left side of the podium. Zipper whispered to Elizabeth, "Did you know the funeral director is a minister, too?"

"A Jill of all trades. How convenient for her. She gets paid twice that way," Elizabeth murmured back.

"Be nice," Zipper scolded.

Elizabeth counted ceiling squares during the service and noticed her right foot hurting a little. She wondered what a bunion felt like. A Bible passage Jean was quoting finally caught Elizabeth's attention: "...Till you return to the ground. Because from it you were taken; For you are dust...And to dust you shall return. Genesis 3:19." Jean's performance in her silky black gown was flawless.

Bored, Elizabeth picked up the Bible that was lying beside her. She thumbed through the pages until she found the verse Jean had just cited, and read it again to herself. She scanned on further through the book of Genesis until she came to the story of Cain and Abel. She hadn't read it since she was a child in Bible School, but remembered it vividly.

> Then the Lord said to Cain, "Where is Abel, your brother?" And he said, "I do not know. Am I my brother's keeper?"
>
> And He said, "What have you done? The voice of your brother's blood is crying to Me from the ground."

She felt the spinning start in her head. Her heart began to beat wildly, as she continued to read:

> "And now you are cursed from the ground, which has opened its mouth to receive your brother's blood from your hand. When you cultivate the ground, it shall no longer yield its strength to you; you shall be a vagrant and a wanderer on the earth."

Elizabeth knew at that moment she was truly doomed. Damned by God himself to forever walk the barren earth, alone and aimless. She began to cry, but it wasn't for Chet's passing. It was for the death of her own innocence.

CHAPTER 55

"What the hell am I supposed to do with that thing?" Elizabeth yelped, as she looked from the passenger side over the back seat, studying the bodacious mock gold urn sitting at Hendrix's feet. He was obviously straining hard not to touch it; but with his long gangly limbs, he could hardly spare the room.

Zipper laughed and shrugged his shoulders. "Put it on your mantle, I guess. That's what they do in the movies."

"I don't have a mantle." She leaned her chin on the heel of her hand and stared at the scenery passing by on her side of the car. She tried to occupy her mind with other things, but the fact that Chet's remains were actually in her car with them was almost too much for her. She imagined them having a car accident and the loathsome ashes spilling out all over her skin. The ashes would whisper "murderer," as they gathered together at her mouth and nose, eventually stopping up her air passages and suffocating her to death. She cleared her throat and glanced at Zipper. His presence calmed her.

Elizabeth saw the upcoming rest area from the highway. It was an old landmark, and most people just used it nowadays to stop and sleep or picnic. "Pull over at this rest area, Zipper. I have to go to the bathroom."

"Here?" He pointed his index finger from the wheel to the area. "The restrooms here aren't very nice. They don't even flush. There is that new rest area coming up in about fifteen miles, can you wait? It would be a lot cleaner."

Elizabeth shook her head. "No. Pull over now. Please. I need to go now."

Zipper drove off the exit ramp and into a paved semicircle drive in front of the small station. It was a little wooden, khaki green building in dire need of a new roof. Both men's and women's restroom signs were posted over the doors in cracking white paint. Zipper parked as close as he could to the entrance.

Elizabeth jumped out, leaned into the back seat, and grabbed the urn. She hoisted it up and kicked the car door shut with her foot.

"What are you going to do with that, Elizabeth?"

"Just dumping the trash, boys. I'll be right back." Her shoes crunched on the gravel as she approached the bathroom door.

Zipper pleaded with her. "Elizabeth, don't do that...let's take his ashes up to the mountains or something. C'mon, Elizabeth." He held up his arms and waved her back toward the car.

"That would give the impression that I gave a flying fuck. Hang on, I'll be right back." She hauled the bulky load to the door marked Women. She pulled on the handle with one finger, then caught the door with her foot, holding it open as she swung the urn inside.

The concrete floored bathroom smelled like an outhouse because that's essentially what it was. She set the urn down under the sink. She ran back to the entrance, stuck her face outside and gulped fresh air. Holding her breath, she went back inside.

There were two stalls, each armed with a cheap green painted plywood door that didn't lock. The commode was essentially an opening cut in a wooden counter, with a token white porcelain lid sitting on top. She set the urn on the space next to it.

She opened the cover, and peered inside the dark smelly hole.

Ick. Very disgusting. Perfect. Elizabeth picked up the urn, held it over the circular gateway to the putrid depths, and dropped it in.

The Voice laughed triumphantly.

We did it, Mama. We finally got him. Burn in hell, you disgusting bastard. Releasing the urn from her hands, she watched the pot splash and plant deep into the heavy sewage. She appreciated the shiny fake gold slimed with feces for a moment, then hurried out of the restroom, gasping for air. No telling what a person could catch if they breathed in the vulgar germs from in there.

As she neared the car, she smiled and announced proudly, "Mission accomplished! Now, that's closure. I should tell your friend Jean, the combo funeral director and minister, just how freeing that experience truly was." After brushing her hands together as a sign of a job well done, she stretched lazily and reached her arms toward the sun.

Zipper and Hendrix both sat very still and gaped.

"What?" She held her palms open and drew up her shoulders. "You two look like you just saw a ghost." She grinned as she got back into the passenger seat and shut the door. "Now, Hendrix, doesn't that give you a lot more leg room back there?"

Neither of the men spoke a word.

"Jeeves, shall we go?" She looked to Zipper and batted her eyelashes.

Zipper started the car and slowly left the rest area, shaking his head all the way out to the highway.

CHAPTER 56

Kyla sipped coffee as she waited for the rest of the old police reports on Chet Strong to come over the fax from Elk Run. She found Elizabeth to have no record, but in searching the archives, the helpful officer from Elk Run had found some assault charges filed against her father, Chet. Sergeant Mattingly's desk was located near the fax machine, and being the snoop that she was, she glanced over the papers and files sitting atop his desk. A stack of manila folders was piled in his out box, and the tab with the name Strong printed on it caught her eye.

Mattingly hurried back to his desk with a puffy glazed doughnut mounted on his index finger and a cup of coffee in his hand. He sat down, flipped his roll onto a tissue and started opening creamers and pouring them in his coffee.

"Why don't you just have a glass of milk?" Kyla teased.

"I usually don't use this much cream in my coffee, but the shit they make down here is so strong that it will eat a hole in your gut if you don't dilute it." He tried to make the coffee and cream swirl and blend with one of those little, skinny, useless plastic stirrers.

"I noticed that you have a file by the name of Strong in your out box. Mind if I ask the first name?" Kyla took a sip of her coffee.

"Elizabeth. Lives over at Park Towers. Her old man died of a heart attack and I had to go over there and tell her about it the other day."

Heart Attack?

"Was there an autopsy ordered?" Kyla asked.

"Naah. He was a drunk and a nobody." Mattingly dipped his doughnut in his coffee and lowered his head to catch the soggy pastry in his mouth.

"What was she like?" Kyla took her papers off the fax and straightened them on the corner of his desk.

Mattingly held up a finger to Kyla signaling her that he had to swallow first before he could answer. "I don't know. Real pretty, nervous, a little rude. She had just gotten home from Vegas. We couldn't even find her to tell her for a couple of days. Why the interest?"

"Oh, I might be working a homicide in her building. I might have to interview her. I just wondered."

"Well, be sure and call first for an appointment. She made it perfectly clear she doesn't like people just dropping by."

"I'll do that, Mattingly. Thanks."

Leaving him to his nutritious breakfast, Kyla made her way back to her office. She sat down at her desk and began to study the old police statements which were both handwritten and typed. The writing was almost illegible, and the quality of the faxed copies didn't help matters any either. Thank God for computers.

Kyla could make out well enough from the reports that on several occasions over the years the police had been called out to Chet's house by the wife Saundra for domestic violence. The first time Saundra called was from her residence in Colorado Springs when she was eight months pregnant. There were lacerations and contusions noted on her face and breasts. Although Saundra had called for help, she went back home to her husband the next day. Sadly enough, it was a cycle so typical of battered women.

Over the next several years, there were more calls from the Strong household, from both Colorado Springs and Elk Run. The violence was escalating; a cracked rib here, a fractured collarbone there, and various wounds and bruises on both mother and child. Once, there was even a report of a cigarette burn on Elizabeth's buttocks. Chet swore it was an accident. After that episode, it took Saundra a whole week to drop the charges against Chet.

Kyla empathized with Elizabeth to a degree. She thought of times when her alcoholic mother, divorced and poor, in an attempt to raise three small kids on her own, would go out and get drunk and bring home some real losers in the name of "finding them a father." Once, when one of her mother's suitors had tried to get little Kyla to come into the shower with him while her mother was sleeping, she ran away and called her grandmother, Emma, from a neighbor's house.

Emma had swooped in and took all her daughter's children into her home, and threatened to fight for custody of them in court if her mother dared to make a stink. She didn't. Kyla knew that her mother was actually relieved to be rid of them. She came around for holidays and birthdays for awhile, then just drifted away. Kyla realized now what a huge sacrifice it had been for her beloved grandmother to take on someone else's three children to raise, but she never once complained.

Kyla's attention turned back to the business at hand. She read the last report in shock and disbelief. *Suicide? Saundra Strong committed suicide? And a nine-year-old Elizabeth Strong was the first one to find her? Oh, my God.*

CHAPTER 57

Elizabeth was at Cleardrive, Inc., packing up her personal things from her office. It wouldn't take her long; she didn't keep much here she needed to take with her.

Doug Weller stuck his head in the door. "Hi, Elizabeth. Got a minute?"

"Sure." She sat down and took a sip of her coffee.

Doug took a seat in the chair in front of her desk. "I just wanted to tell you I'm real sorry to hear about your father."

"Thanks, Doug." She threaded her hands together in front of her.

Doug tried crossing his chubby legs, but finally settled for linking his ankles together. "You leaving for awhile, huh?"

She combed through her hair with her fingers. "Doesn't take long for news to travel in this place, does it?"

"Nope. The office grapevine travels at the speed of light. Well… I'll sure miss you. I won't have an office goddess to compare my pathetic sales record to, so I can punish myself by overeating and drinking excessively."

She smiled at him. "Your sales record is far from pathetic, Doug."

Doug reddened a little. "I'd give you a hug goodbye, but I hear you bite."

She breathed in deeply and managed a smile. "You're probably safer not to anyway."

Doug got up from his chair. "Well, I know you're trying to get out of here. You take care, okay?"

"Okay, you, too." Elizabeth pulled out a stack of index cards from her middle desk drawer. "Heads up!" She called, and tossed the bundle to him. Doug's right hand snapped out and caught it. "Those are some leads that desperately need working. Most of them are fairly solid."

Doug's eyes widened. "But, these are your leads. You're coming back, aren't you?"

"The trail will be stone cold by then. Work 'em. And buy yourself a decent tie." Elizabeth smiled.

Doug immediately took the rubber band off and flipped through the cards. "Thanks, Elizabeth. I don't know what to say."

She felt a disturbing lump in the back of her throat. She smiled. "Your expression speaks volumes, Doug. Now skidaddle. I have to pack."

Doug finally turned, waved, and waddled out the door.

Elizabeth had just resumed her packing when she heard another gentle knock at the door. Maggie opened it just far enough to pop her head into the office.

"May I come in, Elizabeth?" Maggie offered a warm smile.

Elizabeth smiled back. "Sure, Maggie."

Maggie stepped in the office just far enough so that the door would clear her as it shut. "I didn't mean to disturb your packing, but I just wanted to thank you for the wonderful evaluation you gave me this time. Mr. Mohr gave me a nice raise last week. It sure will come in handy."

Elizabeth smiled and took in another deep breath. "That's great! I'm glad. You deserve it, Maggie. You are an exceptional office manager. Please, sit down; if you want to."

"Thanks." Maggie, nervously smoothed the sides of a belted floral print dress that enhanced her plump hips, walked up to Elizabeth's guest chair, and sat down.

"I'm sorry to see you go, but I think I understand why you're leaving." Maggie's face looked sad.

Elizabeth placed a paperweight in her box, a sales award from last year. It was a beautifully cut and polished royal blue fistful of agate, and had an engraved brass plaque with her name on it. "It's just a leave of absence, Maggie."

Elizabeth didn't tell her that she had actually tried to quit this morning, but Mr. Mohr wouldn't hear of it and had talked her into a three month leave of absence, with use of the Mercedes and a partial draw against future sales if she needed it. She didn't. Her careful financial investment program had served its purpose; she could live very comfortably for a long time.

"I know, but I'll still miss you." Maggie fidgeted her fingers through her permed, blondish hair.

"Oh, Maggie." Elizabeth placed her reading lamp carefully in the box. "I just need some time to myself. My father's death and all."

"Yes, of course," Maggie said.

Elizabeth had never realized how much leeway people allowed you for the death of a parent.

Maggie sat up straight and fumbled with her hands in her lap. "I hope you will relax and take care of yourself. But, Elizabeth, don't take this wrong or anything, but, you know—spending too much time alone can do things to your head."

"I beg your pardon, Maggie?"

"Well, I just know that after my mother died, I had to leave the house to go to work every day or go stark raving mad at home. I missed her so much. I just want you to be okay, that's all."

"Yes, well...I appreciate your concern, Maggie, but I've got a little money saved up. I'm going to do some traveling; go see the world before I'm too old to enjoy it."

Maggie laughed nervously. "Oh, yes, Elizabeth, you are really getting ancient."

"I feel old, Maggie." Elizabeth sighed deeply. "I feel so very, very, old."

Maggie got up and approached Elizabeth with open arms and an impending hug expression on her face. Elizabeth didn't dodge her. It felt good resting her head on Maggie's pudgy shoulder, and being enveloped in two strong, loving arms.

CHAPTER 58

Elizabeth found it impossible to sleep at home. Sometimes she would doze off, only to be awakened by images of the dead marching through her mind like impatient soldiers. Her eyes constantly patrolled the bedroom in the dark, fully expecting to be haunted by one or all of the people who she had murdered. A few times, she thought she recognized the ghostly bust of her father hovering over the armchair in her bedroom, but finally convinced herself it was just the glow of streetlights creeping in around the edges of the curtains, casting eerie shadows on the wall.

She tried to cheer herself with thoughts of exotic travel and freedom from the rat race, but Elizabeth still felt no happiness. Instead, she felt only dread. Although she was sure she had become emotionally incapable of being effective at her job, she also knew that, like Maggie had said, not working at Cleardrive would only give her industrious mind more time to spin webs of fear and insecurity.

She had isolated herself in her apartment for several days now, opening her door only long enough to reach for the newspaper. All she had done was watch mindless sitcoms on TV, smoke, and drink brandy. She was waiting for an answer to come, for something to appear to show her the next step. None came. The void in her head was the only place she could bear to be, and even that was most endurable in the dark. Darkness was a warmer, more forgiving place to be, much safer and infinitely more comfortable than the day. Elizabeth often sat in the dark just smoking and thinking, watching the glowing ember of her cigarette cast a warm blush over her body.

What-if scenarios of her future played out in her imagination, but she couldn't imagine herself in any of them for very long. There was no order to her life anymore. Elizabeth, early on and by no choice of her own, had learned to live life by her intuition, trusting to make decisions strictly by what she felt in her gut. But she sensed no inner guidance lately. Just as the Bible passage had predicted, God had demagnetized her inner compass, dooming her to be a solitary aimless wanderer upon the earth. Her life felt meaningless, flat, and one dimensional. Each moment led painfully to the next, and the next, seemingly with no end to the hollow loneliness she felt blowing through her insides like a cold north wind.

Elizabeth had lost the sense of herself and her identity, and there was no peace. After tossing and turning all night, she finally sat up on the side of the bed and looked at the clock: 2:47. Sighing deeply, she grabbed her robe and headed for the pack of cigarettes lying on the kitchen counter. The moonlight shining in from the glass patio doors lit her way as she padded from the kitchen out to the balcony.

As she leaned over the railing of her terrace smoking a cigarette, her eyes went to the bench across the street. An attack of cabin fever suddenly passed through her. The night air felt like refreshing cool water pouring over her skin, and she had to get out and walk in it. Flipping her cigarette butt to the wind, Elizabeth left the balcony and detoured to her bedroom. She pulled on her favorite pair of jeans and slipped on a tee shirt. Tying her tennis shoes, it occurred to her this was the first time she had been dressed for two days. She shrugged, fastening her shoulder holster and Magnum snugly to her body; she slipped on her jacket, locked the door behind her, and went out into the night.

As she crossed a deserted Speer Boulevard, she could hear traffic on distant downtown streets moving and occasionally honking. A few sirens split the air. Dogs barked. This time of day took on a magical quality; it wasn't really night and it wasn't really morning. It was a mystical in-between time that felt neither threatening nor real. The soothing breeze held her like she was on the inside of a feather pillow, brushing soft and tinglingly against her skin.

She sat on the bench enjoying her outing, when her ears perked up at the voices of some young black men approaching her on the sidewalk. They were laughing and cussing at each other, generally being loud and obnoxious. Elizabeth saw glints of the streetlight bounce off their eyes as they noticed her. The noise of the small gang quieted as they advanced, their faces appearing to be studying her with interest.

A young black man wearing a bomber jacket started the exchange. "Say, say, say...what we got here, Homies? Look like we got us a stray white peach—know what I'm sayin'?" He had an athletic build and wore a baseball cap backwards on his head.

"I be definitely knowin' what you're sayin', brother." The fattest member of the trio hooted with laughter. "She's so cute, can we keep her?" He wore nothing under a black leather vest that was zipped up over a bulging stomach. His huge, ebony biceps stuck out of the armholes like tree stumps.

Elizabeth sat quietly, observing. She slithered her right hand in under her jacket, quietly unsnapping the strap that held the Magnum in place.

The giant in the bomber jacket pursued the subject. "You ever had white meat, Ratbait?"

"Yes, yes! As a matter of fact, gentlemen, I have, and it is delicious. And those white bitches, they love it, too. Those white boys got little wienies, ain't that right?" Ratbait pointed at Elizabeth like he expected her to answer, then turned back to her first tormentor. "What they say, Shovel, once you go black you don't go back?"

All three men laughed and catcalled.

Shovel quit snickering and leaned in closer to Elizabeth. "Say, little white bitch, want to have some fun with some well-hung brothers?"

"No, thanks. I've had all the fun I can stand lately." Elizabeth waited, alert, noticing how low the waistbands of their jeans rode on their pelvises. She wondered what kept their pants from falling down.

Shovel put his hand over his heart and frowned. "You refusing us? I think you might be dissing us." He turned to his companions. "What you think, pardners, is the bitch dissing us?" Shovel moved in closer to Elizabeth.

Elizabeth was not afraid. She looked Shovel directly in the eye. "What does that mean, anyway? Dissin'... dissing... what the hell kind of word is that?"

"Dissin. You know, disrespect. Dissin! And that's what you be doing to us. You be disrespecting the Shovel." He waved his arms around as he talked.

Ratbait fed Shovel's agitation. "The bitch is definitely dissing us, brother. Definitely."

The three men looked like hungry vultures circling as they moved closer.

"Disrespecting you?" Elizabeth fingered the cold steel under her jacket. "Just because I am sitting here minding my own business? You think I have nothing better to do than to sit here and figure out how to disrespect a Shovel? That is really fucked up thinking. You're fucked up. I suggest you move on, boys."

"Boys? Fucked up thinkin'? Now the white bitch is definitely disrespecting us. The bitch say the Shovel is fucked up. Now, you know she gotta pay for that. Meat, show her your business."

The third wiry black man, obviously Meat, snapped his wrist and swung open a long silver blade. He put a menacing leer on his face and started toward her. Leaning down close to her, he floated the sharp cool steel over the tender skin of her neck, its tip coming to rest firmly under her chin. Meat throatily whispered, "I never had me a white woman as pretty as you before. I usually like blondes best. So far, that is. Don't get me wrong, I am open to you changing my mind...mmmmm...and you are fine. We gonna enjoy each other." Meat grabbed her breast with his left hand and squeezed it like an apple. "Oh yeah, Baby, now, you be sweet, hear me? Get up nice and slow and start walking. We gonna go take a little ride. Don't test me, bitch. It would be a shame to mess up those pretty eyes." His lips moved towards her face.

Elizabeth fumed as she felt and smelled his hot breath spraying her cheek. His breath stank. His long, serpentine tongue shot out and sloppily licked her cheek. She took that moment to make her move.

With lightning speed, her left elbow shot out and caught him hard in the groin. Doubling up with pain, he groaned loudly and grabbed for his crotch. In one smooth motion, Elizabeth stood up, brought the Magnum out, and shoved it hard against Meat's temple.

Shovel and Ratbait froze in their advance when they saw that she had a gun.

The Voice rooted her on. *Do it. Do it, Elizabeth. He disrespected you. That seems to be what it's all about, to make people pay that have disrespected you. No one will care if this piece of shit bites the dust. Just do it. It will calm your nerves.*

As Elizabeth entertained the thought of wasting him, she caught sight of Beulah from the corner of her eye. The old woman had climbed the riverfront steps only high enough for her red-hatted head to be visible from the bench. When Beulah saw that Elizabeth was glancing toward her, she stepped up another step toward the top of the stairs, her hands gathered up to her chest as if praying. Her quiet presence somehow seemed to give Elizabeth the strength not to pull the trigger.

"Drop the knife, shitbag," Elizabeth spoke through clenched teeth. Immediately, she heard a clank on the sidewalk and the knife came to rest in front of her foot. She kicked it to the side, away from her assailants. Elizabeth talked slowly and clearly as she maintained the pressure of the gun on the side of his head. "Listen real good, you fucking punk. I was just sitting here, on this bench, minding my own business."

Meat made a feeble attempt to wriggle free. "Sorry man, c'mon. Let me go now."

Elizabeth brought her knee up hard in his groin. He groaned loudly in protest and again doubled over hard. She had no patience for his whining. "Shut up! I'll let go of you when I damn well please. Now, when I do decide to let go of you, I suggest you get the hell out of here fast before I change my mind. Believe me, it would be in your best interest. You think I won't shoot you? If you try anything, and I mean anything, I will blow your fucking head off."

Meat could barely talk, only managing a muffled plea. "Okay, okay, man. Be cool. Be cool. I was just playing wid cha." The boy's pleading eyes sneaked toward his buddies for help. Under the streetlight, Elizabeth saw the whites of his eyes and the trapped look that played over his face.

Elizabeth spoke with authority to the bystanders. "You two, get the fuck across the street. Now!" She didn't have to tell them twice. It was apparent they could tell this crazy white bitch meant business.

They fled across Speer Boulevard and quickly hid behind a tree, waiting for their partner.

Elizabeth turned back to her immediate hostage. "Okay, you worthless shithead. Put your hands up in the air and back away slowly. And remember, I still have my finger on the trigger and I'm not afraid to pull it. I could plaster the contents of your stupid head all over this fuckin' sidewalk and not blink an eye." She paused a moment and ground the barrel of the gun harder into his temple. "Believe me, Meat, when I tell you I got nothing to lose. Now, get the fuck out of here!"

The instant she removed the steel from his head, the frightened boy immediately backed up with his hands held high above his head, and skipped to turn around on his feet. He broke out in a dead run, traveling in a zig zag pattern across the street toward the other two bullies who were hiding behind a tree. Ratbait's big butt was hanging out from behind his hideaway and Elizabeth fought an impulse to shoot at it. As soon as Meat caught up to them, the other two fell in behind him, and they were out of sight in seconds.

CHAPTER 59

Elizabeth anxiously looked after them long after they had disappeared, half expecting them to come back any second. The air felt different now, like its pleasantness had been all stirred up and disturbed. She reluctantly returned the gun to its holster and deflated on the bench. A blinding headache was inching up from the base of her skull and it didn't help matters to know Beulah was going to want to talk to her.

Elizabeth urgently sought the solace of the void in her head, the place where she had survived the last few days. The door leading to the comforting silence slammed in her head. The slamming would not end. All of the mental escape hatches she had built for herself banged shut as she approached them, leaving her alone and naked under the glare of the floodlight from her own soul. Resting her elbows on her knees, she held her head in her hands, desperately trying to stop the noise and the spinning.

"Oh, my. Just like my Shelby you are. You make life so hard for yourself. So much harder d'an it has to be."

Elizabeth knew Beulah was there, but was still startled to hear her voice. She squinted to avoid the glare of the streetlight and looked up to find Beulah hovering over her. She felt curiously glad to see the old woman. "I was just out here, minding my own business. Why can't people just let me be? I just want to be. Beulah, why can't I just be?" Elizabeth put her face back in her hands.

"I don't know, girl." Beulah stopped to pick up the switchblade that Meat dropped, and swung it shut. She dropped it into her fanny pack and sat down beside Elizabeth. "D'e Lord, He moves in mysterious ways, He does."

Elizabeth looked at her inquisitively. "You really think there is a God, Beulah? Sometimes I think the earth is just Somebody's big stupid ant farm."

Beulah smiled wisely. "I don't think so, girl. D'at's not what He says when He talks to me."

Elizabeth's expression was disbelieving. "Right. He talks to you. What does He say?"

Before she answered, Beulah sat up straight and stared blankly off to the west. The sky had turned a deep navy blue and it was just barely light enough now to see the silhouettes of the mountains. "Oh, t'ings. He tell me to watch over peoples I love and be real good and I'll see my Shelby again someday. He tell me no matter what happens, everything gonna be okay."

Elizabeth answered in a skeptical tone. "He used to tell me that, too, Beulah. He lied."

Beulah smiled faintly; her weathered hand lovingly reached out and took a wisp of hair hanging on Elizabeth's cheek, and tucked it behind her ear. "He didn't lie, little one. You quit listening."

An old car pulled out from a side street onto Speer Boulevard, and barreled toward the two women. The tires squealed on the pavement as the automobile made the turn. It looked to be about a '67 Chevrolet Impala. Whatever the model, it was in burning need of a new muffler. It cut across three lanes of traffic and slowed as it neared the bench.

"Hey, white bitch!" An angry male voice yelled out. "This is for you!" The long barrel of a gun poked out the window from the back seat and a flash of fire burst from its end. Beulah grabbed a shocked Elizabeth and pulled her to the ground behind the bench.

On the soft grass, Beulah spoke to her calmly and firmly. "Keep rolling, little one. Jump off de ledge to de sidewalk."

"Can you—" A fresh round of fire bounced off the ground beside her head. "Shit!" The near hit woke Elizabeth out of her fog, and she snapped alert.

"Move, girl!" The old woman rolled to the ledge and disappeared. Elizabeth followed. The old car's brakes screeched and she heard three car doors slam.

"C'mon!" Beulah pulled Elizabeth after her. "Hurry!"

They ran away down the bike path. Elizabeth had been right about the cigarettes. Beulah could almost outrun her.

Beulah stayed on the path towards downtown until they got to the bridge. Then she ran up the side of the slanted cement embankment like a monkey. She was obviously younger and in better shape than she looked. Beulah stopped at the corner of the bridge and lowly called out. "Huey! Hey, Huey, you up here?"

"Yeah, Beulah, I'm right here." A male voice answered. "What's up?"

"You gotta hide us, Huey. We got some gang boys after us. Dere's a bottle in it for you. We gotta hurry d'ough, d'ey comin' fast."

"Well, okay, Beulah, my friend. But this'll cost ya a quart instead of a pint."

"It's a deal." Beulah agreed and waved Elizabeth closer.

Huey pointed behind him. "Crawl in those blankets back there. I'll see what I can do."

Heavy foot traffic pounded up the path. "Hey!" A young male voice screamed out. "Where is your white ass? I want to show you what happens when you pull a rod on me! Where you at, bitch?"

The men had slowed down their running near the bridge. Ratbait complained, "Man, I gotta stop. I'm gonna have a heart attack."

Shovel griped at him. "If you would get your fat ass out and run once in a while, you wouldn't be so fuckin' outta breath. You a big ole fat ass and a bad shot, Ratbait. Shit, man. Where'd those bitches go?"

As the gang walked by on the footpath under the bridge, Beulah and Elizabeth were wriggling under some blankets and sacks Huey had piled up in the little space that he had claimed for himself. As she disappeared under a scratchy old Army blanket, Elizabeth's foot hit an empty beer bottle and sent it clanking and rolling down the embankment toward their would-be assailants.

"Whattsat?" Shovel looked up towards the noise and called out. "Hey! Who's up there?"

"Just me, Huey. Sorry about the bottle scare, I'm just a clumsy old man. Hey, uh...you boys got a drink? I really need a drink."

"Ain't got no booze, old man." Shovel put his hands on his hips and looked around as if talking to Huey was wasting his time. "You seen a couple of white bitches run by here?"

"I can't see shit, man. It's dark and I need glasses I can't afford. But, I heard 'em running by here like a herd of elephants a couple a minutes ago. Hey, ain't that information worth a buck or somethin'? C'mon. I'm old and thirsty."

"Forget you, man! C'mon, let's go. Those bitches are long gone. They ain't worth all this trouble. We'll find 'em. We put the word out on the street."

Elizabeth, sweating and itching, waited breathlessly until she heard the old car peel out before she came out from under the blankets. It was the first time she noticed how bad they smelled.

Beulah popped her head out of her side of the covers. "D'anks Huey. I'll be back later wi'd your bottle. Still on gin?"

"Anytime, ladies. Always glad to help damsels in distress. Yep, Beulah, gin's my poison. I'll be here, except for lunch. I'm goin' down to the mission today and get something to eat. My innards are starting to feel pretty raggedy."

The two women stood and straightened their clothes around themselves. Beulah pulled off her red knit hat and smoothed her thin silver hair over her head. Their was a balding spot on the back of her scalp.

Elizabeth wasn't sure what to say, so decided to keep it short. "Thanks, Beulah. I'm going to go home now."

"Are you crazy in de head, little girl, or you just got a bad dea'd wish? D'ose boys, dey'll be watchin' for you. You can't go back d'ere now. I'm going to take you to Zipper's house. You'll be safe d'ere."

"No, no, I can't go to his house at this time of day. He won't be up for a while, and—"

Beulah interrupted authoritatively. "D'en you will come to my place until it's a good time to go. Dat's where you need to be, girl. You need some help wid yaself."

Elizabeth gaped at Beulah. "Help? Help? That's what you think I need? Help? I've been on my own all my life and I don't need nobody's help now. I don't need anybody."

"Okay, okay, I know." Beulah gave her a gummy grin. "You come, Elizabeth. You come with me now. You can't go back d'ere right away."

Elizabeth stood for a moment, looking at Beulah's face and considering her options. She deduced that since she was actually running away with a bag woman from gang members, her options were probably limited. She felt completely at the mercy of the winds. There was no order left in her world.

Silent most of the way, she followed Beulah down the bike path to an exit near some railroad tracks. They were walking in an area somewhere behind Union Station. The air smelled of black, tarry oil.

"Where are we going?" Elizabeth asked impatiently.

"It's just a little ways further."

The sky was beginning to lighten, making it easier to see railroad ties and pieces of iron lying on the ground waiting to trip her. Beulah finally turned toward a white concrete building that looked like it had been abandoned years ago.

Beulah took a key that was hanging from a piece of string around her neck and unlocked a large padlock hanging from a hasp on the door. The door led to a space about the size of a small hotel room. The high windows had steel bars around them, and the door was steel as well. Someone had wanted to make sure Beulah was very safe when she slept at night.

Beulah excused herself to go to the restroom, a skimpy space equipped with a toilet and a shower adjacent to the larger room. Elizabeth took the opportunity to look around. There was a twin bed, where Sugar, the stuffed pink bunny, sat in the middle of a flimsy white chenille bedspread like a princess. A metal reading lamp, mounted on a flexible stem, sat atop a small wooden desk, and was situated on the opposite side of the room. There was a beige metal folding chair tucked in front of the desk. A grocery cart was parked in one corner, filled with grocery sacks and a large clear plastic bag, partially filled with cans.

There was one small metal framed picture on the desk. She walked over to get a better look at it. Leaning down, she saw it was a photo of a girl who appeared to be about twelve or so. It looked like a standard school photo, taken at an age when a tentative adolescent girl doesn't know whether to smile or not. The girl was pretty, the face cheerful and bordered with straight, long, brown hair. The eyes were big and caramel colored, much the same as her own. When Beulah opened the bathroom door, she smiled when she saw Elizabeth looking at the picture.

"D'at's Shelby. D'at's my daughter, my baby girl."

"She's very pretty. You must miss her."

"Her passin's like an open wound in my side dat never heals," Beulah answered matter-of-factly.

"I'm sorry." Elizabeth felt bad and tried to change the subject. "Pretty nice place you have here. I didn't know they had condos in this part of town."

"Condos? Oh—hah—okay, good one." Beulah shot her a quick smile. "Zipper owns d'is here building. He wanted me to have a little place. I don't need it really. But it's nice to have when I get real tired."

"What were you doing out so late tonight, Beulah?"

Late? Girl, dat's early! Dat's de best time to get cans, right after de clubs close. You wait till morning like most of 'em do, d'ey already be picked over."

"Oh, yes, I suppose that's true."

"Yep, it is." She caught her hands and clasped them in front of her. "How did you make d'em boys so mad, anyhow?"

Elizabeth explained the events leading to the confrontation.

"Oh, I see. What was you doin' outside at dat time of night, girl?"

"It's a free country. Can't a person just go outside and get some air?"

"No, ma'am. Not anymore. You know dat. You trying to get yourself killed, aren't ya?"

"No, Beulah, Why would I do that?"

"De light's gone plumb out of your eyes, girl. Plumb out. We got to get you to Zipper's so he can help you get your light back. Now, lay down here on dis here bed and get some sleep. I'll be back after while, okay?"

Exhaustion overruled Elizabeth's protests. She did as she was told and curled up in a ball on the twin bed facing the wall. Beulah covered her with a thin brown blanket and tucked Sugar in by her folded arms. Elizabeth looked up her and smiled. "Thanks, Beulah." She took the threadbare pink bunny into her arms, and held it close. Elizabeth fell asleep almost immediately.

CHAPTER 60

Kyla had been looking through the file she had compiled on Elizabeth Strong when the intercom light lit up on the telephone. She pressed the button quickly. "Yes?"

"Detective Gillespie, it's Dr. Ming from the coroner's office on line three."

"Thanks, Leo." Kyla hurriedly picked up the receiver. "Hi, Dr. Ming."

"Good morning, Detective Gillespie. I am calling about the results of the Brad Richmond autopsy." Dr. Ming paused for a moment. "It has been determined by the National Center of Infectious Diseases in Atlanta that the victim died of anthrax poisoning. They called the Chief Medical Examiner this morning, who is also the State Epidemiologist. The Colorado Public Health and Environment Office has also been notified. They are setting up quarantine of his apartment as we speak."

"Anthrax? Oh, my God! Are we going to start seeing this stuff on the streets?" Kyla asked.

"Oh, I certainly hope not, Detective Gillespie. I will send out the report to you directly."

"Thanks, Dr. Ming. Oh, by the way, what's the incubation period for this stuff?" Kyla asked nervously.

"They estimate an average of three days."

"Thanks again." Kyla sighed a breath of relief. It had been over a week since she had been in Brad's apartment. She must have gotten lucky.

After calling Tracy to make sure she was okay, Kyla went directly to her boss's office with her news of the chemical protection gear, the gun, and the video of Elizabeth she'd collected from the mini-storage lot. She also told him what she knew about Brad and Elizabeth's botched date.

After listening to her report, Chief Brown's order was short and to the point. "Pick her up for questioning. Take Zanelli with you, and get some backup. Shit! When the media gets a hold of this, it's going to be a zoo around here. The Feds have already called me this morning. Looks like it's going to be a long day."

Kyla hustled out of the Chief's office and headed straight for Zanelli's desk. "C'mon!"

Zanelli, an Italian machismo type who took himself seriously, had a little trouble with Kyla barking orders at him, and gave no indication that he was moving anytime soon. "What's up?" He asked in his usual gum-chewing laid-back manner.

"I'll tell you on the way," Kyla grabbed her keys from the middle desk drawer. "Let's go, Zanelli. This is big, I'm not kidding."

Zanelli, obviously intrigued, quickly grabbed his jacket and fell in behind Kyla. They rushed out of the building and into her car.

❖ ❖ ❖

"Detective Gillespie. How nice to see you again." William, the concierge, said a bit sarcastically when Kyla and Zanelli entered the front lobby.

"And you, Bill. I'll need you to stand by in case we need a key to an apartment."

William sounded a bit snide. "Please call me William. I didn't want to eat lunch anyway. Besides, if it's the Richmond apartment, the Feds have already sealed off the floor."

"Thank you, William, but that's not the apartment I was speaking of," Kyla said as the elevator doors closed.

Kyla rung Elizabeth's doorbell while Zanelli hung back a little ways and off to the side, his gun drawn.

There was no answer.

"Zanelli, you stay here and secure the area. I'm going to go call the boss."

She went back downstairs to use the pay phone in the lobby.

Her boss was clear in what he wanted her to do. "Kyla, the Feds want this perp caught immediately. I called Judge Watson and we are on our way over with a search warrant. Stand by. I'm sending you over some help. I'll have them bring you and Zanelli some protective gear. Do not enter the apartment without it."

Kyla hung up and went back to the concierge station.

"I'll need the key for Elizabeth Strong's apartment. A search warrant is on the way."

William crossed his arms and leaned forward on the counter towards Kyla. "Well, I'll need to see it before I give you a key. It's my duty to protect the tenant's privacy. This isn't a police state yet, is it?"

Kyla recoiled at the remark, detesting it when people made offhand derogatory remarks about the police. She would like to see them go out on the street and put their butts on the line some time. Kyla had been questioning herself lately why she spent her days protecting assholes like this against other assholes. It was a question that was getting harder and harder to answer. "No, not yet," Kyla answered, holding her temper in check. "Is there a storage area? I'll be needing that key as well."

"Yes, of course."

The search team showed up with a warrant in about twenty minutes. Kyla was impressed. She rarely saw the wheels of justice spin so quickly.

The team, all suited in gas masks and vinyl gloves, tossed Elizabeth's apartment, hitting all the possible places she might have hidden the biological agent. Zanelli quickly picked the .38 caliber pistol out of the underwear drawer, but they found no evidence of any toxic substances. The ricin had been removed from the medicine cabinet since Kyla's clandestine visit.

When the Feds arrived, they started pulling the place apart, and Kyla felt she could do better down at Elizabeth's storage unit in the basement. The key William had given her was useless. The hasp had a sturdy combination lock on it. After a trip to a squad car, she lopped the lock off with bolt cutters, and began looking through the contents of the boxes.

Sitting on the floor, Kyla shuffled through a box filled with old yearbooks, poems, and diaries. In scanning the papers, Kyla began to get a rough feel for what Elizabeth might have been like growing up. She read through notes, looked at school papers, and report cards. Elizabeth had been an exceptional student. As she thumbed through a notebook, Kyla's eye caught a title that read, *Please Daddy.* Upon closer observation, she saw that it was a poem Elizabeth had written long ago.

Please Daddy

My daddy took me to the fair,
He bought me a hot dog and a cone,
"Oh what fun! " I say to him,
Then I saw I was alone.

I looked and looked and looked for him,
I found him at the beer place.
Please daddy, let's go win a bear.
He gave me a mean blank face.

Here kid, here's five bucks,
Go get your picture taken.
Can't you see I'm busy here?
He said with his hands shakin.

Come with me to ride the rides
They go so fast and high.
Please daddy, I'm afraid to go alone,
I whimpered with a sigh.

I brought you here, didn't I?
You always were a brat.
You never appreciate anything,
Now go on! Vamoose! Scat!

I went and got my picture taken.
I sat up straight and proud.
"What a pretty girl!" the picture man said,
I almost laughed out loud.

I went back out to the fairgrounds,
And bought cotton candy on a stick.
If this is supposed to be so fun,
How come I feel so sick?
~Elizabeth Strong, age 12

Kyla had a few tears in her eyes by the time she reached the end of the poem. She knew exactly what Elizabeth was saying, although, after a time, Kyla had a stable home with the beloved grandmother that she had lived with. Elizabeth had had no one to turn to but her father growing up, and he'd betrayed her again and again.

Elizabeth must have had to grow up like a wild animal, making her own rules as she went along. Kyla shut her eyes and sighed. *But for the grace of God...* Kyla sent a silent blessing to her grandmother, Emma.

Zanelli came rushing downstairs calling her name. "Kyla! Where are you?"

"Over here, Zanelli. What's up?"

"Guess what they found in a fake library book in Elizabeth's apartment a few minutes ago?

"What?"

"A vial of anthrax and one of ricin. They were even conveniently labeled for us. The Feds are rushing the samples out for testing now. They're relieved it was such a small stash."

Kyla tucked all the papers she had been looking at back in the box and got up off the floor. She stretched as to shake off the tension she felt.

"Well, it's all over but the crying, Zanelli. Let's go."

CHAPTER 61

After the vials of anthrax and ricin were found in Elizabeth's apartment, there was an around-the-clock stakeout ordered at her building. The feds were in on this one, and they wanted Elizabeth Strong caught immediately. When they checked at Cleardrive, Inc., the police discovered that Elizabeth had taken a leave of absence. When she didn't show up at her apartment for two days, they decided to thin out and split shifts. Kyla was supposed to be home sleeping right now, but she was too nervous; she decided to drive out to Elk Run and poke around instead.

Kyla caught Ron, a painter and Chet's old boss, in front of his house as he was getting out of his truck. He agreed to answer a few questions.

"Do you know Elizabeth Strong?"

Ron took off his baseball cap and scratched a balding head. He had a fine white spray of paint on his right cheek. "No, not really. I just saw her off and on as she was growing up. She wasn't a friendly kid."

Kyla crossed her arms. "Were they close, Chet and Elizabeth?"

"I don't think so. Once she left home she never came back, until recently. He used to paint for me once in a while when he was sober, and he'd talk about Lizzie sometimes, and how hard he was trying to get to know her again."

"So, do you know, were they working things out?"

"I don't think too well. He said she was a tough nut to crack. Real cold. But then she just up out of the blue came carting him out a practically brand new computer one day. I thought that was strange."

"Thanks, Ron. You've been very helpful."

❖ ❖ ❖

A great way to spend her day off, she thought, wearing a gas mask and looking through some dead guy's house. Judge Colby had provided Kyla a search warrant to Chet Strong's house, although he hadn't been sure if she even really needed one, since the only name on the deed of the house was Chet's and he was dead. It had previously been in Chet and Saundra's name, but she was dead, too. The judge had spent more time figuring out whether or not he had to make the paperwork up, than it would have taken to just have done it from the start. Kyla grew impatient at the snail's pace of the small town judge, but held her temper in check. She sweetly convinced him that it wasn't worth any phone calls, and he finally issued her the search warrant.

Kyla reached through the small window pane she had busted and opened Chet's back door. It took her into a laundry room with an old washer and dryer, a gray metal shelf filled with oily and paint-splattered work boots, and dirty clothes lying all over the floor.

She walked through the mess and found herself in the living room, which wasn't so tidy either. Old food and bottles still sat on the coffee table, and she was sure the place would stink if she could smell it. It was the first time she had appreciated her awkward chemical mask. Obviously, no one had been in the house to clean the place since Chet's death.

It was probably a good thing no one had been in here, as Kyla suspected there was an anthrax connection to this case, too, but since Elizabeth had Chet cremated, she couldn't prove it unless she found something else. Kyla was looking for a tie, something that might link Chet and Brad's murders together. Walking slowly through the house, she stayed alert to anything that might catch her attention.

She wandered down the hallway to the back bedroom, looking for anything that seemed out of place. When Kyla entered the back bedroom, she saw that the computer was on. She turned her flash-light on the back of the computer tower, and hurriedly checked the computer's serial number. It matched a receipt found in a desk drawer at Elizabeth's apartment. She looked around at the many boxes stacked around the room. It looked like it might have been a little girl's room at one time. Probably, it was Elizabeth's old bedroom.

Kyla walked over to one of the cardboard boxes on the top of one of the piles and pulled the flaps open. They weren't taped shut. She looked inside. A cigar box that had intricate curly designs drawn on it with a black magic marker, probably in an attempt to make it special, sat on top of some other things in the box. It looked the most interesting. Kyla took the box out and sat down on the bed with it. She couldn't get over the feeling that this was a very private thing she was doing, but, after all, she did have a search warrant. It still didn't seem right; it felt like she was eavesdropping on a very private past.

There were a few photos lying on top of a diary and a pad of paper. Some pens and pencils rattled around in the bottom of the box when it moved. There was a little green pom-pom made of yarn with white paper eyes and feet pasted on it. A homemade price tag was stuck on it that said 25 cents. On the top sheet of the pad of paper it looked liked there were some names with orders for other pom-pom people in other colors. Apparently, young Elizabeth Strong had been somewhat of a budding entrepreneur.

Kyla picked up one of the pictures and looked at it. It was a small girl, maybe about nine or ten, in pigtails, standing beside a mutt of some kind. Kyla turned it over and looked on the back. "Beeper, my friend," was printed on the back. She looked at it for a moment and picked up another picture. It was the same girl smiling and standing in front of a scrawny Christmas tree with a large doll that was almost as big as she was.

The next picture looked like it could be a senior picture cut from a high school year book. The name beneath it read Saundra Owens. It must have been Elizabeth's mother. There was another picture of an older Saundra that was taken outside in front of a picnic table somewhere. The person standing beside her had been cut out. Kyla assumed it had been Chet .

There was an envelope sticking out from under the diary in the bottom of the box. Kyla lifted up the little beige book with the tiny delicate gold lock and pulled the envelope out from underneath it. Elizabeth's name was written neatly on the outside. Kyla gently lifted the flap on the envelope and pulled out the paper that was inside. She carefully unfolded it and began to read. Tears began to gather in her eyes as Kyla realized it was Saundra's suicide note to her daughter. By the time she got to the end of the letter, Kyla was duly shaken.

She sat on the bed and looked around the room and felt depressed. She could almost hear the voices of a tortured past ringing in the room. She had to get out of here. This place gave her the creeps. If Elizabeth did kill this bastard, maybe she would look the other way. Kyla knew she couldn't, but wished she could.

She replaced the cigar box and turned back to the computer. *It's still on. That's odd.* She sat down in front of the computer. She tipped the trash can and looked into it. There were a few papers wadded up. A beer can. A diskette mailer. Kyla dug the mailer out of the can and thought back to Tracy's having told her about Brad's receiving a diskette mailer, too, right before he died. She pulled another plastic bag out of her jacket pocket, dropped the mailer inside, and zipped the top shut.

In the age of electronic communication, not that many people sent disks in the mail anymore to transfer information. It was mostly done over the computer through e-mail. An idea flashed through her head: *Could it be the disk? But how?* With vinyl-gloved hands, she pinched the disk out of the disk drive and dropped the disk into a plastic bag and sealed it. Kyla peered at it, and noticed some white powder clinging to the side of the plastic. *Oh my God! Anthrax!* She popped up from the folding chair so fast she sent it clattering to the floor. Kyla immediately reached for her cellular phone and called her boss.

CHAPTER 62

Elizabeth woke with a strange woman standing beside the bed she was lying in, studying a syringe that was poised in her right hand. Elizabeth's eyes felt itchy and she ached all over. She tried to speak, but her tongue was dry and sticky, and stuck to the roof of her mouth. She finally pulled it free and managed to croak out some questions. "What is that? What are you doing to me? Who are you?"

The woman stopped to look over at Elizabeth and smile. She looked fairly young and had a white lab coat on over her jeans. "It's okay, Elizabeth. My name is Penny, and I'm your nurse. This is just a little something the doctor ordered to help you rest." The nurse flicked her index finger against the body of the syringe. "Are you thirsty? Would you like some ice chips first?"

"Fuck your ice chips!" Elizabeth sat up. "Answer my questions! I don't want to rest, and why in the hell would I have a nurse? I want to know where I am! Where's Zipper? What's that stuff you've been giving me?"

Penny looked at her with compassionate eyes. "SSsshh...calm down...you just need to rest now, Elizabeth, and this will help." The nurse slowly approached her with the needle.

Throwing the sheets back, Elizabeth stumbled out of the bed, away from the nurse. She suddenly felt dizzy and grabbed the wall for support. Penny rushed over to help her.

Elizabeth began yelling and flailing. "No! Don't touch me! Zipper! Zipper! Someone is trying to kill me! Help! Help!"

The door flew open and Hendrix came running into the room. He stopped right after he entered the door, assessing the situation, and saw Elizabeth crouched against the far corner of the bedroom wall, auburn hair strung down over her face, and her eyes were wide and wild. Her breath came in short gasps. Hendrix approached her slowly and spoke to her in a calm, tender voice. "It's okay, Elizabeth. This is Penny, the nurse Zipper hired for you. She is a very nice lady and has been taking very good care of you for a few days now. You were very upset when Beulah brought you here, don't you remember?"

"No! Stay away! You're lying, Hendrix! Where's Zipper? I don't remember being here yesterday! Somebody must have brought me here after they drugged me. What's happening to me? They're after me!" She looked down at her feet, her eyes blurred with tears. "What's in that syringe?" Elizabeth looked to Hendrix and glared. "Hendrix, tell me the truth, does Zipper want me dead?" Elizabeth flattened against the wall, looking warily at both of them.

"No! No, of course not, Elizabeth. Zipper cares about you very much. You need some help, that's all, and he's gone right now to talk to some people about a place for you."

She barked at him in disbelief. "A place? What do you mean, a place for me? You can't kennel me like a dog! Tell me what you mean by a place, Hendrix. What? Tell me!"

"Settle down, Elizabeth. It's just a little clinic off somewhere private. Some place for you just to rest a little while, to think things through, that's all."

"No! No! No!" Elizabeth shrieked, "I can't be locked up anywhere!" She made a reckless run for the door and Hendrix caught her midway there and held her firmly between his arms. Trying her best in her weakened state to wriggle free, she made it difficult for Hendrix to hold her steady.

"Elizabeth, please! It's not like that! It's just for a rest. Come on ahead, Penny, I got her."

The nurse came forward with the syringe and stuck the needle quickly into Elizabeth's arm. In a few moments, Elizabeth felt woozy and weak. The last thing she knew, Hendrix was carrying her over and placing her back in the bed.

❖ ❖ ❖

The next time Elizabeth opened her eyes, Zipper was sitting in a wooden straight back chair at the side of the bed, his face in his hands.

"Hey, Zip," she said quietly.

He looked up, startled, and smiled. "Hi ya, little sister, how are you feeling?"

"Much better, now that you're here. Where's Hendrix?"

"He's spending the night with his mother. It's her birthday. His sister is having a party for her, so he's just going to stay at her house so he doesn't have to drive back tonight. He's probably having a few brewskis."

"I wouldn't blame him if he got shitfaced. I think I freaked him out. He probably thinks I'm nuts."

"Nah, he don't. You're just under a lot of stress. He thought he should stay here tonight, but I told him to go on, that we'd be just fine. How are you feeling?"

"Like hell. What is that stuff they were giving me? It really knocked me out. What's this talk about a rest Hendrix was talking about? What's going on here? Can I have some water? My mouth is so dry."

Zipper shook his head. "Hendrix has a big mouth. He should have let me talk to you about it first. He can be so insensitive." Zipper reached to the end table and got the glass of water that was sitting there. He bent the white flexible straw so that she could take a sip.

Elizabeth lifted her head and sucked on the straw hard and swallowed. "Thanks. Well, what is it? Where is this place?"

"I was talking to a guy who knows a quiet place in Maine you could go to for awhile. There would be no questions asked. It's kind of a family place, if you know what I mean. It might be good for you to get out of town anyway."

Elizabeth's eyes brightened a little as she got an idea. "Let's just go back to Las Vegas, Zip. We can have fun again! That was so much fun. I could move there!"

Zipper smiled and patted her hand. "I don't think that's such a good idea right now, Elizabeth. You need to be in a place where you can gather your thoughts. Someplace where you can have some quiet time to put your life back together again."

"And exactly how do I put my life back together again? What type of life adhesive do they suggest I use? A new career? A relationship? Kids? Booze? Sex, drugs, and rock 'n' roll? What? Everybody has a vice that keeps them going from one day to the next. What shall mine be, Zipper?"

"Faith, maybe? That's the only thing I can figure out that works for me."

Elizabeth's face sobered. "Faith in what?"

"I don't know for sure. Faith that there's a reason for everything. Faith that there's something bigger than me up there that knows what they're doing and that tomorrow's gonna be a better day. Hell, I don't know, Elizabeth. I'm not the right person to ask that question."

"Why not? You're qualified. You've made yourself a nice little family here, Zip, even if it does look weird. You have a lot of people that care about you."

"So do you, Elizabeth."

"No, not really. I've always been on the outside looking in. I've tried to fit in, but I really never did. I just made myself look like and act like people expected me to. I don't know if I even know myself very well. Like, I don't know how I killed those people, Zipper. It doesn't seem real. My God, Zipper, I actually killed real people." She brought her hands up in front of her face and stared at them. "With these hands. My hands. I'm doomed. God said so, Zipper, remember at Chet's service?"

"There, there, Elizabeth," he patted her hand, "let's not think about all that right now. You're not a bad person. Just rest now, okay?"

"But, Zipper, what am I going to do?"

Zipper smoothed her hair to the sides of her face. "SSshh, rest now. We'll talk later, okay?"

Elizabeth relaxed a little and looked up at Zipper as he rose to leave. "Okay, I'll try. And Zipper?"

"Yes, Elizabeth?"

"I love you."

Zipper smiled and bent down to kiss her on the forehead. "I love you, too, little sister." He quietly left the room, leaving the door ajar. Elizabeth waited patiently in the bedroom until she thought that he had had enough time to fall asleep in front of the television.

Elizabeth crept out of bed and began looking for her clothes. She wondered where the nightgown she had on had come from. It wasn't hers. It looked like something Hendrix probably had picked out. Opening the closet door, she found her jeans and tee shirt hanging on a hook. Her gun and shoulder holster were nowhere to be seen. She opened every drawer, in every piece of furniture in the room. She rifled through the closet looking for them. No gun. *Damn!*

Elizabeth slipped on her jeans, noticing they hung loose around her waist. *And to think I spent all that time running, when I could have just been going nuts to stay thin!* She smiled, then remembered her situation, and her lips fell into a straight line. She tightened the laces on her tennis shoes and tied them in neat bows. *Maybe a little rest somewhere out of state wouldn't be so bad.* She would give it some thought. But, she certainly wasn't going anywhere without her mother's music box. It was the only thing she had left of her mother and she wasn't going to leave it behind. It was simple enough. She had to go back to her apartment and get it.

Elizabeth crept to the crack in the bedroom door and peeked out at Zipper. He was stretched out in his recliner with the newspaper lying across his chest and his head lolled to one side, asleep. She waited until she heard the rumble of his snoring grow steady, then she crept out of the bedroom, across the dining area, and entered the living room. As she got up even with Zipper's chair, her heart pounded when his head rolled from one side of his chest to the other. Luckily, he didn't wake up.

She clenched her teeth and squinted as if it would help her open the door to the outer hallway more quietly. She snuck out the slim opening and looked back in at Zipper before she shut it again. He was still sleeping like a baby. Elizabeth smiled, quietly shut the door behind her, and slipped out into the night.

CHAPTER 63

"And the world will be better for this
That one man scorned and covered with scars
Still strove with his last ounce of courage
To reach the unreachable star."
~The Impossible Dream

After she entered her apartment, Elizabeth turned on a lamp and looked hard at the surroundings. Oddly enough, they looked rather unfamiliar to her. Stark. Cold, really. Very modern, with lots of sharp edges, like the jagged knives she had inside of her. Unblunted pieces of life had ripped wounds into her soul, that would never heal, never be whole, no matter what she did or who she killed.

Elizabeth walked through the dining area to the mahogany credenza, and felt its smoothness; its coolness. *Thanks for everything, Mr. Holy Gatekeeper of Vices.* Smiling faintly, she remembered the night she named it that. It was just hours before she killed her first victim. Elizabeth wondered if it all could've turned out any differently. She doubted it.

She walked over to her computer and ran her fingers over the keyboard. It no longer held an attraction for her. She did not turn it on. On the way into her bedroom, she paused over the marble-topped dining room table and put her palm down on the sharp chill of the surface. It felt good on her hand. She sat down in one of the chairs and put her cheek down on the cool, polished stone. From where she was sitting, she could see a glimpse of the lit Denver skyline. Elizabeth allowed her head to lie there for a few minutes and enjoyed the sheer simplicity of the moment.

After she retrieved the treasured keepsake from her dresser, Elizabeth cradled the music box and turned, gently winding its key as she walked out to the balcony. She lovingly placed it on the patio table, and opened the satiny wooden lid. As the tiny ballerina spun around on the glass, Elizabeth smiled.

Mama.

The spell was broken by a hard knock and a loud voice at the door. "Police! Elizabeth Strong, open up!" Startled, Elizabeth stood up and stared blankly toward the noise. She wondered how they had known she was here; she had been so careful.

She heard Beulah's wise voice resonate in her head. *"Run, run, run, but anywhere you go, d'ere you are."* Elizabeth smiled at the old woman's simple wisdom. Maybe Beulah was right. Maybe life was no more complicated than appreciating a fat cinnamon roll in the morning and talking to a stuffed pink rabbit. Maybe it's just that simple after all. She took the security bar from the inside bottom of the patio door and brought it outside, sticking it between the sliding doors,giving herself a little more time. She heard a faintly familiar voice yelling from the hallway.

"Elizabeth! This is Detective Gillespie, open the door, please! I want to help you! Open up!"

After a few moments, a loud crack sounded and the outside door flew open. Footsteps filled the foyer, but Elizabeth didn't hear them. She had climbed up on the wrought iron railing and was blankly staring at the ground. *Our Father, who art in heaven, hallowed be Thy name.*

"No, Elizabeth, don't! Wait, please! Let me help you!" The familiar voice yelled somewhere behind her.

Thy kingdom come. Thy will be done, on earth as it is in heaven.

She vaguely heard the noise behind her, but Elizabeth tuned it out and continued her prayer. Her fingers were pointed in a steeple under her chin.

...For Thine is the kingdom, and the power, and the glory, forever. Amen.

Hands pounded on the patio door and frantic voices pleaded with her not to jump. Elizabeth briefly glanced backwards. She felt serene. The people behind the door reminded her of mice in a jar, pawing the glass to get at her. She grinned. Just as the large panel of the patio door shattered from the impact of a dining room chair, Elizabeth leapt into the air.

With her arms spread wide at her sides, Elizabeth soared from her cement perch. At first, she thought she might be scared, but she was amazed at how peaceful she felt, flying so high above everything. The cool wind felt so good on her face.

As she sailed through the air, she turned her head to the side, and there was Mama, floating next to her, smiling. “I'm glad you've come, Elizabeth. I've missed you so much.”

Elizabeth felt happy and loved.

Me, too. Now I finally know what freedom feels like, Mama.